A handsome duke, earl, soldier, rake or gambler...
Ready and willing to give pleasure...all night long!

Five sensual short stories
set in the glittering salons and
bedrooms of high society.
Five brilliant, favourite authors
to delight and tempt you...

SCANDALOUS Regency NIGHTS

CAROLE MORTIMER
ANN LETHBRIDGE
BRONWYN SCOTT
MARGUERITE KAYE
CHRISTINE MERRILL

MILLS & BOON

Harlequin Mills & Boon Limited, Eton House,
18-24 Paradise Road, Richmond, Surrey TW9 1SR

SCANDALOUS REGENCY NIGHTS © Harlequin Books S.A. 2011

The publisher acknowledges the copyright holders of the individual works
as follows:

At the Duke's Service © Carole Mortimer 2009
The Rake's Intimate Encounter © Michèle Ann Young 2009
Wicked Earl, Wanton Widow © Nikki Poppen 2010
The Captain's Wicked Wager © Marguerite Kaye 2009
Seducing a Stranger © Christine Merrill 2009

ISBN: 978 0 263 88720 4

009-0211

Harlequin Mills & Boon policy is to use papers that are natural,
renewable and recyclable products and made from wood grown in
sustainable forests. The logging and manufacturing processes conform to
the legal environmental regulations of the country of origin.

Printed in Great Britain
by Clays Ltd, St Ives plc

CONTENTS

At the Duke's Service   9

The Rake's Intimate Encounter   63

Wicked Earl, Wanton Widow   113

The Captain's Wicked Wager   207

Seducing a Stranger   271

Carole Mortimer was born in England, the youngest of three children. She began writing in 1978 and has now written over one hundred and fifty books for Harlequin Mills & Boon. Carole has six sons, Matthew, Joshua, Timothy, Michael, David and Peter. She says, "I'm happily married to Peter senior; we're best friends as well as lovers, which is probably the best recipe for a successful relationship. We live in a lovely part of England."

At the Duke's Service

CAROLE MORTIMER

Author's Note

Welcome to the sensual and exciting world of **The Notorious St Claires**!

Angelina and Alexander's love story, as the matriarch and patriarch of the St Claire family, is where the story all began and it was great fun matching wits between these two strong-willed lovers.

Do look out for:

The Notorious St Claires—Historical romances
THE DUKE'S CINDERELLA BRIDE
THE RAKE'S WICKED PROPOSAL
THE ROGUE'S DISGRACED LADY
LADY ARABELLA'S SCANDALOUS MARRIAGE

The Scandalous St Claires—Modern™ romances
JORDAN ST CLAIRE: DARK AND DANGEROUS
January 2011

THE RELUCTANT DUKE
February 2011

TAMING THE LAST ST CLAIRE
March 2011

I hope you enjoy the new St Claires!

CHAPTER ONE

St. Claire House, Mayfair, London

"WOULD YOU KINDLY explain who you are and what you mean by coming here uninvited and taking me from my dinner guests?"

Miss Angelina Hawkins rose slowly to her feet as a tall, arrogantly forceful man strode into the cavernous entrance hall where the butler had requested she wait whilst he informed his employer of her arrival.

Whilst she waited for this man. Alexander St. Claire, the ninth Duke of Stourbridge.

A man who, as an acquaintance of her late father, was not at all as Angelina had imagined him to be whenever she had thought of him these past three years. Pleasantly so. She had been prepared for a man of middle years, perhaps running to fat, with a face florid from an overindulgence of port.

But this man could be aged only thirty years at the most.

And his face, though admittedly hard and aristocratic, held the same chiseled beauty of an archangel Angelina had once viewed in a painting at one of the art galleries her tutor, Miss Bristow, had insisted "my young ladies" visit in an effort to broaden their education.

It was a decadently handsome face, one stamped with authority as well as arrogance, with a firm, unyielding jaw, and dominated by the darkest, most beautiful eyes Angelina had ever beheld.

Elegantly dressed, his shoulders were wide beneath the tailored black evening coat, his waist narrow, and his thighs and legs long and muscled in black silk breeches.

Yes, Alexander St. Claire was very handsome indeed. "I am come, Your Grace," she informed him huskily, almost overwhelmed by how instantly taken she was by his good looks.

"Come?" he echoed sharply. "Come where?" The scowl on his brow deepened with his increasing irritation.

She gazed up at him guilelessly. "Here, Your Grace."

"Without a doubt." He gave an icy inclination of his head. "What the devil do you mean by it?"

"Do not be cross with me, Alexander!" She moved to press herself against him, her head resting on the broadness of his chest as her arms moved lightly about the slender waist hidden beneath the fine material of his black evening coat. "Miss Bristow did caution me to remain patient and wait until you came to collect me, but I could not wait any longer, Alexander, and decided to take matters into my own hands and come to you instead!"

Alexander stood stiff and unyielding under this

overfamiliar onslaught of feminine softness, as he felt
a faint stirring of memory at the mention of a female
called Bristow. He had the distinct feeling he had heard
that name before. But for the moment, with firm breasts
pressed against his chest, slender arms about his waist
and the soft rose perfume wafting from the golden curls
peeping from beneath her bonnet, he was having difficulty
remembering exactly when and where…!

Not that it mattered at this particular moment. What
mattered was releasing himself from this young woman's
far from unpleasant hands upon his person.

Alexander straightened to push her from him abruptly.
"Now see here…"

"Excuse me, Your Grace…?"

He turned a scowling face in the direction of his butler.
"What is it, Thompson?"

Thompson became uncomfortable under Alexander's icy
stare. "Should I inform your guests that you have been…
called away on business, Your Grace?"

"His Grace will rejoin his guests in but a few moments,"
the young woman reassured Thompson before Alexander
could speak.

He cast a look at this very forward and beautiful young
lady. She was perhaps nineteen or twenty years, dressed in
a traveling gown the same peach color as her bonnet. The
golden curls beguiled, and her eyes were the clear blue of
a summer sky. With a sprinkling of freckles across the
bridge of her tiny nose, and a mouth— Ah, her mouth!
Surely no respectable young lady should have such a sin-

fully decadent mouth! Those lips so full and pouting that they begged to be kissed and to kiss in return…

Damn it, who was this chit to come here and interrupt Alexander's evening entertainment, addressing him so familiarly by name, whilst at the same time evoking such fantasies that Alexander's perfectly tailored breeches now felt uncomfortably tight?

She smiled up at him, seemingly unconcerned. "I understand your need to return to your dinner guests, Alexander. I am tired from traveling these past two days, anyway. And of course, it would not do for you to introduce me to any of your guests," she accepted good-naturedly. "I assure you I shall be quite happy to wait in one of the private salons until you have finished dinner and are free to join me."

Alexander's head was starting to spin. Who was she…? From where had she been traveling these past two days? And why did the name Bristow seem so irritatingly familiar? Until he had answers to his questions, Alexander was reluctant to return to his guests.

"Wait there, Thompson," he ordered, as the butler would have moved to do this young woman's bidding. Meanwhile, Alexander's dark gaze never wavered from the creamy and irritatingly enchanting perfection of his intruder's face. "Exactly who are you?" he demanded of her impatiently.

That blue gaze widened. "Angelina Hawkins, of course. Although I would much prefer that you call me Angel. Your Grace." Belatedly she made a polite curtsy.

Alexander stared down incredulously at her bent head.

Angelina Hawkins…! The illegitimate daughter of Benjamin Hawkins and his mistress? An illegitimate daughter whose existence Benjamin had confided to Alexander on his deathbed almost three years ago?

It had been bleak and stormy on the night Alexander was ushered into Benjamin's hushed bedchamber. The older man had suffered a fall from his horse in an even worse storm two nights previously, resulting in injuries that would ultimately prove fateful. Alexander had sat at Benjamin's bedside and listened to his tale of love and passion for the mistress who had been carried off by a fever but three days before. Benjamin's distress at her loss was such that he had no desire to continue without her; hence, the deranged horse ride and fall that had sealed his own fate.

But there had been more. There was a child from the alliance. A daughter, named Angelina.

With both of her parents gone, and no other relatives who could take her in, Benjamin feared what would become of her, and had requested that Alexander see that suitable arrangements were made for her. A request that Alexander, distraught at his friend's rapidly failing health, had readily agreed to do.

But he had assumed that the girl was no more than nine or ten years of age, and had requested that Hopkins, his man of business at the time, place her in a school where she could board until she reached adulthood. At which time Alexander would turn his attention to arranging a suitable marriage for her, to a parson or some such. Someone who would not question her family background too deeply.

Obviously the chit had decided to take matters into her own hands by appearing here uninvited this evening!

"You really must run along back to your dinner guests, Alexander," Angelina now told him dismissively. "Thompson and I shall sort out where I am to go."

The last person to instruct Alexander St. Claire to "run along," had been his nanny when he was but five years of age—no one would have dared to do so in the four and twenty years since then!

That this—this young woman had done so was intolerable. Unacceptable. As was the fact that she was here, in his home, at all, and acting as if she had a perfect right to be here!

Alexander drew in a sharply hissing breath. "Angelina—Miss Hawkins—"

"Did I not tell you I would prefer you to call me Angel, Alexander," she chided mischievously.

Alexander blinked. This young woman was no angel. More like a devil sent from hell to plague him!

He reminded himself that, in fact, he did not have the time for this conversation with Angelina Hawkins now. His dinner guests were political allies and their wives, and Alexander had already been absent from their company longer than was polite. He would find out the answers he required later. "Thompson will indeed show you to the blue salon." He turned to give the butler a pointed stare before moving his reproving gaze back to Angelina. "I will join you there once my guests have departed, and then we shall talk further on this matter," he assured her grimly.

Her eyes widened. "Talk, Alexander? But I had thought—"

Alexander did not care to hear what this young woman "thought"—although her overfamiliarity and habit of launching herself into his arms at will was beginning to give him a fair indication of what some of those thoughts might be!

CHAPTER TWO

ANGELINA WAS HAVING the most wonderful dream. Of lying on a bed. Of being held in Alexander's arms. His strong, muscled arms...

Her own arms moved up over his shoulders and her fingers became entangled in the dark thickness of his hair as she pulled him down to her and pressed her parted lips against his, before kissing him with warmth and passion.

Alexander, having finally rid himself of his last guest at almost two o'clock in the morning, had entered the blue salon to find Angelina fast asleep on the sofa. His efforts to wake her had proved fruitless. As it was already so late that any chance of removing her from the house, without causing a monumental scandal, was out of the question, he had decided that he had no choice but to carry her up the stairs and deposit her in one of the bedchambers on the floor above.

Only now he found himself being pulled down beside

her as he placed her upon the bed! Her arms encircled his shoulders and her fingers threaded through his hair as she pressed her warm, parted lips against his. To both his dismay and delight, her actions sent a fiercely hot lick of desire coursing through his body.

"Xander?" Angelina groaned in protest as he pulled back in shock at his response. Her blue eyes were reproachful as she raised sleepy lids to look up at him. "Do you not wish to kiss me?"

Alexander scowled down at her as he was prevented from rising to his feet by her fingers still linked together beneath the loosened hair at his nape.

Angelina had removed her bonnet some time before falling asleep, revealing her gloriously golden curls. Her brow was smooth and creamy and her deep blue eyes were looking up at him in seductive invitation. Her mouth was full and sensual, and her neck long and slender above the full swell of her breasts, the low neckline of the peach gown having slipped so that it almost revealed her nipples.

"Kiss me, Xander," she encouraged throatily as she pulled him toward her once more.

Beautiful and willing as Angelina undoubtedly was, Alexander knew he ought to stop this right now. To demand an explanation for the obvious invitation in her behavior.

Perhaps he had overindulged in the port following dinner and his wits had momentarily deserted him? Or perhaps it was just that the invitingly sensuous pout of Angelina's lips cried out to be kissed? Just as the slender curves of her body begged to be crushed against his much harder ones! Whatever the reason—or perhaps excuse—instead of pushing Angelina Hawkins firmly away from him and leaving the bedchamber as he knew he should, Alexander found himself unable to do anything but draw her more fully into his arms.

Angelina moaned low in her throat as she felt the firmness of Alexander's lips against her own, parting them to deepen the kiss as he pulled her roughly toward him.

Oh, how glorious it was to be kissed at last! By Alexander. It was so much more intimate, so much more arousing, than Angelina had ever imagined a kiss to be, and she found her neck arching in invitation as Alexander broke the kiss to seek out the hollows of her throat with his lips.

"Touch me, Xander!" she invited breathlessly, taking one of his hands in hers and placing it against one of her aching breasts. They swelled beneath the material of her gown, their tips swollen and sensitive as she felt the palm of Alexander's hand against her.

But it was not nearly close enough, Angelina decided, as she ached for the feel of that hand against her flesh. She shifted the artfully designed gown and the material moved accommodatingly lower, exposing her breast fully so that her nipple pressed urgently against Alexander's fingers.

Alexander's gaze moved down sharply, feeling the bareness of Angelina's flesh against his hand, desire coursing fiercely through him and causing his already hard and pulsing erection to throb anew as he looked at the fullness of her exposed breast with its tight rosy nipple. Momentary madness came over him as he started bending his head to take that luscious bud into his mouth—

Dear God…!

Alexander pulled back abruptly, jaw clenched as he straightened Angelina's gown determinedly, before pushing her firmly away from him.

He ignored her seductive pout this time, to rise sharply to his feet, and moved purposefully away from the bedside, hands clasped firmly behind his back as he took several deep, controlling breaths before he dared face her again. "I have no idea where you… That sort of behavior is totally unacceptable, Angelina!" he finally rasped in his most disapproving tone.

Disapproval for himself, as much as for her…

He may never have set eyes on this girl before tonight, may have ignored her very existence these past three years except to pay her school fees, but Benjamin Hawkins had nevertheless placed her under Alexander's protection. He doubted that his friend had ever envisaged that it was Alexander himself Angelina might need protection from!

"How is my behavior inappropriate?" Angelina gave Alexander a quizzical stare as she sat up to swing her feet down onto the rug beside the bed."I am sure we will touch each other much more intimately than that once I become your mistress."

"Once you are become my what?" Alexander glowered down at her in shocked disbelief.

"Your mistress, Alexander." Angelina smiled. "I assure you I have applied myself most diligently to my lessons these past three years whilst a pupil at Miss Bristow's school."

At last, Alexander knew where he had heard the name before!

At the time of Benjamin Hawkins's death, Alexander's own father had also recently died, and Alexander had found his time much occupied with his newly elevated status as Duke of Stourbridge.

Even so, it had been remiss of him not to have at least visited Angelina after the death of her parents. Perhaps if he had done so he would have realized that she was not a child at all, but a young lady of fifteen or sixteen years! As it was, he had left all the arrangements for Angelina Hawkins's schooling to his man Hopkins. Something the elderly man had later happily assured Alexander he had done by placing her in what he believed was a "suitable" school in Brighton.

But suitable for what?

CHAPTER THREE

ANGELINA STOOD UP from the bed, an apologetic look on her face. "I had thought to surprise you by arriving so unexpectedly, but I see now that I should have remained patient and waited for you to come for me." She reached up to touch the hardness of his clenched jaw. "Do say you are not cross with me, Alexander."

A nerve pulsed where her fingers had just touched. "I am not cross with you—"

"You are everything that is good and kind!" She beamed up at him warmly.

Good or kind were not descriptions Alexander—or, indeed, anyone else!—was accustomed to hearing in connection to himself.

That Angelina thought him to be so was most unsettling.

Alexander gritted his teeth. "What I am is most displeased with the—the teachings of Miss Bristow!"

Angelina frowned her dismay. "Did I not kiss you properly, Alexander? Were my caresses not to your liking?"

"Of course they were to my liking," he snapped impatiently. "That is not at all my point—"

"I am so glad that I pleased you, Alexander." Angelina gave a delighted laugh. "Indeed, Miss Bristow considered me so able a pupil that I have spent the year since reaching my eighteenth birthday instructing the other girls rather than being one of their number!"

After this recent example of Angelina's capabilities Alexander could well believe it!

He was a man of nine and twenty years, experienced in the many ways of lovemaking. But Angelina Hawkins, with her warmth and lack of all inhibition, let alone guile, had awakened a desire in him unlike any he had ever known before.

Or, indeed, should be feeling now!

"These lessons you mentioned..." He paused, searching for the correct—the most discreet!—way of posing his next question. "Were they only of a theoretical nature, or did practice enter into these—these teachings...?"

"Oh, they were purely theoretical," Angelina assured him lightly. "Miss Bristow was at great pains to point out to all of us that one's virginity was a precious gift to be given only to one's intended protector."

Dear God...!

This woman, at nineteen years of age, with all the theoretical knowledge of lovemaking, if not the practice, spoke and behaved with a candidness that was becoming more and more difficult for him—for any man!—to resist.

"I believe I shall very much enjoy living here with you, Alexander." Angelina seemed unaware of his erratically brooding thoughts as she looked appreciatively at the elegant furnishings of the bedchamber.

Angelina live here with him? At St. Claire House? Impossible!

"That would be most unsuitable, Angelina," he answered her, with an increasing impatience for this situation. "It is far too late for me to arrange for you to go elsewhere tonight, but you must leave here first thing tomorrow morning."

"Why must I?" She frowned her disappointment.

What was to be done with this young woman? Alexander wondered with frustration. The school in Brighton—School? It sounded more like a bordello, with Miss Bristow as its patroness!—had obviously educated Angelina in a way that was most unsuitable for marriage to the parson Alexander had vaguely envisaged arranging for Hawkins's daughter once she reached maturity!

A brothel was what Angelina was most educated for!

And how long after being forced to resort to such an occupation, Alexander wondered, would it take for Angelina to lose her infectious candidness and beguiling warmth of affection? Before she became jaded and hardened by the lack of love and warmth in such relationships?

Perhaps he could provide her with a dowry so that she might marry within society—

No, that would not do, either. Any man of means who might be persuaded into marrying Angelina would necessarily have to be told of her background. Besides, there was

Angelina's undeniable knowledge—even if that knowledge was not of a practical nature—of all things sensual...!

His mouth thinned as he answered Angelina's question as to why she couldn't stay. "There is no woman in residence here to act as your chaperone."

"Why should I need a chaperone, Xander, when I am to be your mistress?" Angel reached up to once again smooth the frown from his brow. "Please do not scowl so, Xander."

He grimaced as he shook his head. "Why do you persist in calling me 'Xander'...?"

Why? Because it was how Angelina was quickly coming to regard him. Not the elderly and debauched Duke of Stourbridge she had always imagined as her protector. But a young and very handsome man, a vigorous man, with whom she would enjoy every sensual delight. A man whom she might love...

She eyed him teasingly. "Does it displease you...?"

"No." His frown was now quizzical. "It is only— It sounds a little odd, when no one has ever before shortened my name in that peculiar fashion."

Angelina laughed softly. "But I am not 'no one.' And when we are alone together like this you must always be 'Xander.'"

Alexander found himself captivated by the warmth in the deep blue of Angelina's eyes. No woman had ever spoken to him so warmly, and with such unaffected frankness. It would be so easy, he realized, to accept all that she offered so freely. So easy to lose himself in her loveliness, to become deeply enamored—

He stepped away abruptly. "I will leave you now—"

"Must you really go…?"

Alexander felt his heart contract in his chest, his gut clench and his breeches tighten as he once again found himself aroused and aching at the invitation writ so blatantly in Angelina's innocently guileless gaze.

He should not have kissed her earlier. Should not have allowed himself to be drawn in by her burgeoning sensuality. "I most definitely must," he stated coldly.

Angelina felt a terrible sense of loss as Alexander turned to leave. It had been so long, too long, since she'd had anyone whom she might love and be close to. "Will you not kiss me good-night first?" she prompted wistfully.

He drew in a sharp breath. "I do not think that wise—"

"I do not care for wisdom!" Angel gave a dismissive snap of her finger and thumb before running lightly across the room to throw herself into Alexander's arms. "I should so like you to stay with me tonight, Xander." She stood on tiptoe to kiss his firmly chiseled lips. Small, lightly biting kisses. "You are so very handsome. So strong and virile. Will you not stay with me, Xander? Hold me? Make love with me?"

Alexander put his hands on Angelina's arms, with every intention of holding her away from him, but instead he found himself once more unable to resist the pull of her sensuality as he drew her close, before lowering his head once again and capturing her mouth with his.

Not a soft or gentle kiss, either, but that of a man who deeply desired the woman whose body was pressed so intimately against his own, the throbbing of Alexander's body increasing to an almost painful degree as Angelina rubbed herself sensuously against the hardened length of his erection.

If he wasn't careful, this young woman was going to drive him out of his wits!

Alexander wrenched his mouth from hers, his eyes dark and stormy as he pushed her away once more. "You must get to bed now. Alone!" he added quickly when he saw her face light up expectantly. "We will talk again in the morning." He marched forcefully from the bedroom to close the door firmly behind him.

Angelina was not at all perturbed by Alexander's abrupt departure. No, she was not perturbed at all. Alexander St. Claire was everything and more that she could ever have wished for in the man who was to be her protector.

So much so that Angelina believed her heart may already have forgotten Miss Bristow's warning as to the wisdom of falling in love with one's protector....

CHAPTER FOUR

"Is it not a glorious day, Xander!" Angelina prompted brightly the following morning as she breezed into his bedchamber shortly after nine o'clock.

There was a stirring beneath the bedcovers. "What the—!"

"But, of course, you cannot see how beautiful a day it is when your curtains are still drawn." She crossed to the windows and pulled back both sets of curtains to allow in the bright sunlight. "There." Turning back to the bed, she smiled warmly at Alexander as he attempted to sit up against the pillows.

The long darkness of his hair was endearingly ruffled from sleep, the deep brown of his eyes slightly unfocused and his face harshly beautiful in the sunlight. The bareness of his chest, with its light covering of dark hair, was also revealed as the bedclothes fell down to his muscled stomach when he sat up abruptly. Making Angelina curious as to whether Alexander might not be completely naked under the bedcovers...

"Good morning, Xander," she greeted huskily as she crossed quickly to the bed to sit down beside him.

"Exactly what time of morning is it?" Alexander's initial confusion with this intrusion into his bedchamber was fast evaporating as he recognized that intruder.

"It is a little after nine o'clock, I believe—"

"Nine o'clock!" he repeated thunderously. "What do you mean by waking me at this time? What do you mean by entering my bedchamber at all uninvited?" he added harshly. "Damn it, Angelina—"

"Angel," she reminded.

He scowled darkly as he omitted to call her anything. "You should not enter a gentleman's bedchamber in this brazen manner, let alone at this ungodly hour!"

She gave him another enigmatic smile. "You are scowling again, Xander."

"Of course I am scowling!" he snapped impatiently. "I have been woken before it is even daylight by a young lady who— Good God, what is it that you are almost wearing?" He had been admiring the long fall of her unconfined golden curls when she suddenly flicked her hair back over the slenderness of her shoulders and he instead noted her attire. Or lack of it!

"Do you like them?" Angelina stood to give an obviously excited twirl so that she might show off her nightgown and robe.

Did Alexander like them? A certain part of his anatomy certainly appreciated the cream-colored garments, most especially the way the already sheer material was made almost transparent by the sun shining behind and through it. Attire surely more suited to a brothel than a bedchamber?

More importantly, to Alexander's bedchamber! "Where did you get them?" he grated through clenched teeth as he held the bedcovers firmly over the swell of his arousal. This young woman was surely going to be the death of him—no doubt from the repeated and frustrated battering his self-control had suffered since she appeared so suddenly in his life the evening before!

Angelina appeared undaunted. "Miss Bristow accompanied me into Brighton and helped me choose them." She beamed happily.

Miss Bristow again!

Alexander was fast coming to the conclusion that he wished to ring Miss Bristow's overly instructive neck!

It was she who was responsible for Angelina's lack of inhibition, and for the low neckline of Angelina's gown and robe as it revealed the half-exposed pertness of her breasts above a slender waist and curvaceous thighs.

Alexander felt himself throb anew as he imagined parting those slender thighs to his avid gaze, his caressing hands, before pleasuring her with his lips and tongue until she screamed—

No, damn it, no!

Angelina was already under the mistaken impression that Alexander intended making her his mistress. If he were to seduce her, as the increasing ache of his penis told him he was so longing to do, then he knew he would be well and truly lost, totally enslaved by her beguiling loveliness!

He viewed Angelina through narrowed lids. "What sort of woman was this Miss Bristow?" Certainly not a lady, if her teachings to Angelina were anything to go by! What had Hopkins been thinking by placing a sixteen-year-old Angelina in such an establishment? Perhaps, knowing of Angelina's background, the man had mistaken Alexander's eventual intentions toward her.

"Oh, she's a wonderful woman, Xander!" Angelina moved to once again sit beside him on the bed. "Very much a lady."

"A lady!" Alexander repeated scornfully.

"Oh, but she is, Xander." Angelina frowned. "She insisted on teaching 'my young ladies,' as she called us, all the social graces as well as our normal lessons. We had to learn to embroider, paint and play the piano before she would even consider telling us about our own sensuality."

Alexander eyed her warily. "Your own sensuality...?"

Angelina gave a husky laugh. "Miss Bristow saw no reason why a woman should not enjoy the bedding as much as the man, and with that in mind—"

"Enough!" Alexander rasped as he held up a protesting hand.

Angel smiled warmly. "Many of the other girls thought some of the things Miss Bristow explained to us to be quite impossible, but I was sure that the right man—you, Alexander—would be interested in ensuring that I also experienced pleasure in our lovemaking..."

"Stop, Angelina!" Alexander said forcefully, realizing

he would have to attend to having Angelina's disruptive presence removed from St. Claire House as soon as possible. If he did not, he was sorely in danger of giving her that "pleasure" she spoke of so openly!

"Well…perhaps not now," she allowed. "But tonight, once we

have become better reacquainted…? Miss Bristow was at great pains to tell us lovemaking should be a mutual pleasure. Of all the senses. Vision. Touch. Hearing. Smell. As well as taste." She licked her tongue slowly over the firm swell of her bottom lip as she said the latter.

Alexander found his gaze mesmerized by the eroticism of her tongue's movement, in that moment easily able to imagine Angelina lowering her head to caress his erection in the same way…

Dear God, he ached intolerably just thinking of Angelina doing such things with him!

"Cease and desist, Angelina!" he muttered agitatedly. "And kindly remove yourself from my bedchamber at once. As I am now fully awake I may as well take my bath." He glared at her.

She stood slowly, the sunlight once again making the material of her nightgown and robe transparent. "Perhaps I might help you with your bath, Xander, and we could become better acquainted in that way? I could wash your back and chest and—other things…" She threw back the bedclothes to fully expose the length of his erection to her avid gaze as she reached out and touched him.

Alexander found the strength to push her hand away and pull the bedclothes back over himself. "As soon as I

am dressed I am going to soundly spank your bottom!"
he warned thunderously.

"Really?" Angelina's eyes widened with interest. "Would
it not be better if we were both to remain undressed when
you did that, Xander? Miss Bristow said that a little pain
during lovemaking—only a little, you understand?—can
heighten the senses and—"

"I believe Miss Bristow has said altogether too much!"
He gave another aching groan.

Angel looked at him with concern. "Are you in pain,
Xander? Can I do anything to help?"

'Xander' was in great pain! He was also in danger of
completely embarrassing himself as visions of putting
Angelina over his knee and spanking the bareness of her
bottom threatened to tip him over the edge!

"My only need is for privacy, Angelina," he declared
gruffly. "Now!" he added with firm emphasis.

"As you wish, Xander." And, as she had the night before,
Angelina pouted her disappointment before turning and
slowly walking to the door.

CHAPTER FIVE

"HAS IT NOT BEEN A happy day, Xander?" Angelina beamed across the small table at him as they dined alone together that evening.

Alexander's gaze glowered over the rim of his glass of claret as he grudgingly acknowledged how lovely Angelina looked this evening in a gown of cream silk, with her golden hair curling onto her bare shoulders.

In fact, Alexander had found it a most frustrating day!

For one thing, it was proving far more difficult to relocate Angelina than he had initially thought.

Having promised Hawkins that he would see to Angelina's future, Alexander could not just throw her out into the street to fend for herself. Neither could he send her to a hotel when she had no chaperone.

Instead, he had decided that perhaps his aunt Elizabeth might be persuaded into having the girl—as long as Angelina was cautioned first concerning any attempt on her part to discuss the finer points of her education with his aunt... Alexander had driven Angelina in his carriage to his aunt's house in Grosvenor Square this morning, only to find his aged relative had unhelpfully taken herself off to the country for the day to visit her daughter, and was not expected back to town until much later this evening.

Alexander did not even entertain the idea of sending Angelina back to Brighton to the dubious guardianship of the overinformative Miss Bristow!

Consequently Angelina had now been at St. Claire House with him for almost twenty-four hours, during which time she had more than capably confirmed her claim to be able to deport herself with all the elegance and charm of a lady.

Andrews, Hopkins much younger replacement, had taken one look at Angelina this morning, when she strolled into Alexander's study uninvited, and completely fallen under her spell, rendering the normally reserved young man virtually incapable of fulfilling his secretarial duties.

The household staff were falling over themselves to accommodate her. So much so that their meal this evening had consisted of Angelina's favorite dishes.

All that was needed to complete the bedlam would have been a visit from one of his younger brothers, who no doubt would have become equally smitten with Angelina's beauty and charm. Luckily Alexander had at least been spared that!

Still, despite keeping himself busy, it had hardly been a happy day as far as Alexander was concerned, and dinner alone with Angelina was making his head ache almost as much as another part of his anatomy had once again begun to do the moment he joined her.

"You are looking tense again, Xander," Angel chided softly before rising to her feet. "I shall endeavor to help you feel better."

Alexander could envisage several ways in which his tension might be eased, but he turned to eye her warily as she moved to stand behind him. "What are you doing?"

She smiled. "One of the girls at school suffered from severe headaches and I learned a way in which I might ease them. Just relax, Xander." She turned him firmly to face forward, before placing her hands either side of his head so that her thumbs rested against his temples and her fingers over his brow. "There, does that not feel better?" she prompted huskily as she rested his head back against her breasts so that she might look down into his face as she continued to lightly massage his brow and temples.

Alexander gave a groan as he kept his eyes firmly closed, dark lashes resting against harshly chiseled cheeks, and his mouth thinned in a grim line.

"You really must try to relax, Xander," Angel encouraged soothingly.

How could Alexander possibly relax when the back of his head was nestled between Angelina's breasts?

He could not suffer this torment a moment longer...!

He had watched as Angelina charmed all about her all day. Listened as her tinkling laugh filled his normally austere and quiet household. All the time wishing that her charm was for him alone. Her delicate laugh for his ears only...!

Now, to have her touch him—!

Alexander jerked away from her caressing hands as he stood abruptly to turn and take Angelina in his arms, pulling her fiercely against him as his mouth captured hers in a kiss that owed nothing to gentleness and everything to the wild clamoring need he had to possess her.

Angel felt a thrill of excitement as Alexander pressed her body fiercely against his as his lips claimed hers, her arms moving up so that she could release the ribbon from his hair and entangle her fingers within his thick dark locks.

The initial fire of his hunger satisfied, Alexander began to flick his tongue lightly against her lips before surging hotly inside the heated cavern beneath, Angelina's tongue meeting his in a duel of desire that could have only one outcome.

Her throat arched as Alexander broke the kiss to nuzzle and then bite the sensitive lobes of her ear before trailing his burning lips down the length of her throat to seek the swelling tops of her breasts.

"Oh, yes, Xander…!" she gasped encouragingly as he impatiently pushed aside the material of her gown so that his tongue might meet one roused nipple. "Please, do not stop…!" She moaned as she cradled the back of his head to hold him against her, her knees buckling slightly as Alexander began to suck oh-so-satisfyingly.

"You have far too many clothes on!" he growled disapprovingly as he raised his head slightly, his breath hot against the cool dampness of her breast.

"We both do," she acknowledged breathlessly. "Lock the door, Xander, so that we shall not be disturbed."

"Angelina—" Alexander's protest arrested in his throat as she stepped back to unfasten half a dozen tiny—and conveniently placed—buttons at the back of her gown, before allowing it to slide down her arms to fall onto the carpeted floor.

Any chance Alexander might have had of putting an end to this dangerous situation fled completely as Angelina stood before him dressed only in her almost transparent chemise, which clearly outlined her firm breasts, and white stockings that stopped tantalisingly short of the nestle of dark blond curls now clearly visible between her thighs.

Until the advent of Angelina into his life, Alexander had always prided himself on his self-control, but he would have to be made of marble to be able to withstand the invitation Angelina's seminakedness now represented.

"The door, Xander," she reminded as she reached up to take the pins from her hair. The riotous golden curls fell down to her waist before she slipped the thin straps of her chemise down her arms to bare her lovely breasts and curvaceous hips, as she now wore only those tantalising white stockings held up with garters of blue ribbon the exact color of her eyes.

The darkness of Alexander's gaze remained transfixed on all that wanton loveliness even as he moved to the door to turn the key in the lock.

CHAPTER SIX

THE TURNING OF THAT lock brought Alexander momentarily to his senses and he gave a shake of his head in an effort to clear it of its riotous longings. "Angelina, we cannot…"

"We will not complete the act tonight, if you prefer that we not do so, Xander. It will be enough for now if we give each other pleasure," she promised huskily.

"What—" His second protest ended abruptly as Angelina moved across the distance that separated them to stand in front of him, the warmth of her nakedness, pressed against him from breast to thigh, becoming his complete undoing as he pulled her into him roughly and his lips once again laid siege to hers.

Even as his kisses deepened, his breathing becoming ragged, Angelina reached up to pull his jacket down his arms and loosen the necktie at his throat, before unfastening the top of his shirt and unbuttoning his waistcoat. She then slide it down his arms before pulling his shirt from his breeches and sliding her hands underneath the material so that she might touch the hot, bare flesh of his back and chest.

Alexander groaned low in his throat as Angelina began to move her hands across that muscled heat, the groan turning to a growl as she ran her nails over the hard pebbles of his nipples nestled amongst the darkness of the hair on his chest. She moved her hands lower still as she followed the path of that soft, downy hair to the waistband of his breeches, caressing the hardness there that throbbed and strained against the tightly stretched material.

Alexander wrenched his mouth from hers. "Angel...!"

His first use of the name she preferred made her bolder still as she released the buttons of his breeches to allow all the pulsing hardness to surge powerfully free, and her fingers curled about him.

"Angel—"

"Sit, Xander." Angelina stepped back to urge him in the direction of one of the dining room chairs, before dropping down onto her knees in front of him.

"Angel, I cannot allow you to— Oh, my God...!" Alexander's cry was one of pure ecstasy as he felt the heat of her mouth on him, his fingers clenching the arms of the chair as her tongue circled the tip of his erection.

Alexander's head fell back, his knuckles white as he continued to clutch the arms of the chair, teeth gritted, jaw rigid, as Angelina began to suck.

It was all Alexander could do to keep himself from instantly giving in to his release. Instead, he suffered the agonies of hell for long, timeless minutes as Angelina continued to alternately lick and suck as her hands caressed him.

How he needed...wanted— "Take all of me, Angel! He groaned as he reached down to thread his hands fiercely into her golden curls that draped so erotically across his hips and thighs. As she took the full length of him into the heat of her mouth he began to thrust his hips until he felt his climax surging in an agony of pleasure such as Alexander had never experienced before.

Angelina instantly drew back, having been told the exact moment to cease the ministrations of her lips and tongue. Knowing that a man took time to recover from climax, if she paused now she would be able to reinvigorate him, to bring him to that peak again and again.

"Don't stop, Angel...!" Alexander murmured achingly.

Angelina kissed down his still-pulsing length, enjoying Alexander's groans of pleasure and renewed hardness as her fingers encircled him, and she began to rub rhythmically up and down until she gave him the pleasure he so sought.

Dear God, how she had pleasured him, Alexander thought as he felt the ache in every part of his body from the fierceness of his release.

A release that Angel had still to attain herself.

Alexander pulled her up so that she now stood between his parted thighs, his eyes dark as he gazed upon the firm thrust of her breasts. "I believe it is now my turn to pleasure you, Angel," he drawled in anticipation.

"Yes, please, Xander," she accepted almost shyly.

Alexander's gaze held hers as he moved his mouth onto one bared breast, Angel's hands clinging to the broadness of his shoulders as his tongue stroked across her hardened nipple. One of his hands moved down below the gentle slope of her waist in search of the nub nestled in the softness of her curls and, upon finding it, caressed her rhythmically until she moaned and writhed beneath him.

Angelina's breathing became ragged and uneven, and she parted her legs to give him greater access, allowing him to slide one finger inside her, and then two, as he thrust into her rhythmically, all the while the soft pad of his thumb caressing the hardened, pulsing nub above until she collapsed weakly against him.

Alexander raised his head to look at her as he slowly slid his fingers from inside her. Immediately he knew he wanted to give her that pleasure again.

He grasped her hand in his as he led her over to the rug in front of the unlit fireplace, laying her down upon its softness, before spreading her legs wide so that he might kneel between them. He thought how beautiful she looked as he lowered his head to rasp the heat of his tongue over the still-swollen place between her thighs, and began to rouse her once more.

Angelina cried out as Alexander's hands moved upward, over her stomach, to cup both her breasts, fingers caressing and lightly pinching her nipples as his tongue pressed against with ever-increasing urgency.

She could feel the rising of her second release as the pleasure became almost unbearable and she arched up into him. Her breathing became shallow as that pleasure centered, pooled, at the place Alexander stroked so rhythmically with his tongue. Higher, and still higher, that pleasure rose, until Angelina felt as if she might shatter into a millions pieces.

"Oh, Xander, please," she choked, her fingers becoming entangled in the dark thickness of his hair as she pressed him harder against her. "Please...!"

One of his hands released her breast to once again seek out the throbbing nub hidden in her curls, stroking harder, and then harder still, as his tongue thrust deep inside her, over and over again.

Angel almost sat up as she cried out in ecstasy, her body meeting Alexander's thrusts as her climax flowed through her, before she fell back, her breathing labored and rasping.

Alexander moved slowly up the length of her body to lie beside her, his head against her breast as his hand moved to curve about its twin, fingers lightly teasing the erectness of her nipple.

Alexander found himself thinking of numerous—no, dozens!—of ways in which he wished to make love with and to Angel.Again. And again.

But where? When? Did he make Angel his mistress, after all? No! He could not—would not—do that to this warmly giving and beautiful woman. What to do with her, then? How could he keep her in his life and at the same not be her ruination? What—

"The reality is much more...exciting than the theory, is it not, Xander?" Angel breathed happily at his side. "It was truly a—a wondrous experience!"

He laughed softly, forgetting the future for the moment. Time enough to decide upon that later. For now it was enough that he held this enchanting creature in his arms. "It was indeed," he assured warmly. "In fact, I have become quite taken with the teachings of your Miss Bristow!"

"Did I do everything correctly, Xander?" Angelina prompted softly.

"Everything!" he assured her with a self-derisive chuckle, as he recalled how completely he had been undone as Angel had kissed and caressed him with her own unique blend of innocence and seduction.

Angelina's face glowed, her eyes shining with emotion. "I am so very glad that I pleased you, Xander."

If Alexander had been any more "pleased" he may have expired completely! As it was, he still could not believe the intimacies he had shared with this young lady. He had never, ever allowed himself release in a woman's mouth before. He had not "allowed" it this time, either, he recalled ruefully; his arousal, the excitement of Angel's mouth and hands upon him, had been such that he had simply been unable to prevent it!

Still, indulging in such licentious behavior in his own home had been both rash and impulsive. Anyone might have found them together—

"Stourbridge!" The loud and imperious barking of his name reverberated through the house.

"Oh, God, no...!" Alexander gasped in protest as he turned to stare toward the locked dining room door.

"What is it?" Angelina looked up at him in concern.

"Not what, Angel, but who!" Alexander corrected

harshly as he rose hastily to his feet and began to pull on his clothes.

"Who, then?" Angelina prompted as she less hurriedly got to her feet.

He fastened his breeches before answering her. "It would seem that my aunt Elizabeth has indeed returned to town and decided to pay me a visit...!"

CHAPTER SEVEN

"SIT UP STRAIGHT AND do not fidget, Angelina." Lady Elizabeth Montague instructed brusquely but not unkindly as the two women sat together in the elegance of her town house drawing room, awaiting the arrival of afternoon visitors.

Angel instantly stilled in rearranging the folds of her cream gown, still somewhat at a loss to know how it was she came to be in residence at Lady Montague's home at all.

The elderly lady had swept into the dining room at St. Claire House the evening before, having been informed by not one acquaintance but several that the Duke of Stourbridge had been seen in his carriage that very morning with a young, unmarried female at his side. An occurrence that she had felt the need to look into personally. "Being seen with a female and having that female stay in his home unaccompanied," Alexander had been informed disgustedly, "were two completely different things!"

Having taken in the intimacy of their situation at a glance—how could she not when Alexander had only had time to hastily don his shirt and breeches, and Angelina's own appearance showed signs of their lovemaking in the untidiness of her hair and lips swollen from the force of Alexander's kisses!—she had ordered Angelina to collect her things immediately as she would be returning home with her instantly.

Such had been the older woman's force of will that Angelina had felt compelled to comply with the instruction. Quite what had taken place between aunt and nephew in her absence Angelina had no idea, but when she returned down the stairs, her appearance suitably tidied and her belongings duly repacked into her trunk, she had found Alexander to be in complete agreement with his aunt's arrangements.

Angelina had personally received no word of rebuke from that lady, either last night or this morning, Lady Montague seeming to attribute any and all blame, for the intimacy of the situation she had so obviously interrupted, to her nephew.

Something Angelina knew she must now correct. "Lady Montague, I feel I must tell you—"

"I would rather you did not, my dear," the older woman assured her hastily. "I saw enough yesterday evening to know the way things are between you and Stourbridge," she added kindly. "The sooner the two of you are married the happier I shall be!"

Angelina's eyes widened in alarm. "Oh, but—"

"The Duke of Stourbridge, my lady," the butler announced

while standing in the doorway, only seconds before Alexander himself strode forcefully into the room.

Angelina was only vaguely aware of the butler withdrawing and closing the door behind him, her attention all on Alexander as he crossed the room to bend and place a kiss upon one of his aunt's powdered cheeks. He looked every inch the haughty duke this afternoon, his hair tied back meticulously, his dark blue jacket and paler blue waistcoat impeccably tailored above cream silk breeches.

At last, Alexander turned to look at Angelina, frowning darkly as her lashes instantly fanned down onto the paleness of her cheeks and so hiding her expressive blue eyes from his gaze.

"What have you been saying to Angel in order to cause this uncharacteristic demureness, Aunt?" he drawled ruefully, his gaze unrepentant as Angelina's lashes rose instantly so that she might give him a censorious frown for his levity in the midst of a situation that was obviously causing his aunt some distress.

"I am afraid that your aunt is under the misapprehension that the two of us are to be married, Your Grace," she informed him worriedly.

"Indeed." He gave an inclination of his head.

"Yes," Angelina confirmed breathlessly. "When you arrived I was just about to inform Lady Montague that I am intended as your mistress and not your wife!"

"Stourbridge!" his aunt prompted in alarm at the same moment as Alexander gave an uncontrolled shout of laughter. "I fail to see anything in the least amusing in this situation!" she admonished severely.

Alexander smiled ruefully. "That is because you are you and not me, Aunt."

She looked scandalized. "Stourbridge—"

"Aunt Elizabeth—" he sobered, his narrowed gaze still fixed intently on the beautiful vision Angelina made in her cream gown "—would you be so kind as to allow Angel and I a few minutes alone in which we might converse privately?"

"Very well. But a few minutes only," his aunt warned sternly as she rose majestically to her feet. "I am expecting dozens of visitors this afternoon, all of them anxious to meet and gaze upon the young lady who has succeeded in capturing the elusive Duke of Stourbridge's heart!"

Angelina waited only long enough for the elderly lady to leave the room before rising sharply to her feet, her expression one of alarm as she beseeched. "Xander, you must put a stop to this instantly!"

"Must I?" he drawled mockingly.

"But of course you must!" Angelina chided impatiently. "Your aunt is under the misapprehension that the two of us are to be married. You must go to her and tell her the truth. That I am to be your mistress—"

"I have always found it wiser by far never to lie to my aunt Elizabeth," he assured softly.

"But you would not be lying in this instance— What on earth do you mean, Xander...?" Angelina now eyed him guardedly.

Alexander's eyes glowed as he looked across at her. As he took in the glorious gold of her hair. The pale beauty of her face. The depth of her blue eyes, the sprinkling of freckles upon her tiny nose and the full and sensuous curve of her lips. As for the fullness of her breasts...!She really was the most exquisite creature.

St. Claire House, the place Alexander had called home all of his adult life, where he had always been perfectly at his ease, had seemed empty and cold today without Angelina's warmth and laughter in it. All of which had told Alexander exactly what his future relationship with Angelina must—had—to be!

He drew in a ragged breath. "I mean, my dear Angel, that it is my intention to marry you at the earliest opportunity."

She gasped. "Xander, you cannot possibly mean to marry me simply because your aunt expects it of you!"

He gave a pained wince. "I do not recall ever saying that was my reason for marrying you."

"But of course it is the reason—"

"You claim to know my thoughts and emotions so well, then?" he mused.

Angelina frowned her consternation with his behavior. "Of course I do not," she assured agitatedly. "But I have been...tutored, groomed, these past three years for the role of your mistress—"

"Not at my bidding, I do most fervently assure you!" he rasped. "Not that I am complaining, you understand?" he added gently as Angelina recoiled at his vehemence. "On the contrary—to date I have found your...tutorage more satisfying than anything I have ever before experienced. So much so, that after only a few hours of being apart from you, I find I wish to repeat it every day—and night—for the rest of my life."

Angelina gave a confused frown. "I fear you must explain yourself better than that, Alexander."

"You have only been with my aunt Elizabeth a matter of hours and already you are starting to sound like her!" His smile was rueful. "Yes, my dear Angel, I have no doubts whatsoever that you will make a formidable Duchess of Stourbridge," he added appreciatively.

"Duchess—!" she gasped."I— What on earth are you doing, Xander?" she protested as he fell to one knee in front of her.

His eyes glowed darkly gold as he looked up at her. "I believe, Angel, that I am endeavoring to propose to you. If you would be so kind as to allow me to proceed…?"

CHAPTER EIGHT

"PLEASE RISE AND cease this nonsense at once, Alexander," Angelina told him anxiously.

Not quite the response Alexander had been hoping for to his first attempt at a marriage proposal. His last, too, he hoped! "I assure you it is not nonsense, Angel," he said gruffly, making no effort to stand. "It is perhaps a little soon in our acquaintance for you to know the state of your own heart—"

"Soon? Soon!" Angelina repeated incredulously. "We have known each other but two and a half days, Alexander."

He raised dark, slanted brows. "During which time we have come to know each other as well, I believe, if not better, than most betrothed couples of the ton do on their wedding days!"

"Oh, please do get up!" Angelina clasped his arm and attempted to pull him to his feet. Unsuccessfully. "You must rise, Xander! What will your aunt think if she comes back into the room and sees you like this?" She shot a nervous glance toward the closed door. "I do not know her terribly well as yet, but I am sure she would not think it at all the thing for the Duke of Stourbridge to be down on his knees in this undignified manner!"

Alexander tried to hold back his amusement—he really did try—but in the end he failed miserably as a bark of laughter broke free, and then another, followed by yet another.

Angelina stared down at him incredulously. "Xander, have you completely taken leave of your senses?"

"Probably." He sobered slightly, although he could not seem to prevent the smile that still curved his lips. Something he found he did all too easily when he was in Angelina's company. "Do you have any idea how adorable you are, Angel? How utterly, utterly unique?"

Angelina ceased trying to force him to his feet to instead stare down at him in wary—if hopeful!—disbelief. Hopeful, because she was very much afraid she had forgotten Miss Bristow's warning completely and fallen in love with the haughty and aristocratic Duke of Stourbridge the moment he walked into that cavernous hallway two evenings ago and demanded to know what she was about, interrupting his dinner party! And she was very sure that she had fallen in love with the Alexander with whom she had made love with and to the evening before!

Could Alexander really be serious in this marriage proposal? Surely he could not, she instantly rebuked herself. A duke did not marry the daughter of a—a—

"My mother was an actress and a mistress of my father," she announced with a challenging rise of her chin.

"I am well aware of the fact." Alexander gave an inclination of his head as he finally rose slowly to his feet and took both of her hands into his own. "Your father, until his death, was one of my closest friends."

Angelina swallowed hard at this mention of the dear and kind man whom had visited her often whilst he was alive. "He was not married to my mother."

"No," Alexander acknowledged softly. "He was unfortunately married very young, an arranged marriage to a cousin, I believe, and so was not free to marry your mother when he met her several years after that marriage had taken place."

"He would have married my mother if he had been free," Angel protested fiercely.

"Again, I am well aware of the fact," Alexander assured her gently. "Angel, your family history is of little matter to me—"

"How can you say such a thing?" she gasped incredulously.

"Quite easily—when it is the truth. I admit, sending you to a school, where you were tutored in subjects most young ladies are never fully made aware of, does not give that impression but...Angel, I had no idea, until you informed me of it two days ago, that you had attended such an academy." His expression was grim. "I had been the duke only a matter of months at the time of your father's death, and he made his request to me to see that you were not left alone and destitute now that both your parents were dead. In my preoccupation with my new duties, I foolishly left the details of your education to my then man of business. Obviously I was not clear enough as to my wishes in the matter." He scowled.

Angelina's eyes were wide. "It was never your wish that I be—be schooled to become your mistress?"

"Certainly not! At least..." His hands tightened about hers. "Angel, it is now my dearest wish that you do indeed become my mistress—but only if you will first become my wife."

She gave a quizzical frown. "You wish me to be your mistress, as well as your wife...?"

He smiled roguishly. "In the usual way of the ton, I believe I would be expected to first take a wife and then a mistress. But in you, my darling Angel, I have found both those things in one saucily seductive woman. Of course, it also helps that I love and adore you," he added matter-of-factly.

Angelina's eyes became even wider. "You love and adore me...?"

"To distraction," Alexander confirmed decidedly. "From the moment I first looked at you, it would seem," he added self-derisively. "I had not realized how empty my home was until after you had left it yesterday evening, Angel. How soulless. You have brought joy and warmth into my life, into my very household, in a way I had never imagined." His eyes glittered darkly.

"I have...?"

He gave a rueful nod of his head. "All these years, I have thought my inability to love to be some defect in my character. That there must be a blank space where my heart should be. After you left yesterday evening, I discovered I do have a heart, after all. And that, with your going, you had taken it with you. I do love you so very much, Angel. Do you think you might ever come to love me in return?"

"Miss Bristow advised against any of us falling in love with our protectors—"

"And, in the normal course of things, Miss Bristow was wise to issue such a warning." He nodded abruptly. "But it is my dearest wish to become your husband, Angel, and not your protector. A husband you will hopefully come to love as dearly as he already loves you."

She shook her head. "It is too late for that, Xander—"

"Never say that, Angel!" He groaned. "I will wait to make love to you again until you feel the same way about me, I swear. I will court you. Shower you with diamonds. Angel, I cannot bear it if you do not one day come to love me in the same way that I already love you—"

"By all means, court me and shower me with diamonds if you feel you must, darling Xander," she acknowledged happily. "But abstinence from our lovemaking is going too far!"

His expression softened slightly. "Then I will make love to and with you day and night until you fall in love with me," he vowed fiercely.

"Make love to me day and night by all means, my darling, but when I said it was already too late to hope that I might one day come to love you, I simply meant it was too late because I already do love you! From that very first moment, too, I believe," Angelina assured softly. "I had not expected the Duke of Stourbridge to be so young. So tall. Or so arrogantly, wonderfully handsome. His features and body so—so incredibly and magnificently formed! Or his lovemaking ecstasy beyond my wildest dreams! I already love you so very much, Xander," she repeated quietly.

"My darling!" Joy lit up the previously austere lines of Alexander's face.

Angelina placed her hands upon his chest as he would have taken her in his arms. "Xander, a duke cannot marry the daughter of a woman who was both an—an actress and a—"

"This duke can certainly marry whom he damn well pleases!" he stated with all the arrogance of that duke, his expression once again softening as he saw how apprehensive his beloved still looked. "Please say you will marry me, Angel. I cannot bear even the thought of living another day without knowing you are to be mine forever!" he admitted gruffly.

Could she? Could Angelina Hawkins, the illegitimate daughter of an actress and a lord, really marry a duke? No, that was not the question. The question was, how could she not marry Alexander, duke or otherwise, when he asked her, when he proclaimed his love for her, when he said he adored her and could not bear to live without her?

Her eyes glowed and her cheeks felt warm. "I do love you so very much, Xander."

"And…?"

She smiled up at him lovingly. "And I did so enjoy our lovemaking yesterday evening."

His eyes glittered with the same remembered enjoyment. "And…?"

"And if you are really sure that you want me—"

"Angel, I have never been surer of anything in my so-far jaded existence!" he vowed fiercely.

"Then, my love, my darling Xander, I wholeheartedly accept your proposal of marriage!"

"Angel!" Alexander drew her into his arms and pulled her down onto the chaise beside him before his mouth claimed hers.

"Your aunt…?" Angelina reminded worriedly as those kisses threatened to spiral into another bout of lovemaking.

Alexander stood to cross the room and turn the key in the lock. "Has plenty of other salons in which she might receive her afternoon guests," he assured dismissively as he returned to her side.

Clothes were discarded. Murmurs and ecstatic sighs followed. A gasp as Alexander thrust into Angel to claim her. A soft and muffled scream minutes later as Angel's pleasure reached its satisfying peak. Quickly followed by Alexander's own achingly ecstatic groans as those inner quakes and spasms caused him to spill himself deep inside her.

"I believe Hawk to be a fitting name for our first son," Angel murmured sometime later as she lay still naked and deeply sated in Alexander's arms. "In order that my own name is not lost completely."

"Whatever you wish, my darl— First son?" Alexander echoed as he sat up slightly in order that he might look down at her. "How many sons are you planning on giving me?" he prompted indulgently, knowing that he could deny this woman nothing. That she did, indeed, hold the whole of his heart in her tiny hands.

"Oh, at least two, possibly three," his Angel assured him lightly.

"As long as we also have a daughter, or two, with your beauty, golden curls and determined nature," Alexander murmured with satisfaction. "Although I think I would prefer that they not attend Miss Bristow's school in Brighton!" he added dryly.

"I have so far heard no complaints from you concerning my own tutelage," Angelina teased huskily.

"And neither will you," Alexander assured warmly. "In fact, I am already looking forward to sharing the revelations of your next lesson!"

Angelina laughed softly. "We have only just begun, my darling," she promised warmly.

Alexander gazed down at her adoringly, utterly sure of his love for this warm and wonderful woman. Knowing that, with her, each day together would be a joy, each night a revelation, to be savored and cherished for as long as the two of them lived....

* * * * *

The Rake's
Intimate Encounter

ANN LETHBRIDGE

Ann Lethbridge has been reading Regency novels for as long as she can remember. She always imagined herself as Lizzie Bennet or one of Georgette Heyer's heroines and would often recreate the stories in her head with different outcomes or scenes. When she sat down to write her own novel, it was no wonder that she returned to her first love: the Regency.

Ann grew up roaming England with her military father. Her family lived in many towns and villages across the country, from the Outer Hebrides to Hampshire. She spent many memorable family holidays in the West Country and in Dover, where her father was born. She now lives in Canada, with her husband, two beautiful daughters and a Maltese terrier named Teaser, who spends his days on a chair beside the computer, making sure she doesn't slack off.

Ann visits Britain every year, to undertake research and also to visit family members who are very understanding about her need to poke around old buildings and visit every antiquity within a hundred miles.

I dedicate this book to my husband,
who is my inspiration

Author's Note

Margaret and Tony knew exactly what they wanted when they met and it certainly wasn't each other. Thank goodness for Lady Falstow! I do hope you enjoyed a peek at the beginning of Tony and Margaret's romance and our brief meeting with the Evernden brothers who appeared in my 2009 Mills & Boon® Historical romance, *The Rake's Inherited Courtesan*. All of my characters become close friends, so I am pleased to be able to invite you to sit down, have a cup of coffee, tea or juice and get to know them.

I love to hear from readers, so please visit me at my website: www.annlethbridge.com, where you can find all my latest news and where you can reach me directly.

CHAPTER ONE

London, 1815

BRUNETTES, BLONDES and even a redhead displayed their mouthwatering attributes while they handled the cards at the green baize-covered tables with the dexterity of Captain Sharps. Tony Darby sauntered ahead of the Evernden brothers into what had once been a ballroom. At each table, fashionable gentlemen leered at their scantily clad banker, or stared at their cards.

Piquet. Whist. Vingt-et-un. Women. All the usual pastimes. Tony sighed as ennui swept through him and then turned to his companions. "This is why you dragged me all the way to Hampstead, Stanford? A gambling hell in a brothel?"

"Indeed," the fair haired and usually cheerful Christopher Evernden said with a grimace. "You've got a lot to answer for, Garth."

On the other side of Tony, Christopher's brother, Lord

Stanford, grinned, his dark eyes unrepentant. "Lady Falstow will have your head if she hears the word 'brothel' in her establishment. The women here are looking for amusement, not money."

"Good Lord," Christopher said. "Is that Lady—"

"No names," Garth murmured. "In this club, discretion is the watchword. One wrong word and we will never darken these hallowed portals again. Look at them. It's a banquet of female desires."

Following the direction of Christopher's stunned gaze, Tony recognized one of London's foremost hostesses, known for her sumptuous dinners and witty conversation. Tonight, the blonde wore a carnivorous expression and a gown diaphanous enough to shame a courtesan.

She caught his glance. Her gaze ran down his length, obvious and assessing. Clearly liking what she saw, she beckoned.

Tony stifled the urge to flee and pretended he hadn't noticed.

Christopher groaned. "I have no interest in playing stud for some bored hausfrau. You promised piquet in interesting surroundings."

"Can it get more interesting than this?" Garth asked. "Look at them. They'll rip your clothes off, they're so desperate."

"The next time I go to White's I don't want to shake some fellow's hand knowing I tupped his wife," Tony said, speaking from an experience that still gave him nightmares.

"Nor me," Christopher said.

"You do the ladies no favors," Garth said. "They are here because their husbands don't give a damn whether they are happy or not." Strangely enough, the usually insouciant Garth sounded rather grim. "And besides, many of them are lonely widows."

"I don't have the ready to set up an indigent widow with a host of hungry mouths to feed," Tony said. Tomorrow morning he had an appointment to view a property, which, if he decided to purchase, would empty his pockets.

"I thought you came into some money," Christopher said.

"Gone." He wasn't going to let the cat out of the bag and let them ridicule his decision to give up a life of idleness. Not until he made a success of it. "If you want gambling and a prime article on each arm, I know a great little hell in the Seven Dials—no limit on play and no commitment."

"Such gratitude," Garth muttered. "I invite you to London's most exclusive club and you prefer Haymarket ware. Do as you please. I have someone waiting upstairs, and I never disappoint a lady."

"Who the hell are you tangled up with now?" Christopher said with a frown. "You'll find yourself on Primrose Hill with a bullet lodged somewhere in your person."

"Nor do I bandy about a lady's name." Garth stalked off down the hall, the slight stagger an indication of the quantity of brandy he'd consumed on the drive over.

Tony smothered a yawn. Garth's legendary exploits among the ton's females had palled long ago. "Let's leave."

Christopher expelled an impatient breath. "I'll wait for

him. He'll no doubt be too foxed by the end of the night to get home in one piece. Join me in a game of whist?" He gestured to a nearby table with three men and a pile of tokens waiting for a winner. "At least it presents a challenge."

"I pity the woman who holds the bank at your table," Tony said.

Christopher laughed. "It's a game of chance. I simply count better than most."

The blonde holding the bank had a lovely face and hard calculating eyes. The kind of woman Tony had found appealing when he first made his bows. "You know, I think I'll wander about for a bit."

"See if anyone strikes your fancy?" Christopher said, his eyes twinkling.

"See if they have any food. I haven't eaten for hours."

Christopher raised a brow. "*Bon appétit.* He headed for his chosen victim and Tony spared a second's worth of pity on those about to lose their money to his friend's mathematical acumen.

He strolled down the hall and peered into a library lined with books and occupied by a couple sprawled on a couch. The next open door revealed a drawing room. No food there either. A young dandy, perhaps no more than twenty, knelt at the feet of a gorgeous creature in a red gown cut low across a magnificent bosom. The severe smoothed-back style of her dark-brown hair emphasized her prominent cheekbones and, along with her almond-shaped eyes, gave her face an exotic look. The boy seemed to be sobbing, while the striking brunette patted his shoulder.

Tony started to back away, but she raised her head and their gazes met. She rolled her eyes heavenward with rueful smile of full lips and a glimmer of laughter in her dark eyes. An instant of connection, yet he was sure he'd never met her before. One thing he knew for certain, her melting brown eyes contained a cry for help. He bowed. "May I be of assistance?"

The boy raised his head. "She won't have me."

"I didn't mean you, you puppy," Tony said. "Madam, may I remove this watering pot?"

The young man sat up then, and fumbled in his pocket.

The woman handed him a scrap of lace. "Use this, Radcliffe. A man with puffy eyes and a red nose is rarely taken with any degree of seriousness."

"A red nose?" The boy sprung from the couch and ran to the mirror between the two tall windows overlooking the square. "'Pon rep. You are right." He dabbed at the offending aristocratic proboscis.

The blatant sensuality of the woman's smile, as she watched the lad, held Tony captive. No wonder she had the youth on his knees at her feet. And her breasts? Well, they were magnificent. Glorious mounds of pale, soft flesh. He didn't need another glance for confirmation. Didn't care to look, because her smile intimated she'd discovered life's greatest jest and hinted that if the right person found the key, she might share the joke. He wanted that key.

"Vanity," she said, with a mock shake of her head at the lad. "It does wonders for a broken heart. I recommend cold water at once."

Radcliffe spun around. "Cold water, madam? Will it not make it worse?"

She laughed, a throaty chuckle with a pulse-quickening effect. *Had he lost his mind?*

"Not at all," she said. "Take the word of someone who has cried many tears." She turned her amazingly liquid eyes on Tony. "Don't you agree, sir?"

Tony smothered a smile as the young man paled. "Without a doubt. As one who has been the cause of many tears."

The woman laughed outright. More heat to his blood. Good God, he'd never met a woman who so instantly aroused his interest. *Aroused.* An unfortunate word, with hardening results.

"Countess, you will forgive me if I go in search of cold water?" Radcliffe asked, returning to stand in front of her, much like a lad before a governess. "I will return. Then you will listen to me."

"Try some ice," Tony said. "I suggest you use it elsewhere on your anatomy. Cool your ardor. Can't you see you are bothering the countess?"

"Am I, Countess?" Radcliffe asked with a boyish smile. Tony wanted to punch him in the mouth.

The woman smiled. "Darling boy, I am old enough to be your mother. Now run along and find a nice young girl of your own age."

Radcliffe pouted. "You are not old enough to be my mother. She is ancient. And girls my age are dull."

The boy needed a lesson in manners. Tony took a half step into the room. "The lady is being polite to protect your manly pride. I, on the other hand, have no such scruples.

If you don't leave now, you might find your nose a deeper shade of scarlet."

The countess's handkerchief held to his nose, Radcliff scuttled from the room.

The countess sighed. "I made a mistake in letting him speak to me alone. I had intended to let him down gently and instead, seemed to have raised his hopes. The dashing of them was hard, I think."

"I apologize for my countryman, Countess."

"Oh *la,* sir. No need for that. I'm as English as plum pudding, born and raised. "

Not plum pudding. Perhaps baked apple with cinnamon or a succulent lemon curd, or a rich honey cake. He pulled back from the images and smiled. "I did wonder, given your lack of accent. I'm sorry, I should have introduced myself. Anthony Darby, at your service." He bowed and as he rose, raised a brow in question. "Countess...?"

She inclined her head and held out her hand. "My deceased husband was a Russian count. I am recently returned to England. I was beginning to think I would require the help of a servant to release me from the poor boy's clutches. Thank you for your timely intervention."

A widow and thus available. Something feral and hungry sharpened its claws in Tony's gut even as he noticed she had not supplied her name. Damnation, he was mad, because instead of bidding her farewell, he took her hand and pressed his lips to the filmy lace covering her fingers.

The view of creamy breasts rising from plush red velvet, and the shadows in their valley sucked the breath from his chest. Even so, he inhaled the subtle fragrance of lavender.

"The pleasure is all mine." He was surprised at the low growl in his voice

She tilted her head, a flicker of amber in warm brown eyes. Interest. Perhaps even challenge. Definitely not fear.

She withdrew her fingers slowly, lingeringly.

He regretted the loss. "I was looking for something to eat. May I escort you to the dining room?" He blasted well hoped food was laid out somewhere, because he needed something to counteract his light-headedness.

"Why not?" she said, rising.

Only then, did the full glory of her figure reveal itself. Full bosomed, tall for a woman—almost his height in fact—and with long, elegant limbs, she embodied each and every aspect of female charm he preferred.

Perhaps he wasn't in such a hurry to depart, after all. Dash it. Hadn't he said less than five minutes ago that he didn't want any commitments? He held out his arm.

Margaret put her hand on the sleeve of the man holding out his arm with élan, felt muscle and sinew beneath the dark blue superfine coat as they walked. An athletic man, as lithe and sleek as a racehorse. Quite beautiful, in fact. Unlike the bear-like Russians to whom she'd become accustomed, this man oozed finesse. And he was tall. Lovely and tall.

She studied his profile. Handsome in that narrow-faced, rather vulnerable English way, he'd looked too young at first glance. On closer inspection, the cynical mouth and the world-weary silver-gray eyes marked him as older. Around her age, or a little older, some thirty summers, she guessed. He glanced at her, caught her staring. The flicker of heat in the depths of his steely gaze had the same effect as too many glasses of champagne on her blood. A dizzy sort of breathlessness.

"I don't suppose you know where we might find supper?" he asked with a heart-stopping smile, his deep voice hinting at seduction. The dark, wicked places in her body responded with a delicious thrill. This man positively created havoc on her senses.

"Aah," she said, indicating the direction. "This is your first visit to Lady Falstow's infamous establishment."

He inclined his head in acknowledgement. "But not yours?"

"No indeed." In a rash moment of utter abandon, she bit back the information that her only previous visit was for afternoon tea. After all, such an admission would weaken the armor of scarlet gown and carefully constructed air of confidence. After five minutes alone with young Radcliffe, she'd decided her wild flight of fancy to experience a little danger, to savor some of the joys she'd missed these past many years, wasn't really her cup of tea. Now she was wondering if perhaps this man could change her mind. It was a long time since her heart had fluttered, and right now it beat within her chest like a caged wild bird. A heady and youthful sensation she'd almost forgotten.

"This must be it," Darby said, ushering her into a room at the back of the house. A table set with epergnes and covered dishes lined the wall opposite the door. Artfully scattered small round tables allowed for groups of guests to talk, while equally tasteful screens permitted an element of privacy for those who wished it.

Margaret tensed at the sight of an inebriated noble plying his female companion with champagne. Couples and groups also occupied some of the other tables. An army of burly footmen hovered throughout the cream and gold painted room ready to intercede, as her ladyship had promised, should matters get out of hand. Margaret wasn't ready for this. She wished they'd remained in the drawing room's seclusion.

Their hostess, a gargantuan figure in a gown of gold tissue, and shimmering with diamonds, circulated among her guests, her plump face beaming, her be-ringed hands gesturing volubly. She surged towards them in a tidal wave of hastily moved chairs. "There you are," she cried. "I heard you'd gone off with young Radcliffe. I was about to send Peter—" she gestured vaguely at one of her minions "—to see if you were all right."

A rush of warmth filled Margaret. It had been a long time since anyone cared about her comfort. "Thank you. As you can see, I am quite rescued already."

Lady Falstow turned her gaze on Margaret's escort. "Darby, isn't it?"

He bowed. "Good evening, my lady. I regret I did not see you when I first arrived."

"Came with the Everndens, did you not? The youngest brother is going to ruin me."

"I hope not, my lady." Darby grimaced as his gaze swept the room. "You have a full house tonight?"

Apparently, he also did not relish the crowd.

"Looking for a quieter spot, are you?" Lady Falstow tapped Darby on the shoulder. "Tell the fellow at the buffet what you would like, and run along to the conservatory where it is quiet."

A perceptive woman, Lady Falstow. Margaret lowered her lashes, fearing her eagerness to flee the room might show. As Darby headed for the food, she pulled her hostess aside. "What do you know of him?" she asked in low tones.

"A younger son, I think. His friend Stanford's a bit of a rake. Not sure I know much about Darby." She frowned.

"Married?" For some odd reason, Margaret held her breath.

The older woman shrugged. "I don't believe so. I'd have warned you off right away, if that were the case."

Margaret winced. She needed more than a guess and Darby was headed their way with a bottle of champagne tucked under his arm and two flutes held in one large hand.

Lady Falstow leaned closer. "Take my advice. If you want to enjoy him to the full, don't play the innocent." She held out a sliver of metal. "This opens the door to the room I showed you. It is up to you whether you use it." The heavily ringed hand caught Margaret's as she reached for the key. "Courage, lass. If you change your mind, ring the bell. You will find one in every room. A footman will arrive in an instant. I promise, you will be fine. Not one of my ladies has ever complained about their treatment in this house."

Swallowing, Margaret tucked the silver key into her reticule before Darby reached her side.

"Now," he said with a smile sweet enough to make the older lady flutter her eyelashes. "Where is this conservatory?"

Lady Falstow fanned her face as if suddenly hot, sapphires, diamonds and rubies winking and glittering. "At the back of the house. Run along. The food will follow in a moment or two."

They wandered in the direction indicated, and Darby opened an etched-glass panelled door.

Margaret gasped. A glass cathedral met her gaze. The domed structure ran the length of the side of the house. Air, warm and moist and redolent with fragrance, filled her lungs. Orange trees, lemons and limes too, lined the walks among splashes of red, yellow and blue blossoms.

"Look at this," Darby said, indicating a long stem crowned with waxy petals of the palest cream and leopard-like spots. "An orchid. Did you ever see anything so delicate?"

"Beautiful," she whispered.

"Like you," he murmured.

She glanced up to see hunger in his eyes, naked and raw. A surge of heat rushed up from her breasts to her face. *Blushing like a schoolgirl, dash it.* And the color no doubt clearly visible in the light of the torchères strategically placed along the walkway. "*La,* sir, a compliment indeed."

He tilted his head as if puzzled by her coquettish tone. Did he see through her defenses to the rapid beat of her heart? He smiled and waved his bottle. "Let us find somewhere to sit. We can open this and talk."

Further on, they did indeed find a loveseat fashioned from bamboo and wicker, and cushioned with chintz, and set in an arbor of vines.

"How lovely," she said.

"A perfect setting," he replied and led her to the seat. While she settled her skirts, he eased the cork free with a gentle pop. Vapor issued from the neck of the bottle. He filled the glasses, not spilling a drop.

"You do that with great expertise," she said.

"Had lots of practice." He glanced upwards. "I didn't dare shoot the thing though that lot." He grinned with nothing of the cynic about his mouth. Her heart tumbled slowly and pleasurably.

She raised her gaze to the gleaming arch of glass. "Oh, gracious. No indeed."

Their voices mingled in laughter swiftly absorbed by the verdant greenery. A companionable sound. Her stomach clenched. A painful longing within the joy of discovery of a kindred spirit. What would it have been like to marry a man with the ability to laugh? She forced the thought aside. Regret had no place in this evening. Lady Falstow had advised her to live for the moment. After all, she'd paid her full dues as a dutiful wife.

Darby handed her a glass of wine. Their fingers brushed. Little shimmers of something hot ran up her arm. A shiver of anticipation ran across her skin.

The quick uplift of the corners of his lips said he, too, felt the spark. "To your beautiful eyes."

"To your lovely mouth," she replied and drank deeply, the champagne cool and tart on her tongue, the bubbles misting her cheeks and the tip of her nose.

"My lovely mouth?" He raised a brow and leaned back against the cushion, his eyelids lowering a fraction as if to hide the heat in his gaze. Not possible. She was veritably scorched.

"I like the way it smiles." Oh, lord, one mouthful of wine and she sounded foxed, when in reality it was he who made her feel giddy. Or perhaps it was the perfume of so many flowers? "You must think me a fool, Mr. Darby."

"Please, call me Tony. And no, I find you…delightful. Uniquely charming."

Her heart beat a little faster. Her skin tingled. This was how it began, the dance of intimacy. Words and looks and sighs. Only she wasn't sure she remembered the steps. Still, she would not sit like the proverbial wallflower and let the music pass over her head.

"Tony." She shook her head. "I think I prefer Anthony. And I am Margaret."

He took her free hand in his large warm one. His gaze dropped to her mouth. "Margaret. It suits you."

"Plain and proper is what my father said." She smiled, remembering her beloved father's face.

"I see nothing plain and proper about you, Margaret." His gaze drifted lower, and once more, betraying heat rose up her neck and blazed in her cheeks. "You cast a hothouse of exotic flowers into the shade." He leaned closer and breathed in slowly. "You smell wonderful."

Carried by his soft outward sigh, the words brushed her

collarbone. Her heart picked up speed, a breath caught in her throat, her lips parted. Things were moving far too fast with this man. She knew nothing about him. Yes, she would indeed live for the moment, but only if the moment was right. She sipped at her champagne, using the glass as a shield. A poor one, to be sure, but a symbolic gesture any gentleman would recognize.

He leaned back with a smile, his hand along the back of the sofa, a hairbreadth from her shoulder. "So, you are recently returned from Russia. How did you find it?"

"Cold." She laughed, because she really did not mean the weather. "My husband spent most of his time at court, but in the summer we traveled to his estate. The country is vast and very different from here."

"In a good way, I presume?"

How did one express five years of homesickness without whining? "I learned a great deal about the land and its people, but I am glad to return to England."

Another question lurked in his eyes. She could see him trying to decide whether he should ask it or not. She asked, "What do you want to know?"

He smiled. "Am I really that obvious? I was wondering if you left ties back in Russia. If you will return there?"

"A politic way of wondering if I have children, perhaps? And *no*. I have no ties and no intention of returning. My husband had more than one heir from a previous marriage. His position at court required a hostess. I learned Russian. I can organize a banquet for a thousand people or a tête à tête for two." Why was she telling him all this? He would think she was looking for another wifely position, when nothing could be further from the truth. "My husband left me a comfortable independence, and I now seek my own amusement."

"Was it really that bad?" he murmured.

The gentleness in his voice cut through her carefully constructed defenses, not something she wanted on a night such as this. "You mistake me. It was not bad at all. The Russian court glitters beyond anything imaginable. The czar is all powerful."

"And many of the people are serfs." He pursed his lips. "I don't see how it can last. Look at France."

The man was talking to her as if she had a brain. She shook her head. "You are right. I do not see it lasting either. And nor did my husband. He advised following England's lead. Alas, I do not see anyone taking up his standard. Certainly not his heir."

"I'm so sorry."

"I beg your pardon?"

"For your recent bereavement. It was tactless of me to remind you."

"Ah, once again you mistake the matter. Konrad died more than a year ago. I mourned his passing, but he was not a young man, he lived a full life, and I fulfilled my duty."

He withdrew his hand from the sofa's back and for a moment she thought she might have given him a disgust of her callousness, but he lifted her hand from her lap. He gently turned it over and bared her wrist of glove with his forefinger, then leaned down to brush the pulse point with his lips. Tingles ran across her shoulders and lifted the hairs at the base of neck. "Now it is your turn for life," he said softly.

Footsteps rang on the flagstones. She snatched her hand back. They jumped apart like guilty children. She laughed.

He grinned ruefully. "Dash it. The food."

She arched a brow. "You said you were hungry, Anthony."

"I'm starving," he said. The low growl in his voice did not speak of bread and meat. Her inner muscles tightened pleasurably. She shivered.

The footman coughed loudly, then appeared round the corner carrying on high a silver tray loaded with several small plates. He dragged a small table from concealment behind the trellis and set the tray in front of them. He unfolded the napkins, placed one on each of their laps. "Will there be anything else, sir?"

Anthony eyed the tray. "Thank you, no." The footman withdrew.

He had selected nothing but the best. Oysters nestled in ice, caviar in a silver bowl, mouthwatering frosted grapes, light temptations designed to sharpen the senses. A hedonistic feast.

Anthony picked up an oyster and held it to Margaret's lips. Tipping her head back, she swallowed the delicate flesh, salty and sweet and tangy with lemon. She licked her lips.

He leant forward and tasted the corner of her mouth with a delicate lap of his tongue. "Delicious."

A flutter pulsed between her thighs. Wicked man. "Me or the fish?"

"Both, of course."

She smiled and heaped a tiny water biscuit with a mound of blue-black beads. The finest caviar, all the way from the Black Sea. She knew, because she had ordered it, sent packed in ice. When she raised her gaze from her hands, she found his gaze fixed on her face, intent, hungry and hot.

"Open," she murmured, the thrumming in her veins growing stronger, more demanding.

He did, and his grin was that of a wolf about to be fed a small tender morsel. She popped the tiny cracker in his mouth and watched him chew, experiencing the delightful burst of salty flavor in her mind as his eyes closed in pleasure.

He picked up his wine glass and held it to her lips, watching as she sipped and swallowed, his chest rising and falling with each deep breath.

How did he breathe so evenly, the wretch, when her heart raced out of control? She reached for her glass, determined not to be beaten. The glass shook only a little as she brought it to his mouth. His eyelashes flicked up as the rim touched his bottom lip, his gray eyes, glinting with more than laughter, met her gaze. Her hand trembled. He grasped her wrist, held her hand steady and drank deep. She felt so weak, he might have been draining her blood.

He took the glass from her slackened grip and placed it on the table. Fine trembles ran through her body, running deep beneath the surface, an ache in her center, a yearning in her heart. The heart she could do nothing about. The rest? Well, time would tell. She managed a smile.

He returned his attention to the platters, his hand hovering above the dainty offerings, looking for the choicest piece. For her. She felt like some medieval lady, with her knight searching his trencher for the most tender cut of meat. He settled on a crescent of pastry. It hovered at her lips, and unable to resist the gentle urging in his expression, she opened her mouth.

Dear God. It tasted wonderful. What was in it, she could not tell. Something savory rather than sweet: spiced meat perhaps. The pleasure was all about him, his look of satisfaction, the slight curl to his lips, the scorch of his eyes. He selected again and again, little bursts of heaven filling her mouth, until she put up a hand in defeat.

He dabbed at her mouth with his napkin. "Crumbs," he said. He refilled their glasses. They chinked them together and drank an unspoken toast that was all about what would happen next. Her pulse beat faster.

"Eat something," she said, her voice husky.

He leaned forward, tilted her chin with the tip of his finger, and pressed his lips to hers, a gentle brush, a butterfly wing of a kiss, a sweet touch of his tongue. Sweet sensations tingled in her breasts, tightened her stomach.

She put a hand on his collar for support and deepened the kiss, swept his champagne-flavored mouth with her tongue. Delicious.

His hand, warm, steadying, strong, came up to her ribs. His thumb brushed the underside of her breast, a tantalizing touch, a sensual promise. A cry of surrender lodged in her throat.

Too fast. Too soon. She felt thrilled, and wicked and completely out of her depth. Today had simply been a testing of the waters. To meet a man she liked so quickly seemed beyond the realm of possibility. Dare she trust the desires of her body, when it knew so little?

He must have felt her slight resistance, for he pulled slowly away, his lids at half-mast, his breathing faster than before, she noticed with a surge of heat.

"There are chambers upstairs where we could ensure our privacy," he murmured. "Should you wish?"

He stood and brought her to her feet.

CHAPTER TWO

HER GAZE SEARCHED his face, looking for something. Tony experienced the most anxiety he'd known in his life. The urge to sweep her up in his arms, to kiss her senseless, to drive out all resistance, pounded in his blood like hammer blows. If she turned him down now, he might well end up weeping at her feet like young Radcliffe. Or putting her over his shoulder and carrying her upstairs.

His groin pulsed approval at the latter vision.

The deuce he would. An English gentleman accepted a no at face value. While it might not suit his baser nature, he wasn't about to force the issue. He'd have to find another way to seduce her into his bed. Or perhaps she was one of those women who preferred teasing over a relationship. Or she wanted a *carte blanche*. He drew back, tensing, as if he sensed the headman's axe about to fall.

"Anthony," she said, her voice hesitant.

He straightened his shoulders, smiled.

"Are you married?" she asked softly.

An unexpected question. He raised a brow. "No."

"Betrothed, perhaps?"

"Not as yet."

"The prospect of a betrothal soon, though," she said nodding.

"Why don't you come out and say what is on your mind?" The growl was back. Damn, but he felt as if he'd fallen afoul of the inquisition.

She waved a hand, her cheeks flushing a shade of pale rose. "I have no wish to engage in anything harmful to another woman. If you have prospects, I prefer to acknowledge our very pleasant conversation and leave it there." The words seemed to come out of her mouth in a rush, the pink on her high cheekbones turned a deeper red.

He ached for her obvious embarrassment and adored her principles. He took the fluttering hand in his. "I have no obligations, I swear it."

She gazed into his eyes for a very long moment. She nodded, as if coming to a decision. "I accept your word." She smiled then, openly. "I apologize. I will not blame you if you have changed your mind." Her gaze lowered to their clasped hands.

"Badly burned, were you?"

She shook her head. "It is over and done, not worth repeating."

"I suppose, since we are laying our cards on the table I should ask about your expectations, from this evening."

"None at all."

He experienced a sensation of dismay, followed by shock. He forced a smile. "Nor hopes for the future?"

"Most definitely not."

She was either a very good liar, or he hadn't made much of an impression. Or was it something else? Why be disappointed when her answers were exactly what he'd hoped? Good grief, an hour ago, he'd wanted to leave.

Now, he wanted to dive into the warmth of her brown eyes, to kiss her eyelids, feel their lashes against his cheek. He couldn't resist. He pulled her close, dipped his head and claimed her lovely full mouth. She melted against him, warm and willing and curvaceous and soft. Pliant. Deceivingly yielding for a woman with a backbone of iron. He tasted her mouth, while his hands explored the sloping shoulders, the wonderfully straight back and the swell of her hips. She arched against his erection and he stifled a groan of pleasure.

Lifting his head, he gazed into her face. "Will you come upstairs with me?"

"Oh, yes," she said. "I would like that very much. There are stairs just beyond the door where we entered."

Ah yes. An organizing woman. She'd forewarned him. "Perfect. Then let us go." He held out his arm.

They strolled along the walkway amid the leafy plants. He matched his pace to hers, needing very little adjustment, he noted with satisfaction. A branch drooped over the walkway, covered in red blossom, an hibiscus. She paused to inhale its fragrance.

"Very little perfume," she said, with a disappointed little grimace, her nose and cheek generously dusted with yellow.

"But lots of pollen." He took his handkerchief from his

pocket. "I know you gave yours to that young puppy, so please allow me." Grasping her jaw, he flicked the yellow grains away. She wrinkled her nose, and he leaned forward and kissed the delectable tip. His body quickened. A mad vision leapt into his mind of her naked flesh covered from head to heel in pollen and him, feather in hand, dusting her off. It was on the tip of his tongue to suggest it. God save him. He hadn't had those kinds of visions since his green youth. Nor had his body roused so hard and so fast.

"This way," he said, making a break for the door before his imagination took him beyond the point of no return.

Nearby, a narrow set of stairs did indeed wind its way up. A servants' staircase, he guessed.

"One floor up," she said, her voice husky. She rummaged in her reticule. "I have the key." She pressed the cool shiny metal against his palm.

How many other men had she led up these stairs, panting those little breaths, her bosom rising and falling in a tantalizing rhythm of feminine music? He didn't want to know. He didn't want to think about it. He'd never cared before, so why this sudden feeling of possession?

He put his arm around her waist, nuzzled her neck below her ear, gorged on the scent of lavender and needy woman. "Lead the way, Countess."

They climbed the stairs like sweethearts, her head against his shoulder, his arm about her waist pulling her tight against his side. Each time she stepped up, she afforded him a glimpse of a well-turned ankle and curve of calf. Slender and shapely. What more could a man ask? Passion? She had that too. The heat of her body burned though his clothes at hip and thigh and forearm. He fought to control his breathing as his blood grew heavy and thick.

He swung open the door and watched in appreciation the sway of her hips as she sauntered in.

Lady Falstow might be an abbess of sorts, but she did not run anything so common as a bawdy house. The suite—for it opened into a sitting room, and beyond lay a chamber he felt sure must be a bedroom—had pale cream walls and a sofa covered in green and white damask. A low table at one end of the daybed held a bottle of champagne in ice and two glasses.

He closed the door with a soft click and she spun around, her slanted eyes wide, like a cat deciding whether to hide or play.

"Would you like some more champagne?" he asked.

"Yes" One corner of her mouth twisted ruefully. "Thank you." She sat down on the sofa while he drew the cork and poured two glasses. He sat beside her. "To us," he said raising his glass.

"To us," she whispered.

"A delightful room," he said.

"Indeed." She took a long sip of her drink and set the glass down. She was nervous. Not quite the sophisticate he'd presumed. That pleased him, strangely enough.

"Give me your hands," he said.

Her eyes widened.

"Please."

She held them out. They shook just a little. He took them in his. "I promise I will do nothing without your approval."

Her gaze rose swiftly. "I did not think you would." Her voice sounded breathless, but her expression remained calm, her eyes dancing again.

"I'm glad." He turned her hands over, placed them on his knee. Three tiny pearl buttons marched up the inside of her wrists. Starting with her left hand, he slipped the tiny beads through the loops one at a time. He pulled the fabric aside, revealing a tracery of faint blue veins in her creamy skin. He brushed it reverently with his thumb.

She drew in a breath.

The soft sound sent a shiver down his spine. Her skin there was sensitive. There would be many more places on her body equally responsive. He looked forward to discovering them all. He brought her wrist to his lips, tasted the fragrant flesh with his tongue. She brushed his cheek with her fingertips, the lace rough against his skin.

He drew off the glove and laid it beside her glass on the table, still maintaining hold of her hand. It trembled lightly. It reminded him of a swallow he'd removed from the cold grate in his bedroom as a boy. Soft, warm, fragile and terribly vulnerable. He replaced it on his knee and went to work on her right hand.

She smiled. "You are good at buttons."

"Mmm," he said, tasting her other wrist. "Lots of practice."

She giggled. "It tickles when you talk."

He finished denuding her hand and handed her the glass. "Sip."

With a raised brow she did and he took a deep swallow of the bubbling wine from his own glass. Tart and crisp, it cleansed his mouth. He drew her to her feet and captured her mouth, tasting cool champagne and warm woman. She tangled her tongue with his with a tiny cry of encouragement in the back of her throat.

Ah, yes.

He cupped her buttocks, pressing his hips to her belly, his thigh against the apex of hers, felt her hips answering pressure against his erection.

It felt good. Very good.

His palm wandered the span of her lovely back, the straight spine, the velvet of her gown soft against his hand. And another row of tiny buttons. Far too many buttons. He cradled her nape bowing her back until he held her weight in his palms.

Desire mounted as she leaned back, trusting he would not let her fall. He warmed in a way that had nothing to do with the heat at his groin, or the lust urging him to strip her naked. It registered in the corner of his mind still capable of rational thought.

The exploration of her wonderful welcoming mouth, the weight of her supple body in his arms, had him on fire. The raging beast of lust wanted to rip her clothes away, to throw her to the floor, hair wild about her shoulders, spread her legs and drive into her heat. Blood pounded in his ears. His heart thundered.

He brought her upright, cupped her face in his hands and gazed into her liquid brown eyes. Amber flame sparked in their depths. She smiled and lowered her lashes. The sweetness in her expression touched his heart. In that moment, she seemed more child than woman. Almost innocent.

"Lovely," he murmured. "May I see your hair down?"

She reached up.

"Let me," he said, filled with a kind of madness that required he serve her. He walked around her with measured steps, the urge for haste beating in his veins, only iron will chaining it fast. The knot at her nape presented an interesting challenge. As did the myriad buttons down her back. With a gentle probe, he located a pin in the luxuriant coil. Tortoiseshell, he saw as he pulled it free. Its companions amid the glossy tresses were more forthcoming. In a rainstorm of pins, copper fire bursting forth wherever candlelight touched, a mass of soft wavy skeins fell to her creamy shoulders, slid halfway down her back and over her breasts.

The strands ran through his fingers, silken ribbons scented with lavender. Rich, and glorious. She glanced over her shoulder, a teasing half-smile on her lips. "Do you approve?"

"Oh, yes, my sweet." He spun her around and swept her up, her wonderful hair trailing over his arms.

Her face alight, her eyes dancing, she laughed. The throaty sound went straight to his groin. In a fever of impatience, he kissed her forehead, her nose, her lips in quick succession. He swept her up and carried her through to the next chamber.

Covered in gold brocade, draped with filmy hangings, an enormous bed dominated a room lit by wall sconces and a blazing fire. A rug of white fur lay in front of the hearth, a chaise-longue occupied the bay window embrasure. Tony had eyes only for the bed.

He set her on her feet. "May I help you with your gown?"

The rough edge to his voice sent pleasurable little quivers racing around in Margaret's belly. Her throat dried. No going back. She'd wanted this. He was lovely. Perfect in fact. Handsome. Gentle, and obviously experienced in seduction. In less than an hour, he had her body humming with tension, strung tight with desire and longing.

Even so, the little pinprick of fear poking around in her mind warned of terrible consequences. A fallen woman. Easy virtue. Wanton. Words of disparagement. All true, to some extent, if she followed this path. And if she didn't? If she called a halt right at this moment and returned to her lonely sensible existence, would she regret it forever?

She had weathered many storms in her life, ridden out the fierce gales of shattered hopes and dreams in absolute calm as good breeding demanded. Here, no duty, no expectations lay in wait to mould her decisions. Only free will. Hers.

His face hovered above her, waiting for her answer, his gray eyes smoky, mobile lips full and sensual from their kisses. A man with a powerful need to conquer, for all that he held it under control.

And if she let him conquer her body, would he also conquer her heart? Could she come out of the adventure unscathed? Incredulous, she let go her breath at the painful squeeze in her chest. Clearly it was too late. He'd already touched her soul. If she weren't careful, he'd leave scars.

But she would not let him think her a pawn to be played at will.

"First you, my dear Anthony." She reached for his cravat.

"It will be faster if I do it," he said, breathing just a little hard.

"And deprive me of the pleasure? I think not."

"Hell," he breathed.

"Don't worry. I know what I am about." After all, her elderly husband had occasionally required her attentions. Konrad had been a considerate husband, always kindly, but other women had hinted at things that led her to believe she might have missed something in the marriage bed. In seeking to learn the truth, she was taking a risk. The thrill surging in her veins made her think it might be worthwhile.

She flipped the ends of his cravat free. The knot proved resistant to her efforts, but he stood patient, his chin elevated, the flickering of a muscle in his jaw the only sign of tension. That and the heat rolling off his body and dashing against her breasts like waves breaking on shore. The knot gave. She unwound the crisp length of muslin free and let it fall to her feet.

Wicked. She swallowed, trying to ease the dryness in her mouth, wondering if she had the courage. Her heart seemed to beat louder in the quiet room. Could he hear it? Sense her nervousness?

She inhaled a quick breath and fumbled with his coat's five gold buttons. He helped her pull the garment over his shoulders and down his arms. It landed on top of the cravat. Next the pearl gray waistcoat. It slipped off easily and she flung it aside. Her breathing became very shallow and rapid. Her hands were shaking worse with each passing moment. If she didn't get this done quickly, she'd be running for the door.

The shirt disappeared into the waistband of his biscuit-colored pantaloons. She tugged it free and undid the buttons at his throat, revealing golden flesh and a sprinkling of light brown hair. She laid a hand flat on his flesh, feeling warmth and a strong steady heartbeat. Her insides quickened. "Bend down," she said.

He laughingly groaned, but did as she bid and she hauled the soft fabric over his head and off. The treasure she had uncovered held her gaze. Delicious arcs of muscle and chords of sinew sculpted his firm flesh. Beautiful. His pectoral flexed as if to prove his strength. His Adam's apple rose and fell with a swallow. She wasn't the only one feeling the stress.

Unable to resist the glorious sight, she ran her hands over the warm flesh of his shoulders and biceps, trailed her fingers through the crisp curls on his deep chest, outlined the ridges of muscle beneath his ribs.

Lovely curves and defined shadows. Hard flesh and supple muscle. Not an ounce of extra flesh or any blurring of the definition of shoulders, waist or hip. Perfect male beauty.

He sucked in a breath.

A thrill tightened her center, deep between her thighs. She rode the sensation as it rippled outward, loosening her limbs, making her breasts feel full and sensitive.

His hand went to the buttons of his falls and she took in narrow hips and lean flanks, gloating at the evidence of his arousal. With a quick flip, she brushed his fingers away. "I'll do it."

"Sweetheart, you are killing me," he murmured, his voice a hot murmur.

"I know." Her voiced rasped.

He cupped her chin and pressed a swift kiss to her forehead. "Hurry up."

Truth to tell, she thought she might die soon herself, if she didn't get him onto that bed. But she would not rush. She'd never have the courage to do this again, and never with anyone else.

The buttons of his falls slid free with little effort, thank heaven. Reveling in the tensing muscles of his stomach at the intrusion of her fingers between fabric and skin, she worked on the fastening at his waistband. The button pinged onto the floor. "Oh dear."

"Not a significant problem." He sounded as if he might be laughing and indeed when she glanced up his eyes were dancing beneath half lowered lids.

She peeled the tight fabric over his hips, down long muscular thighs to his knees.

His erection sprang free, larger than she'd expected, hard and proud, curving up to his navel.

She knelt to remove his shoes, her cheek brushing his arousal.

"Hades," he said. "Woman. Enough." He toed his shoes off and stripped off his pantaloons and stockings in seconds.

She sat back on her heels and looked up at him. She'd seen statues in museums that didn't hold a candle to this man.

A sound rumbled up from his throat, a frustrated growl.

She laughed. In a flash he had lifted her to her feet.

"No more teasing. You've had your fun. Now it is my turn. Be prepared to suffer the torments of heaven."

Slowly she turned her back to him. She bowed her head and let her hair fall forward, a curtain to hide her heated cheeks. "If you please."

He traced the line of her dress across her spine, a gentle abrasion of her skin, then briefly pressed his lips to her nape. She shuddered, whether in terror or delight she wasn't sure. Nimble fingers released the buttons down her back. A quick jerk and the bow holding the lace for her stays unraveled. Strong practiced fingers pulled them free of their eyelets. Despite the warmth in the room, her back tingled with the touch of cool air as he pushed the gown off her shoulders and down her arms.

She swallowed. Turned to face him. For she had never been accused of cowardice. His gaze lowered to her breasts, covered only by her chemise, a gauzy muslin shift edged in fine lace. The wonder and awe in his face brought a smile to her lips. "I see you are not disappointed."

He glanced up then, and grinned. "No indeed. *J'adore.*" He dropped to one knee, pulling the gown over her hips, untying her petticoat. His movements, though quick and strong, were not quite as controlled as before. "I am at your feet."

"Literally." She laughed. She had never felt so beautiful in her life, or so alive. She ran her fingers through his hair, shorter than fashionable, but shining. Light brown with hints of gold.

"Step out, please, madam." For all of his politeness, his service as her maid, there was no mistaking the words for anything but a command. A request to make haste.

She stepped over the pile of crumpled red fabric pooled at her feet, and he whisked it away, tossing it across the room.

"Sit," he said, still on one knee and gesturing at the bed.

With raised eyebrows, she complied.

One foot at a time, he removed her slippers with an economy of movement that had her heart pounding in her chest. He shot them after the dress. He ran a hand up her calf, caressing, shaping, then brought her to her feet wearing naught but her chemise and stockings and her emerald choker. "Gorgeous."

He cupped her bottom in one large hand, the other went around her shoulders, and he scooped her up and deposited her on the bed as if she weighed no more than a kitten.

She felt kittenish, flirty, lighthearted and terribly wanton.

He nuzzled her throat, licked her ear, making her whimper approval. He straightened, gazing down at her with hot quicksilver eyes.

Her nipples hardened and her breasts ached for his lips and tongue.

"It seems to me," he said, his grin wicked. "You are overdressed."

The words, the roughness in his voice, drew her insides tight as if a chord between them had shortened or twisted. A jolt of pleasure made her gasp.

He laughed. "God, you are so responsive."

"Anthony," she said. "Lay with me."

He shook his head. "Stocking first, madam." A warm hand caressed the sole of her foot. A knuckle massaged the arch. A strong thumb rubbed the ball of her foot.

"Mmm. Now you are the tease," she said.

"This is serious business," he said, dropping to his knees beside the bed. All she could see was his shoulders, his nape, the glint of gold among toffee-colored waves as his hands shaped her ankles, squeezing and rubbing her calves before straying up behind the backs of her knees. A finger eased beneath her garter.

He leaned forward, breathed on her thigh, warm and moist and blazing sensation. More sensation than she ever imagined. Her insides melted, grew hot, quivered.

He tugged at a garter with his teeth. It came undone. Slowly he slipped off her stocking. Then the other garter.

"Lovely," he said. "Beautiful legs. A feast for the eyes."

"Please," she said, wanting him skin on skin, inside her.

"Soon," he murmured. "My sweetly veiled. Patience." He pressed his palm against the inside of her thigh.

She swallowed, feeling the blush rush to her face, yet relaxed at the gentle pressure, let her thighs fall open.

He stroked her inner thighs, up and down, gentle sweeping caresses of both hands now, each pass reaching higher, closer. Her woman's flesh tingled, expecting his touch, wanting the weight of his hand. She reached down and caught his wrist, place his hand at the juncture of her legs.

He drew in a soft hiss of breath. "You are bold. Demanding." Pressing down with heel of his hand, he increased the pleasure.

Her stomach rolled slowly. This man knew how to please a woman. She purred her approval.

The touch disappeared. She lifted her head, frowning, and he grinned as he climbed up on the bed. "I'm not going anywhere."

"Good," she murmured.

He kissed her then, sweetly, a light brush of mouth on mouth. A whisper. She nipped his bottom lip and he thrust his tongue into her mouth. She sucked it. He groaned. The sound arrowing sweetly to her core. He took control of the kiss, tangling his tongue with hers, ravishing her mouth, plundering with his tongue until she felt dizzy.

He broke away and in one swift and ruthless move, pulled her shift up her body. She lifted her arms and head, and he pulled up and free with one hand, while capturing her wrists with the other.

"No escape for you now." He gazed into her face, his eyes dark like the smoke from an open fire. Mysterious, promising heat, and yet waiting for permission.

Had he sensed it then, her cowardice? If she told him no, he would stop. For a little while longer, she had the control. But this was the point of no return; his eyes said so.

Whatever happened tonight, she would never see him again. Couldn't. It would be too difficult to hide her feelings. Feelings one should not have for a casual lover. And if she would never see him again, she might as well have something worth remembering. She smiled.

He captured her mouth, while his free hand went to her breast, teasing the nipple, rolling it, squeezing hard enough to cause sensual pain. She gasped into his mouth.

He broke away, trailed little kisses down her jaw, her throat, licked at the small hollow at her shoulder, blazed a path to the rise of her breast. Sensations swirled through her blood, leaving her languid, yet tight as a bowstring. She stroked his back, his arms, his wonderful shoulders. Warm and wet, his mouth took her breast. His tongue played with her nipple, licking, flicking, swirling.

He suckled.

Her insides clenched so hard, she almost tipped into bliss. Not quite. So close. "Sweet heaven," she gasped, pressing up with her hips, reminding him of her other need.

First one nipple then the other, he kissed and suckled and tormented, until she thought she might go mad.

She bit his shoulder and he groaned and chuckled softly. "Are you ready for me?"

She managed a nod.

"Let me see." He reached between them, caressed her woman's flesh, eased a finger inside then another, gentle probing. So good. Not nearly enough. She arched her back.

"Ah, sweetheart," he said. "You feel wonderful. Hot and wet and ready." He nudged her legs apart with his knee, and guided himself to her entrance. She felt the head of him, bathing in her moisture, tracing her cleft, touching that special place that seemed to make her crazy with lust. Her mind darkened, focused only on that one small place, every fiber of her being centered on the tension.

He thrust forward. Hard. Huge. To the hilt.

He withdrew. Pleasurable friction.

She lifted her legs, clenched around his waist and hung on for dear life.

He thrust into her deep and hard, again and again the tempo increasing with each thrust. The sound of damp flesh coming together. Murmurs of pleasure and cries increasing desire.

Nothing else in the world. Desire spiraling higher. Hot flesh. Soft moist sounds. Kisses.

Tony thought he would unravel at any moment. Her inner muscles clenched around him, drawing him deeper with each penetration, until he hung on to control by a thread. Dark-honey eyes drew him into their depths as her body held him fast. She clung to his shoulders, his hips, meeting each thrust with a gasp in the back of her throat that made his balls clench. Passion filled her face. Her body accommodated his like a sweet sensual glove. He was in heaven.

She lifted her head and nibbled his ear. The tickle went straight to his groin. He thought he might go right over the top. Not without her. She deserved everything he had to give and so much more.

Three hours, he'd been hard. Since the moment they'd met. If she didn't find her release soon, the back of his head might explode.

He brought his hand between them. Felt for that hard little nub of clitoris, watched her face until her eyes widened, then rubbed hard fast little circles, found the rhythm and watched her melt into abandonment with such a feeling of tenderness it almost stopped him cold.

Closing his eyes against the emotion, he drove into her body, hard and fast, seeking release and the best of deaths. She stroked him, nuzzled his neck, welcomed him into her heat, and then she shattered, her internal pulses of pleasure kissing his shaft. He broke through into white light and mind-numbing bliss, falling into wonderful warmth.

Somehow he managed not to collapse. He remembered to breathe. His heart pounding, he hung over her, saw her arms fall away from his shoulders, her eyes glaze, her lips curve in satisfaction.

He felt like a hero.

God help him.

He eased out of her and rolled on his side, pulling her

close, holding her as if he could keep her there for all time. He stroked her shoulder, kissed her ear, felt her tiny shiver. His groin gave a happy little pulse. Once wasn't enough. He had the feeling that no matter how many times he made love to this woman it would never be enough. Something inside him ached at the thought of never seeing her again. And the thought of another man touching her wasn't to be born. Had she truly driven him mad?

It hit him like a horseshoe to the temple. This was what he'd been seeking all along. Bricks and mortar were only a fraction of the permanence he sought. Without a heart at its center, a house would mean nothing. He'd never believed in hearts as anything but a pump for blood, but the ache in his chest was all about her. He knew instinctively, illogically, that without her, the land would mean as little as the rest of his life.

Dear God. If he wasn't badly mistaken, he loved her.

"May I call on you?" he murmured into her wonderful mass of lavender-scented hair.

She turned her head, her brow furrowed, her eyes regretful. "I don't think so."

The pain of her rejection hurt worse than a fall from a horse at full gallop, worse than the bite of a well-honed rapier. Rather, it seemed to explode in his chest like a barrel of gunpowder.

He drew in a long breath. He'd asked. She'd said no. She offered nothing beyond this one encounter, and he'd gladly accepted.

But it hadn't been an outright no, had it? He lifted his

head and smiled into her lovely face. "I'm not easily put off."

Her eyes swam with tears, even though she smiled back. "Please. Don't say something we will both regret later."

Those tears gave him hope.

He nestled her into the crook of his shoulder. "Then we will talk about it later."

She sighed as if she hoped he would not, then closed her eyes.

He gazed down at the dark sweep of lashes, at the pale skin taut over exotic bones. He wanted to wake up to this vision every day. Nothing else would ever meet this need.

Somehow he'd persuade her to change her mind. He'd find her. They'd talk. Get to know each other. He'd make her see he wasn't a frippery fellow who didn't know his own mind or his own heart. He would not let her go without a fight.

Margaret knew she'd slept, but not how long. The aftermath of bliss, the languor, the melting limbs had taken her by surprise.

She opened her eyes and stared at the canopy, felt his breath on her cheek, the weight of his thigh across hers. This was what she'd missed by being the dutiful daughter. How unfair.

Her heart ached. Not for the past, but for something larger, something as solid as a mountain, something as deep as a chasm. It was loss.

He'd asked her to see her again.

He should not have done that. For a moment, she'd almost said yes. Fool. Had years of obedience, rigid duty, self-control been for naught if this man could crumble her will to dust? For years, she'd submitted to the strictures of her life because Konrad had said that on his death she would never be dependent on anyone again. He'd kept his word. How could she consider giving up her freedom?

Except, somewhere deep inside, youthful hopes and dreams stirred into wakefulness, as if they had slept for a very long time. Painful with longing as they stretched and unfurled, they offered more than duty, they promised joy. If only she dared take the risk.

Beside her, Anthony shifted. "Awake?" he murmured, and traced her jaw with his finger.

She couldn't help her sigh of pleasure at his touch. "Yes. It is time for me to leave."

"Will I find you here tomorrow?"

Her heart skipped a beat. She quelled its enthusiastic reply with a frown. "I will not return."

He gazed into her eyes, searched her face. "Did I offend in some way?"

She'd wounded him. The pain was there in the shadows clouding his eyes. She wanted to beg his forgiveness, but did not trust herself to speak of it, in case she cried. "Of course not."

He stroked her back. Her skin danced under his finger-tips, begged for more. She almost groaned out loud. "It is better this way," she managed to say.

He was silent. Angry? She turned to look at him. His eyes were smiling. "I will find you, countess."

Her heart soared in the most ridiculous manner.

He slid out of bed and gathered up their clothing from the far corners of the room. Silently he helped her dress, lacing her stays, buttoning her gown, kneeling to help her into her stocking and shoes, even retrieving her pins from the floor in the other chamber. On the dressing table, she found a brush and while she fixed her hair, he dressed swiftly. As she finished, he came and stood at her shoulder.

Faces side by side, they stared at their reflections, hers dark, his fair. He put a hand on her shoulder and turned her to face him.

His mouth brushed hers. Delicate, tender, no more than the brush of a butterfly wing.

A promise? Or a gentle farewell. Tears were hot at the backs of her eyes. She would never see him again. Must not, if she truly wanted her freedom. And yet it no longer held the bright allure of a distant star that she could see every day in her marriage. Right at this moment, the future looked bleak.

"Are you ready?" he murmured.

Was she? He gave her no chance to answer, for he opened the door and escorted her along the corridor to the staircase leading down to the entrance hall.

Two young men, one saturnine leaning against the wall, the other fair and looking at his watch, glanced up at their descent.

"Darby," the fair one said, his eyes opening wide as they reached the ground. "I thought you'd forgotten us." He sent a telling look to the dark gentleman, who had straightened. The Evernden brothers, no doubt. Anthony's friends.

Anthony signaled to a lackey to open the door. "May I drive you home?" he asked her softly.

"No need," she said, smiling, wishing she could kiss him goodbye. "My carriage is waiting."

"It would be," he said. A rueful twist to his lips, he bent closer, his breath tickling her ear. "You can't hide from me. I'll find you. You will be mine."

Her heart picked up speed, beating out longing and wild hope. Should she listen? She wanted to. Apparently madness had invaded her blood. She whisked out of the door, before her tongue could say anything incriminating.

"Who is that?" one of the young men asked.

"My future wife, though she doesn't yet know it," Anthony said, loudly enough for her to hear. "The love of my life."

Her breath caught in her throat, her stomach took a long slow roll of happiness. She stopped. A smile took control of her lips. Glancing back over her shoulder, she caught the full effect his cat-who-ate-the-cream grin and wanted to laugh. She raised a brow. "We haven't had our courtship yet."

He bowed with a flourish, then gazed into her eyes. "We will, my love."

My love. Her heart swelled, filled with a bubble of the purest joy. It grew so large, she thought it might carry her away like a hot air balloon. With steps as light as girl in the first blush of youth, she ran for her carriage. *The love of my life.* She savored the words, and foolish tears ran down her face.

Anthony would move mountains to find her. He'd said so with his eyes.

"Home, John," she called to the coachman, as the footman opened the carriage door.

Home to prepare a welcome.

* * * * *

Wicked Earl, Wanton Widow

BRONWYN SCOTT

Bronwyn Scott is a communications instructor in the Puget Sound area and is the proud mother of three wonderful children (one boy and two girls). When she's not teaching or writing, she enjoys playing the piano, travelling—especially to Florence—and studying history and foreign languages. You can learn more about Bronwyn at www.nikkipoppen.com

Author's Note

This story was fun to write, especially since I wrote it during the autumn and apples are such a big deal in the Pacific Northwest where I live. Herefordshire, where this story takes place, is the Orchard of England, even today. Cider enjoyed a popular existence in Herefordshire since the Middle Ages, but it wasn't until the nineteenth century that farmers banded together to make it possible to transport cider to the cities and make it a more lucrative industry outside of the region. Today, sixty-three million gallons of cider are produced in Herefordshire, accounting for over half of the cider produced in England.

I hope you enjoy the story of Killian Redbourne and his feisty heroine, Rose Janeway. Peyton Ramsden, the Earl of Dursley, is on hand to help Killian with his awkward inheritance. You can read more about Peyton Ramsden in *The Earl's Forbidden Ward,* already available through Mills & Boon® eBooks!

Drop by and say hello at www.bronwynswriting.blogspot.com

Bronwyn

CHAPTER ONE

Fall, 1830, Herefordshire, England

KILLIAN REDBOURNE'S kisses could make a woman swoon. They had in fact done just that two weeks ago at the theater where a Mrs. Dempsey had been caught in his arms performing said feat (a stunt many suspected she'd engineered herself). Such was the latest rumor that had accompanied him down from London.

Rose Janeway was not proud that she'd succumbed to the inclination to gossip, but it was all the people of Pembridge-on-the-Wye knew of the man who would be earl. She excused her weakness on the grounds that no one had actually seen Killian Redbourne in fourteen years, not since his last quarrel with the Earl of Pembridge and no one had expected to see him again. After all, he wasn't the heir, merely the cousin of the heir in case the unthinkable happened. But the unthinkable had happened. The heir had died a few months ago without securing the succession and the old earl had never recovered from the blow.

Tired of living with the reality that his prodigal nephew would inherit, the old earl had shuffled off his mortal coil and surrendered to the inevitable five days ago. And here they all were: a motley assortment of villagers, farmers and herself, gathered at the grave of the earl in the chilly October wind, drawn in small part out of respect for the passing of the resident peer and in larger part by the lure of seeing the rumors incarnate.

News filtering down from the big house held that Killian Redbourne and a friend, Lord Dursley, had arrived late last night in a black-lacquered carriage with wide glass panes and elegant lanterns for night travel. The carriage had been pulled by a superior set of four matched gray horses, no expenses spared and the trappings of luxury self-evident. That would have to change. If he wanted to succeed around these parts, he'd best put a damper on such a blatant show of wealth. Harvests had been poor and the day laborers who worked them even poorer these last three years.

The object of her ruminations (and truth be told, the ruminations of everyone assembled at the funeral) stood across from her, separated only by the width of the open grave. Over the edge of her prayer book, Rose covertly surveyed the rumors made flesh, concluding that in this case, the rumors might indeed not suffer from over-exaggeration even if her own rather heated imagination did. She'd been without a man four years now and the absence had been wearing on her lately. She'd even contemplated the notion of taking a lover. It was all very hypothetical. No one had appealed as a likely candidate, although since it was hypothetical, Killian Redbourne would certainly be a viable nominee.

In theory, he definitely possessed the potential to make a woman swoon. Taller than the other men gathered, Killian Redbourne drew the eye and riveted the mind. He wore his hair longer than fashionably suitable, although today, out of respect, he'd tied it back with a tasteful black satin bow reminiscent of an earlier age. His broad shoulders filled out the greatcoat to advantage, the coat itself left open to show off long legs in riding breeches tapering into high boots, offering hints of a trim waist and a well-muscled torso. Temptation of an excellent physique aside, Killian Redbourne's best asset was his eyes; dark coffee orbs framed by long black lashes that flashed with a suggestion of laughter, and they were laughing now.

At her.

She'd been right and duly caught.

It seemed unfair that she'd been the one caught when everyone else was getting away with it. A slow sensual smile spread across his lips, igniting a certain aching warmth deep at her core and a wicked fantasy.

What would it be like to take a man such as him to her bed and ease the loneliness of the nights? Images raced through her mind of him naked and aroused, rising above her, his dark hair falling forward, his eyes hot with desire, his body slicked with the sweat of his exertions.

Across from her, Killian Redbourne winked in concupiscent conspiracy as if he knew precisely what she'd been thinking. Rose blushed. How could she not? Her thoughts were hardly fitting for a funeral. But their eyes held. Why not stare openly? There was no sense in looking away now. The damage was done.

It wasn't the first time a woman had stared at him. The fairer sex had been staring since he'd turned fifteen and the blacksmith's daughter had lured him behind a haystack. Women had been trying to catch him ever since.

He was thirty-four now and had no more intention of being caught than he had back then. It had become something of a game for him over the years. The risks had been higher in recent months, the pursuit more ardent once his prospects as the Earl of Pembridge were assured. Even so, his ability to keep his heart separate from his encounters had risen proportionately to the increased need for evasion.

Killian studied the striking woman, letting a slow smile take his mouth, the smile that said he was aware of her scrutiny and was most ably returning it. She was slightly taller than most, with a firm, high bosom (his preference) and long legs (also his preference), and her hair, what he could see of it beneath her bonnet, promised to be a rich shade of red-gold. All in all, a very nice package.

To his surprise and delight, her forget-me-not-blue eyes did not look away. Perhaps this visit to the hinterlands of Herefordshire wouldn't be without its comforts after all. The earl's funeral had inconveniently drawn him away from some deuced excellent hunting and he was eager to get back to it. But in the meanwhile it appeared Herefordshire had its own charms.

Beside him, his traveling companion, Peyton Ramsden, the Earl of Dursley, nudged him none too gently in the ribs, reminding him flirtatious shenanigans had no proper place at a somber occasion. Well, maybe not for Peyton. Peyton didn't have a reputation for the shocking to uphold.

It hardly mattered to Killian what the people of Pembridge-on-the-Wye thought of him. No doubt they'd been living on speculation and hearsay for years in regards to him. He'd hear the reading of the will, consult the steward who'd been running the estate for ages, give him instructions along with an address of contact and be on his way in two days—tops, the pretty woman across the grave site notwithstanding. Still, two days was a long time to be alone when one was Killian Redbourne.

CHAPTER TWO

"I, RUTHERFORD Michael Redbourne, fifth Earl of Pembridge, being of sound mind and body on this day, the fifth of September, in the year eighteen hundred and thirty, bequeath my earthly estate and all its entailments to my nephew and heir, Killian Christopher Redbourne...."

Killian tapped impatient fingers on the small table beside his chair in the private study of Pembridge Hall, seat to the Pembridge earls for five generations. With an eye to expediency, he'd requested the solicitor read the will immediately following the funeral. The sooner everything was signed and the title officially transferred the better. His uncle had never liked him, nor he his uncle. There was no need to stand on the pretense of grief and delay realities.

Killian had no title of his own, his father being a second son. But he'd never coveted Pembridge for himself, never wanted to trade places with his cousin, Robert, who'd grown up with the assurance of a place in society. Killian was proud to have made his own way in the world, his birth allowing him to straddle a delicate fence between the world of the ton and the world of trade. Now, his inheritance firmly entrenched him on one side of that fence. At the age of four and thirty, he was an earl, whether he wanted to be or not. If his uncle could have chosen, he would have preferred *not*. It was grim consolation to imagine his uncle turning in his grave at the thought of his black-sheep nephew inheriting lock, stock and proverbial barrel.

The solicitor stopped reading, the ensuing silence drawing Killian's attention. "Is that all? Are you finished?" Killian inquired. The solicitor was looking at him oddly over the rims of his wire spectacles as if he were expecting some kind of reaction. Admittedly, Killian had not given the reading his entire attention; he had saved some of that for introspection on his uncle and some of it for the lovely woman at the ceremony. But what he *had* heard was all as expected, quite de rigueur as wills went: a listing of assets to be considered as the entail and an outlining of debts requiring payment.

The man coughed. "Mr. Redbourne," he began, then hastily corrected himself, "Lord Pembridge, I said the estate is penniless."

That got his full, undivided attention. Killian raised an eyebrow in challenge. "I beg your pardon?"

"The estate, milord, is, in the common vernacular, without a feather to fly with."

Killian sat back in his chair, letting the unexpected news penetrate. Those were words no businessman liked to hear. He had not anticipated this. He'd always imagined

Pembridge as he'd known it during the infrequent visits of his youth: vibrant with bustle and consequently financially viable. "How is that possible?"

The solicitor steepled his hands and assumed the tone of a bored schoolteacher re-explaining basic principles to an errant student. "Harvests have been poor these last few years and there hasn't been enough work available. Tenant revenues have decreased and cottage rents have gone up to compensate for the loss. Workers have been displaced and 'living in' on the larger farms has faded out in these parts. It has not helped that your uncle invested heavily in farm machinery that limited the need for laborers. There simply hasn't been enough money in rents to keep the estate running beyond a minimum. Surely, you've noticed such economic changes even in London?" The last was said with a patronizing tone that Killian did not like. He did not care for the solicitor's obvious perception that he did nothing more than fritter away time and money in debauched city living. In fact, his life was quite the opposite. He was up early most mornings and to bed late, overseeing his shipping line. His recent hunting trip was a rare exception to the usual hustle of his day.

Killian fixed the solicitor with a hard stare. Politics over the succession of the new king and the subsequent election that needed to follow had kept him in London all summer. He was all too aware that without new reforms, the situation facing rural England was only going to get worse. "Mr. Connelly, I am well aware of the social and economic situation facing the country these days. I was, however, unaware of how those conditions had affected

Pembridge. My uncle—" Killian gestured meaningfully to the papers spread on the desk. "—did not communicate with me on such matters."

Duly reprimanded, Mr. Connelly made a great show of shuffling papers and ahemming. "Quite so," he said, regaining his composure. "However, the fact remains that the estate hasn't a penny once the bills are settled."

Killian dismissed the concern. When something in business cost more than it was worth, it was minimized or sold off. Since entail prevented selling, that left minimizing. "No matter, I don't plan to stay here. We'll shut the house up and that will decrease expenses immensely. I have my own funds, which are considerable in their own right, to fill in any gaps."

Mr. Connelly gaped at him. "But milord, what about the tenants? What about the farm? They will be penniless too. As the lord goes, so does the peasantry."

Ah yes, noblesse oblige. Killian sighed. He'd never cast himself in the role of a peer before, not even after Robert had died last spring. But surely his business skills would be suitable for remedying the circumstance. "I'll tour the estate and assess their needs. I'll see what I can do to provide for them." *Even if it means dipping into my own reserves.* He was a businessman, but that didn't mean he was heartless.

In his mind, the situation was easily resolved. He would take care of the remaining tenants, see them off to a new life or make provisions for them to continue here, and be away, not in two days, alas, but surely within the week. With Peyton here to help him, it would go quickly, but they were both strangers. Gaining an entrée with the locals might be tricky given the reputation that preceded him.

Inspiration struck. "Is there anyone here who is well-acquainted with the people? Perhaps someone who could ease my way with the tenants and villagers?" The last thing Killian wanted was to come up against the stubborn pride of farmers. It would slow him down immensely.

The solicitor took off his glasses and rubbed the bridge of his nose in thought. At last he said, "Mrs. Janeway would be able to do that, milord. She's run things here pretty much for the last two years since the old earl stopped going out on account of his bad leg. She knows everyone, visits the sick, takes food to the shut-ins, runs her own farm since her husband passed. Best apples in the county."

A paragon indeed and a widow to boot. Killian could imagine what this Lady Bountiful looked like right down to the eternal widow's weeds and steel-gray hair scraped back into a no-nonsense bun. Lovely. Not only had his uncle interrupted his hunting season, he'd saddled him with a broken estate and now a bossy Mrs. Janeway.

He'd been wrong—his uncle wasn't turning over in his grave. No, his uncle was laughing his bony arse off.

CHAPTER THREE

THERE WERE WORSE DAYS for a ride. The wind of yesterday had died down and the sun had deigned to shine. With a blue sky overhead and the crispy crunch of fall leaves beneath the gig's wheels, Killian was happy to be out of doors, even if it meant he was on his way to collect Pembridge-on-the-Wye's model citizen, the Widow Janeway.

The estate's gig could only seat two and Peyton, no doubt seeing a way to avoid the task of going, had generously volunteered to stay behind and look over the books. Killian turned at the fork in the road and tooled the gig down the short drive leading to the Janeway grange.

In the drive, he pulled the gig to a halt in front of a neat, well-kept brick-and-timber house and jumped out, reminding himself the day was beautiful even if Mrs. Janeway was not.

A knock on the heavy door of the grange brought his fears to fruition. A stout, gray-haired woman answered the door, wiping her hands on an apron.

"Mrs. Janeway?" Killian inquired with all the charm at his disposal, only to find it didn't work. The woman skewered him with an assessing eye, looking him up and down with a slight air of disgust. He assumed her disgust stemmed from having been interrupted on what was clearly baking day judging from the smear of flour on her cheek and the voluminous apron.

"Dressed awful fancy for work, aren't you?" She jerked her chin to the left behind the house. "Mrs. Janeway's out in the orchards. You can see if she's still hiring."

The door shut before Killian could give his charm another try and disabuse the woman of the impression he was looking for employment. All the same, he was relieved; Mrs. Janeway, whoever she was, couldn't be worse.

The orchard behind the house hummed with an activity that took Killian quite by surprise. Apple trees spread in long straight rows, ladders against their trunks, their branches alive with pickers. Calls rang up and the down the rows for basket runners to come collect full bushels. Even children were employed to gather up apples that had fallen or been shaken onto the ground.

He'd forgotten the time.

For the last fourteen years, he'd been a city man by necessity, his kind of business more efficiently conducted near banks and the Exchange. He'd forgotten the rhythms of the country. It was October, and to the people of Herefordshire it was time to pick the apple crop. At the sight of such industry, a deep-seated desire for the satisfaction of manual labor, of seeing the physical results of one's efforts, stirred. Something that had lain dormant since he'd left his father's home began to awaken in Killian.

He asked a passing basket-carrier for Mrs. Janeway and continued on his quest, although now it seemed unlikely Mrs. Janeway would be able to accompany him on any rounds. A tour of his tenants would have to wait.

But things were looking up. He found Mrs. Janeway atop a ladder, her mind engrossed in the picking, her long legs and delectable derriere encased in a tantalizing pair of trousers. Things were looking up indeed, and not all of them had to do with ladders. Mrs. Janeway was turning out to be quite a surprise. He'd not expected a tree-climbing paragon.

"Hallo down there, I need another basket." She called without looking.

Killian grabbed up an empty basket at the base of the tree and passed it up, appreciating the view, a more than apt compensation for the harridan who had met him at the door. "Mrs. Janeway, might I have a moment of your time?"

She turned to take the basket and halted, momentarily stymied upon recognition of who stood at the bottom of her ladder. The expression on her face clearly indicated her rushing thoughts: how did one greet a peer when they showed up at the harvest?

Mrs. Janeway passed down her basket and nimbly descended, apparently having decided since there was no known protocol to cover such a contingency she'd behave normally. She stripped off her heavy gloves and reached a hand up to pull off the cap she wore, red-gold hair tumbling in a rich waterfall over her shoulders, blue eyes challenging his right to interrupt her harvest.

It was Killian's turn to be surprised for the second time since entering the orchard. Mrs. Janeway, the village paragon, was the woman who'd stared so boldly at him yesterday. Hmmm. Events were taking an interesting turn.

He gave her a slow smile of acknowledgement. "Mrs. Janeway, I feel as if we've already met."

"Looking for work, Pembridge? I haven't got any. There's barely enough to go around as it is." Rose replied coolly, ignoring the implication that he was going to make her accountable for yesterday's unguarded moment.

"Looking for *you*, actually. I'm afraid I'd forgotten what time of year it was. I've caught you at a bad time but I'd appreciate it if you could take a stroll with me. I've a proposition for you and it won't take long."

His dark eyes danced with deliberate mischief. Proposition indeed. He'd used the word on purpose, she decided. Well, she wouldn't bite and give him the satisfaction of having made her all hot and bothered with his innuendos. Not yet anyway.

"I won't even pretend to match wits with you, Pembridge. I would be out of my depth in no time. No doubt you've made a career of such dazzling wordplay in London while I've sharpened mine not at all. However, a proposition implies there's something in it for me, so I'm willing to listen."

Rose gestured toward a quiet place at the corner of the orchard where they might talk in relative privacy and she could keep an eye on the activity. The crop had ripened late this year and every day before the frost counted if the apples were to be saved. If he expected to be taken inside for tea and scones, he'd be sadly disappointed.

He was not fazed by her business-like demeanor. "Are you really so indifferent, Mrs. Janeway? Yesterday, I rather thought you weren't." His voice was low and private, far too seductive for the orchard.

She was conscious of his eyes on her as they walked. Her first line of defense was being eroded with astonishing speed. She was well aware that she had the full sum of his attentions. Acutely so. The woman in her fired too easily to the flattery of his scrutiny. Her fantasies were within her reach if she dared.

She opted for the truth. "I'm not indifferent, as you well know."

"I'm glad to hear it, Rose." He'd paused ever so slightly before saying her name. *That* did unnerve her. A bolt of want shot through her at the sound of her name on his lips, intimate and personal.

"Is this your proposition?" She asked, trying to regain her equilibrium. Sparring with Killian Redbourne was an undeniably heady experience.

He shot her a teasing glance and she saw an appreciation for her bold, honest wit. "Rose, I don't have to bargain for a woman's affections."

"Well then, what do you have to bargain for?" Rose

fired back, matching his tone with a light sauciness of her own.

They reached a quiet niche of the orchard, out of earshot and out of the way of wandering eyes. He stopped and turned so that he stood very near her, close enough that she could smell the spices of his toilette.

"I need a guide to show me around and help me meet everyone. My uncle's solicitor, a Mr. Connelly, suggested you would be best suited for that role. It should not take more than a day or two."

It was as she'd feared. He had no intention of actually being the earl. He was going to claim the title and go without a thought for what he left behind. Pembridge-on-the-Wye needed more than a handsome face.

"And then you're back to London, just like that?" Rose snapped her fingers, the light sassiness that had peppered their encounter earlier overcome by the reality.

"I have my own business to look after," Killian explained.

"There's plenty of business here to look after too." Rose reprimanded sharply.

It did the trick. The playful charm was instantly muted in his eyes. Good. Life in the country was serious business these days. There'd been reports of machine-breaking in Kent and swing riots in East Anglia. Another bad harvest was all it would take for the unrest to spread here where there were more laborers than farms that could employ them.

Her hands were on her hips and she was conscious of the

defiant picture she must present in her trousers and boots. "These people will expect you to look after them."

"I've heard you're doing a superior job of that." Pembridge broke in. "They don't need me."

"I'm just the squire's widow. I can bring them food baskets and hold their hands when they're sick. But I can't solve their real problems."

"And I can?" Pembridge queried, putting her on the spot. If he was going to force her to spell out his duty to him then she would.

"If you can't, then no one can. Have you wondered why so many people turned out for the funeral yesterday in the middle of the apple harvest?"

"Curiosity, I suppose, if your behavior is anything to go on."

Rose snorted. "It takes more than curiosity and respect for protocol to drag a farmer away from his crops at harvest. They came because you're their last hope."

Pembridge leaned back against a tree trunk in casual repose, his legs showing to advantage in his buckskin trousers and high boots. They were as long as she'd imagined yesterday beneath his greatcoat and far better muscled than her imagination gave them credit for.

"Bravo, Mrs. Janeway. You should be an actress. Although I must admit, while your performance is inspiring, it feels rather over-dramatic."

Rose gestured to the orchard beyond them, her agitation rising. "There hasn't been a good harvest since 1827. Last year there was snow in October. Even if legislation in Parliament and the Enclosure Laws weren't conspiring against the average farmer, the issue of the weather would be enough to cause these folk grave concerns. At this point, it's not a matter of making economies to get through the winter. It's a matter of *surviving*. For some of these families it's not a foregone conclusion that they'll make it. That's why their children are out here working alongside them."

"I will meet with them. I will do what I can for them to see them settled for the winter. Let that appease your conscience. But Mrs. Janeway, I do not intend to be an earl in residence. I rather doubt anyone thought I would be, whatever other expectations they had. I haven't been here in fourteen years."

"You're here now." Rose said coldly, disappointment swamping her. The disappointment was all her own. Unlike the others of Pembridge-on-the-Wye who'd given up, she'd hoped the new earl would take an active interest in the estate, that maybe he'd have some magical solution to their problems. They needed an additional source of income that could last beyond the harvest.

Pembridge gave a curt nod. "Good day, Mrs. Janeway, I seem to have let you down. That was not my intention." He moved past her, probably wanting to get away from her company as fast as he could. No wonder. By all social standards, she'd behaved abominably. She had no right to scold a peer. But Rose had never been one to bow to social mores when right was on the line, and it was on the line now.

"You haven't let me *down*, Pembridge. You've merely lived *up* to the rumors. I am at fault for stupidly wishing for more. I imagine that's the difference between expectations and hope."

She regretted the harsh words the moment they slipped out of her mouth. If she hadn't alienated him already, she'd surely done so now. She barely knew him and it was unfair to make him the whipping boy for her shattered hopes.

Pembridge paused in his departure and turned back to face her. Rose squared her shoulders. She could not take back the words. She deserved whatever he said next. There was an unmistakable look of challenge on his face and she braced herself.

CHAPTER FOUR

ROSE WATCHED PERPLEXED as Pembridge shrugged out of his coat and slowly rolled up the sleeves of his white shirt, an expensive one, made of fine lawn. Men around here didn't have such shirts except perhaps a lucky few who saved them for church. Surely he didn't mean to work in it? If not, what did he mean to do?

A horrible thought came to her. Did he mean to spank her? She hadn't been spanked since she was four, and she'd deserved it for talking back to the minister. *You deserve it now,* a little voice prompted. *You never did know when to keep your thoughts to yourself.*

Pembridge stepped towards her and she instinctively backed away, although a wicked thrill replaced her initial reaction at the prospect of a spanking. Her cheeks flushed at the image of her own naked buttocks on display across his lap.

He laid his jacket over a low limb of the tree; her eyes

followed his every move. His hand tested the strength of the branch. "Good solid wood."

Rose sucked in her breath. Dear lord, what was happening to her with all these heated, sordid thoughts? She hoped he didn't have any inkling of the lust he was stirring in her beyond that which he already guessed at.

He cast a brief glance at the sky overhead, blue and sunny. "Snow in October, you say? I'll take your word for it. In that case, you'll need all the help you can get."

That was not at all what she'd expected to hear. It took a moment to drag her thoughts away from spanking. "What do you mean to do?" He was not nearly as angry as he should be after that stinging retort of hers.

"My dear Mrs. Janeway, I mean to change your lowly opinion of me." The Earl of Pembridge favored her with a dark-eyed wink. "It may surprise you to note that I am not entirely unaccustomed to labor, although you and Mr. Connelly seem inclined to believe I live the raciest of lives. I hate to disappoint you, but between mistresses and gambling dares, I manage to help off-load cargo from my ships in London." He gave a jaunty bow in her direction, a laughing smile on his lips and sauntered off into the depths of the orchard, scooping up an empty bushel basket as he went, his shirtsleeves rolled up.

Rose watched him go, manly swagger and all. What a man! He exuded sexual possibility at every turn—each look, each word a seemingly calculated attempt at seduction. Yet, she sensed an honest man beneath the winks and slow smiles. A man who didn't claim to be more than he was, who liked women and took opportunities to enjoy them. There was intelligence beneath the surface too. He'd built his own business after all.

It put her in something of a quandary to feel such an attraction to the man who could save Pembridge-on-the-Wye and wouldn't. Pembridge-on-the-Wye was her passion. She wanted it to be his too, because he had the connections and the ability to do something here. And yet, he wouldn't stay. While that was good news for any potential affair (it would be best if her lover could simply disappear after they were finished. Lingering would create complications), it went directly against her larger priorities.

That was putting the cart before the horse. He wasn't in her bed *yet*. Still, Rose couldn't help but feel such an event was inevitable. He wanted her, had indicated that he found her interesting. Even after her scold, he'd not run away from her. He'd walked with the cocky assurance of a man who knew he was going to get what he wanted.

A man like that was dangerous to the feminine mind. She'd do best to keep an eye on him and that would be no hardship at all.

As surprises went, this was the most pleasant one she'd had in some time. It was also the most distracting. Everyone had recognized Pembridge immediately and shyness had fallen over the orchard like a blight. Wonderful. The stubborn man had found a sure way to destroy productivity. They'd never get the crop in at this rate and while Rose wasn't worried about snow this year, she *was* worried about frost. There was a bite in the air suggesting the first frost was not far off. But Pembridge was cognizant of his effect on the orchard and moved immediately to dispel it with his easy manner. Within a half hour, all was miraculously restored to its proper order and Rose breathed easier.

It appeared he'd been telling the truth about off-loading cargo. Unafraid of hard work and heights, he volunteered himself for the taller trees, agilely climbing up and down the ladders with athletic grace. He carried filled bushel baskets on one shoulder with ease. Rose saw him stop on numerous occasions to relieve women struggling with heavy baskets; he was a gentleman and a laborer all neatly rolled into one exquisitely male package.

Pembridge was indeed undeniably male, a fact made self-evident by the sweat of his efforts and the thinness of his shirt by late afternoon. More than once, she stopped to admire the play of his muscles through the perspiration-soaked shirt as he lifted and hauled. He hadn't the usual stocky build of the laborer, but the muscled leanness of an athlete. He bent to retrieve an apple from the ground, his buttocks flexing at the motion, setting sinful notions running throughout Rose's head, enough to start a slow heat low in her belly. Again.

Rose blamed her unseemly fascination with him on the rumors. She never should have listened to the gossip. It was only natural to wonder about such things when so many of the rumors surrounding him were sexual in tone. But she'd rather not be so consumed by them out in public.

From up near the house, she heard her housekeeper, Mrs. Hemburton, ring the bell, signaling the end of the work day. Mrs. Hemburton would have cider casks out with plenty to drink before the workers headed home. There would be a short bit of socializing over the cider, a chance to celebrate the day's labor before it was too dark to travel.

It was a good day's work too that they'd put in, Rose noted, taking stock of the trees as she trudged through the rows. By the end of the week all would be harvested, safe and sound. She was lucky; her apple harvest had been good. But she knew many around her who had not had the yields they'd expected.

Pembridge was already at the casks, surrounded by men as if he were another local at the pub. His shirt was dirty (probably unsalvageable) his dark hair loose from his queue. The utterly masculine sight of him sent a small jolt of desire through her. The image of a hard-working man was a potent one. She tamped it down with a reminder; this was only one day. He still meant to leave as soon as he possibly could. He had no plans to make a long-term commitment here. His long absence and his estrangement from his uncle proved he viewed Pembridge as nothing more than an unwanted inconvenience. To be fair, he was not the cause of their suffering, that had been in place long before he'd come.

And when he looked at her with those laughing dark-brown eyes and sensual smile, she couldn't think of anything but the pleasure he promised. It gave one ideas and set one's mind to wondering what it would be like to be indulged by such a demigod of a man. Why not seize what the moment provided?

And then what? Moments had consequences. Reality

intruded. An earl might dally with a squire's widow while rusticating in the country, but nothing more. What did she expect would happen after an affair? He might not be the marrying kind now, but his title was new yet. He'd have to change his mind sooner or later and beget an heir. When he did, it would be with some suitable London girl with rank. These were crazy thoughts indeed.

Rose took a mug of cider to clear her thoughts and waited for the crowd of workers to ease away. It was clear she was not the only one affected by the earl's presence. There was a wave of energy among the people gathered for cider. He'd certainly boosted morale. She feared it may also have boosted their flagging hopes for change. A man of power who worked beside them was an intoxicating prospect.

"You did well today." Rose approached him as the last of the workers disappeared down the lane. She needed to make peace for her earlier behavior, regardless of her mental dilemma.

He turned his slow smile towards her. She couldn't help but smile back. His charm was contagious. "Why, Mrs. Janeway, is that an apology?"

Rose laughed, catching the teasing tone beneath his drawl, and met him head-on. This was the second time he'd held her accountable for her bold actions. "Do you never let a woman forget her foolishness?"

He considered her for a moment with thoughtful eyes. "I like a woman who can be honest with herself, Mrs. Janeway, as you were yesterday. You didn't look away even after you'd been caught in the act."

"There seemed no reason to stop since the damage had been done." Rose tossed him a coy glance and gave him back a taste of his own wit, "After all, I told myself, he doesn't seem to mind."

She was actually flirting with the enemy. No, *enemy* was too strong a word. Pembridge wasn't opposed to her—just the opposite, in fact. He wanted her. It was just Pembridge-on-the-Wye he was opposed to.

Pembridge laughed outright, his laughter a rich, full-bodied sound that filled the night air and wrapped her in its warmth. How long had it been since she'd laughed with anyone? There'd been so many cares of late, and only she to carry them.

"Mrs. Janeway, you are a delight. Thank goodness your wit is not sharper or it would cut me to threads. As it is, I will bid you good night and retreat with what dignity is left to me."

"No, wait." Impulse came to Rose sudden and swift. She didn't stop to think. "Now it is my turn. *I* have a proposition for *you*." That got his attention. His eyes perused her face in a casual study that caused her to flush. Perhaps she'd been too bold this time.

"I like the sound of that, Rose." He was back to first names with her and she was mightily encouraged.

"Stay for dinner. Mrs. Hemburton has made shepherd's pie and I hate eating alone. It's the least I can do for your services today."

"And the most?" He'd stepped closer to her, his eyes on her lips, creating the sensation that he was already kissing her in his mind.

"The most? I'm not sure I follow." He was hunting her again with his eyes, as he had in the orchard, hot and direct, making it impossible for her to think straight.

"You said dinner was the least you could do. What is the most?" Was he intentionally opening up a seductive gambit? Or perhaps he just couldn't help himself? Flirtation must come naturally to a man like him. Heaven help her, all the logic in the world could not keep her fantasies at bay. She ran her tongue over her suddenly dry lips. "Mrs. Hemburton baked fresh sugar biscuits today as well. We can have them for dessert with pears from the orchard."

He took another step towards her, his voice a soft, low tease. "I prefer something a bit tarter for dessert, something with a little bite to it."

Rose's heart hammered in erotic excitement. His kisses weren't the only things that could make a woman swoon. But she didn't want to appear over-eager. She wasn't out of her depth yet when it came to matching wits. "I think we'll leave that open to negotiation."

CHAPTER FIVE

THE ONLY THING STANDING between her and the promise of
unbridled pleasure was shepherd's pie and sugar biscuits.
He was leaving the 'negotiations' of what was to come
up to her, she realized. She'd scolded him, worked him
hard, ruined his shirt, insulted his lifestyle and somewhere
during the day he'd decided he wanted her anyway.

Did she want him? The primal woman in her clamored
yes. A man like Killian Redbourne was a treat to be savored
even if only for a night and, who knew, maybe she could
change his mind about leaving. But that was a dangerous
fantasy. If she chose to embrace such whimsy, she'd be
opening herself up to great hurt. Her heart would be at
risk, she could see the inevitable now if she went down
that road. It would be all too simple to love a man like
Killian.

The soft light of the candles in the dining room served
to enhance his looks, and Rose was tempted to forego the
shepherd's pie altogether. He'd taken time before the meal

to sluice off the day's grime at the pump. She knew because she'd watched him from her window upstairs, biting her nails as he'd stripped out of his stained shirt, all glorious, naked muscle in the light of the rising moon. Now, he sat across from her in an old shirt rummaged from a trunk in the attic, his dark hair loose on his shoulders, turning the shade of a polished walnut thanks to the combined efforts of candlelight and water droplets.

"You look like a highwayman." Rose ventured.

He gave her a skeptical stare, mischief at home in its usual place in his eyes. "I hope not, unless of course you mean the romanticized highwaymen in the ballads. Real highwaymen tend to be dirty and ill-kempt." Rose laughed at that and took a bite of the shepherd's pie.

He gave her a bone-warming smile. "Today, *you* looked like a highwaywoman in your trousers and shirt and those high boots you wore." He chewed and added as an after-thought, "Very appealing. Very *distracting*, if I might be so bold."

"At least we both have future careers in crime assured."

Pembridge laid aside his fork and sat back in his chair. "I may be reduced to that. The estate is broke. I haven't told anyone else, except Peyton of course. I'm not sure I want word to get out and create more panic than is neces-sary. But I thought you should know."

Because she'd accused him of not caring, of treating the responsibilities of the estate callously, Rose thought. "I didn't know." It was a throwaway line. What else could she say? Perhaps she had been hasty in her conclusions.

Pembridge lifted one shoulder in a shrug, dismissing her guilt. "The estate could be faring well and I still wouldn't be staying. Even if I wanted to stay, I'm not Rumpelstiltskin. I can't spin straw into gold for these people. I have my own fortune from business ventures, but it's not of the magnitude needed here."

Rose smiled wanly in agreement. "The only gold around here is red-gold." He raised his eyebrow in question and she explained. "The apples in my orchard are called Redstreaks. Local legend has it that a Lord Scudamore brought the pips for Redstreaks back from France with him in the 1600s. They're known for their reddish-golden hue."

"Like your hair." Killian said softly, reaching across the table to wind an errant curl about his finger. "It's the most original color I've ever seen, not blond but not really red." He gave her a hot look and dropped his voice. "It makes a man wonder if perhaps all your hair is lucky enough to share the same hue."

One well-placed remark and dinner was over. Sugar biscuits would have to wait. There would be no more negotiations, although in truth, Rose knew she'd reached her decision long before she'd invited him to dinner.

Killian rose from the table and extended his hand to her, the gesture both blatant and eloquent in its message; *I want you. Tonight, I will be your lover and you will be mine.*

Rose took his hand and all it offered. She let him lead her upstairs, the brace of candles in his hand casting their shadow along the staircase wall, his other hand gripping hers with his warm strength.

In her room, he quietly shut the door behind them although there was no one to see or hear. But the very act of doing so created an intimate sense of privacy that said he was hers alone and she was his.

He came to her, bending slightly to kiss her at the base of her ear and to whisper, "Watch me, Rose." He drew back, his eyes holding her to the request, and slowly began to remove his clothes.

The shirt went first, button by button, until his torso was revealed in all its anticipated glory. She'd only seen his back at the pump. He was beautiful, all sculpted muscle, the definition of his abdomen tapering to the trimness of his waist.

"Come help with my boots."

There was a familiar intimacy in helping a shirtless man remove his footwear, Rose thought, tugging at the boots. They gave easily and he ordered her back to the bed, his hands already at the waistband of his trousers, pushing them down his hips and kicking them off his legs.

What legs they were, shaped by long hard muscles. He must have spent ages in the saddle to have calves like that, thighs like that. Her eyes moved up his legs to his rampant masculinity—proof, had she needed it, of how desperately he desired her.

Wonder filled her, peaceful, inexplicable wonder that a stranger could provoke such a reaction in her and she in him. She was a practical woman, an earthy woman. She'd lived around the cycles of the seasons her entire life. She knew the power of the harvest. It was no coincidence that so many babies; foals, calves, and lambs were born in the spring. Humans mimicked their pattern as well. One had only to look at the plethora of summer birthdates in the parish register to see the lure of the harvest season.

Perhaps she and Killian (it was impossible to think of him as Pembridge in the intimacy of the moment), were nothing more than strangers looking for the succor of another's body.

He was reaching for her, drawing her to him. She could feel the heat of his naked body, but her curiosity would not rest. "Why do you want me? You hardly know me." She whispered.

"I know you better than you think." His breath feathered against her ear, his mouth moving to take her mouth in a long kiss. She opened her lips to him, letting his tongue tangle with hers until she was caught up in the need rising between them, the kiss growing stronger, more insistent as it progressed. His hands worked the bodice of her gown loose, shoving it off her shoulders before his warm hands took her breasts in their palms. She moaned against him, feeling the power of his erection hot through her clothes. She wanted release from the garments, from the pressure building inside her.

He gave it to her, sliding her gown to the floor and making quick work of her under things so that she stood naked with him. He bent her back towards the bed. "Lie down for me, let me see you."

She started to protest, suddenly uncomfortable. She'd never been openly, blatantly naked with her husband.

They'd relegated their lovemaking to the dark anonymity that existed beneath the blankets.

"You're too beautiful to hide," Killian coaxed, coming down beside her on the bed. He ran his hand the length of her body, from breast to hip, hip to that most private place and there his hand rested in the red-gold arbor of her curls, gently exploring, teasing.

"Touch me too, Rose." He encouraged. "I'm as much yours as you are mine."

She needed no further invitation. Her hands ached to touch his body, to feel the paths of his muscles beneath her fingers. Her own hands traveled downwards as his had until they found the length of him. His eyes lit with desire at the contact, a groan of appreciation escaping him.

She stroked him, learning his rhythm until he begged for mercy. His pleasure made her audacious and suddenly she couldn't wait any longer. She widened her legs and whispered, "Come into me, Killian."

No other summons was required. He growled and moved over her at once, entering her in one fierce thrust. She bucked hard against him, his penetration full and intense. It had been ages since she'd taken a man into her body and her

body welcomed him as if in homecoming, as if he had always been meant to be there. She gasped in delight and felt him tense.

"Did I hurt you? Do you need me to stop?" She heard the grit of restraint in his voice and doubted he could have stopped even if she wanted it. She didn't. Stopping was the furthest thought from her mind. Passion had her in its throes. She could only think of going forward to the great paradise each thrust of Killian's brought closer.

She raised her hips, urging him onward until they were there, on the crest of their desire. She had only time to gasp once more and they were at the top, hovering in the wake of a shattering bliss, and then they were falling together towards peace and oblivion.

CHAPTER SIX

THE GRAY SHADOWS OF morning teased Killian into waking. He stretched, arching his back in well-rested satisfaction. Then it hit him—where he was, what he'd done and with whom. Rose. But the bed felt empty. A quick roll to his side confirmed his suspicions. She was already up. Her side of the bed was cold, suggesting she'd been up for quite some time.

It couldn't be later than seven o'clock in the morning judging by the pale light. But he was in the country now. The country kept different hours than the city and this was a working farm. Crops and harvests didn't grow on banker's hours.

Killian sighed, blowing out a deep breath of air and fell back on his pillows. Yes, he was in the country now and more than the hours of the day were different. The social rules were different too, in some ways more lax and in other ways more strict. Would the residents of Pembridge-

on-the-Wye permit him to dally with their Widow Janeway
without imposing negative consequences on him or her?

He was fairly certain he could get away with it. But
Rose? The last thing he wanted was to leave her under a
cloud of censure while he simply departed back to his life
in the city. *Departed.*

So much had changed in the span of one day. Yesterday
morning he'd been eager to leave Pembridge-on-the-Wye.
He'd gone searching for a woman who was supposed to
help him expedite that goal. Instead, he'd ended up picking
apples and this morning he was in no immediate hurry to
leave.

Last night, he'd expected to remain detached from the
encounter beyond the physical gratification it brought and
yet, making love with Rose had touched him far beyond
that. She was a generous lover, giving herself over entirely
to their mutual pleasure. Beneath the sheets, his cock
thrummed in remembered knowledge of it—the way she'd
touched him, the way she'd opened to him and unabash-
edly joined him in mutual climax. He'd been with women
he'd known a short time and women he'd known much
longer before they'd coupled. But in neither instance, had
he ever felt the way he'd felt last night. It had been more
than simple physical pleasure. He'd felt connected in some
fundamental way with another human being, and he found
he wanted to feel that way again.

This was not going as planned. Usually bedding women
he was attracted to and knew little about worked out well
for him. He'd get up in the morning, ready to walk away.

Last night had started that way, but it hadn't ended with his regular level of detachment.

He'd told her he knew her better than she thought. Maybe it was true, and maybe it was just something a man said to get what he wanted. After last night, Killian doubted the latter and was puzzled by the former. What did he know about Rose Janeway? She was a widow with vast orchards she personally worked herself if yesterday was any testament. And she was beautiful. That was the list. The list of things he *didn't* know about her was far longer.

He didn't know her favorite color, her favorite food, her likes or dislikes. He knew none of the things friends know about one another. And yet, they'd shared an intimacy that exceeded friendship. It was strange how little time had been needed to stoke his desire for her to a fevered pitch. Stranger still were the remnants of that possession. Usually when he took a woman on short acquaintance, his ardor was quickly cooled. Not so in this circumstance. He wanted her again and with such immediacy he was about ready to go in search of her and drag her back to bed. When it came to Rose Janeway, his ardor was far from slaked.

Hard to say if he would have acted on that impulse. He didn't get a chance to find out. The door to the bedroom opened and Rose entered, shutting the door with her hip, her hands wrapped around a basket of folded clothing. She looked enticingly fresh in a dark-blue skirt of heavy fabric for everyday wear and a white blouse, her hair draped over one shoulder in a tight braid that lay provocatively against the swell of her breast.

"No trousers today?" Killian queried, wondering if she'd notice the tenting bulge beneath the sheets.

"I've come up to change."

Ah, no help for him there. He was already imagining the buttons of her blouse coming undone one by one, each one revealing a larger show of the cleavage beneath. His hands already itched to hold the weight of her breasts in his palms.

Rose set the basket down at the foot of the bed. "I unearthed some more clothes in the attic for you. I thought you might like them for work."

It was a nervy statement. Leave it to Rose to so masterfully introduce the prickly topic of 'what next' with the subtle offer of a shirt and trousers. He knew precisely what she was asking him.

Killian found he liked her presumptions. Perhaps it was a sign she didn't think as poorly of him as she had the day before if she was thinking he'd stay and help pick apples. He knew too, this was not just about apples. She was offering him her bed for the duration of his stay; an offer that had merit and one he'd gladly accept.

But he had to tread carefully here too. Too many assumptions on her part might lead to a precarious situation when he prepared to leave. He *was* going to leave. It was a foregone conclusion. The only question was when.

Certainly not before I drink my fill of this woman. His body throbbed. Even the simple act of watching her fold laundry and put it away was painfully arousing. She stretched up to put a stack of clothes on top of the wardrobe, the reach drawing the fabric of her blouse tight against her breasts. But the reach was awkward for her to manage easily, even with her height. Without thinking, Killian threw back the covers and went to her aid, steadying the teetering stack of linens.

"Thank you." She said, her color suddenly rising beautifully in her face as her eyes took in his naked body and obvious state of arousal.

Killian shrugged, at ease with his own nakedness and body. He turned to face her fully, utterly unashamed and smiled at her, his eyes sparkling with an unspoken question.

Her blue eyes darted towards the window, uncertain. "The workers will be here by eight." She stalled.

"We don't need very long, I think." He dropped his gaze to her lips in deliberate contemplation. "I'm already undressed and you were going to change anyway." He bent to kiss her, to silence any other half-hearted protests and because he couldn't wait any longer to do otherwise. She melted into him, assurance that her protests were pro forma at best, that she wanted him too.

He bunched the hem of her skirts in one hand and rucked them to her waist, seeking the wet heat of her core. She was long past ready, making him wonder what exactly she'd planned to do all along when she'd come up to the room. It was clear neither of them were going to wait for her to undress.

A moan of distress escaped her lips and her attention momentarily focused on the window. He heard it too, the sounds of a wagon jangling into the drive. He'd not survive the day if he didn't take her now. He'd not experienced apple picking with an erection, but he didn't think it would be pleasant, let alone easy to explain. "Don't worry." His voice was ragged.

He maneuvered her against the flat surface of the wardrobe doors, her arms tight around his neck, and lifted. Instinctively, her legs wrapped about his waist and he thrust deep inside her, her excited cries muffled against his bare shoulder. He could feel the desperate nips of her teeth against his skin, an intoxicating delight of erotic proportions. Killian pumped once, twice more, the pressure of his culmination rough and savage as it built. He felt her convulse around him and he let himself go.

They were both breathing hard in the aftermath, her eyes wide with wonder, a certain elation coursing through him at having been the one to put the wonder there. Killian pushed a strand of loose hair back from her face, his hand caressing her cheek. "I'll go down first," he murmured, latent desire still evident in his voice. "It will look as if I merely arrived early and am awaiting you. Take your time."

Killian let her down gently and grabbed his borrowed shirt from the bed. With a little luck, she'd take him at his word and take time to change. With more luck, it would be enough time for the well-kissed puffiness of her lips to go down. If not, he'd soon find out how tolerant the citizens of Pembridge-on-the-Wye could be, because there was no mistaking the look on Rose's face for anything other than what it was: the look of a woman who'd been well loved.

CHAPTER SEVEN

WHEN HAD SHE BECOME such a wanton? She'd always been an honest woman (as Killian had phrased it) about her passions. But never had she indulged them so thoroughly. Just the remembrance of last night was enough to heat her cheeks.

Rose quickly undid the buttons of her blouse and sponged down her skin with a cool cloth. She rinsed the cloth in the basin on the washstand and washed her face, trying to restore some calm to her racing body. She had workers waiting in the orchard for her command. She had crops that needed picking. There'd been no time for a morning dalliance, and yet here she was, struggling to cover up the signs of having been well and thoroughly tumbled. The mirror over the washstand didn't lie.

Rose slipped into her work shirt and pulled on her usual trousers. But even the manly garb carried its own reminders of the passion that had ruled her judgment of late. Killian thought the trousers gave her the air of a highwaywoman, an air he rather liked. Her mind, her room, was full of reminders of Killian's presence. His ruined lawn shirt lay folded in the basket she'd brought up, along with his trousers. The smell of his sex lay heavy and alluring on the sheets. She would never be able to look at the old wardrobe again without recalling what they'd done there.

Rose tugged her boots on with a fierce pull. She had to get the apples in. They were far more important than a bout in the sheets with Killian Redbourne. They would be here, providing for her, long after he was gone. Handsome is as handsome does, and Killian had no reason to stay beyond the deal they'd struck. Really, seeing as how things had turned out between them, his leaving was for the better. They could have their nights of passion without any tedious strings attached. She told herself to think of how awkward it would be to see Killian regularly after what they'd shared, knowing he had no plans of building on that night and she had no right to expect it.

But knowing and doing were two different ends of the stick. Rose knew herself well enough to know she would indeed expect what he had not promised if he stayed around. Knowing he was near would only serve to raise her hopes. How could it not, when last night had been every woman's fantasy? It had certainly been *her* fantasy. He'd been a lover nonpareil who'd given her the whole of his attention. She'd seen it in the depths of his eyes, felt it in the stroke of his hands, the caresses he lavished on her body, exploring her, learning her as if she were the most priceless of treasures. With him, it had been more than a sex act done for the purpose of procreation. With him, it had been a search *for* and a claiming *of* pleasure, the ultimate pursuit of mind and body. Wanton or not, she wanted it to be that way again, something extraordinarily different than the practical couplings she'd shared with her husband. Nightfall could not come fast enough.

Over the next few days, Killian knew he was only moderately successful in keeping his thoughts on his work. Any time Rose was near, his attention strayed. Once he nearly fell off his ladder. Another time, he'd almost collided with a basket carrier who happened to cross his path. It was all for a good cause, though. Rose Janeway fascinated him. She was a woman who was not bound by convention. Perhaps it was the freedom of the countryside that made such a lifestyle possible. During the day, she was an admirable leader directing the activities of the extensive orchards. By night she was extraordinary lover. Killian found himself counting the hours until sunset, eager to hold her.

There were so many ways to make love and she was open to them all. One night, he'd come upon her unawares as she bathed. It had been the height of voyeuristic eroticism to watch the water sluice over her body, her washcloth moving over her breasts and between her legs. He'd watched until his own arousal was at its peak and then he'd carried her to the bed, dripping wet.

He could not always wait until after dinner or until they reached the bedroom. There'd been a night when the sight of her in a soft pink wool dress had been the undoing of him. He had not waited for the meal to be finished before the table had been engaged in double duty.

Other nights, their need had been too great to wait beyond the shutting of the front door. She'd shaken with desire as he shoved down her trousers, baring her bottom and thrusting deep within from behind while she cried out her release bent over the arm of the sofa.

It wasn't just the sex that made his time with Rose so memorable. In the night, they had time to talk, time to think about something besides apples. Sometimes talk was serious. He'd asked about her husband, curious to know what kind of man had married Rose Janeway. She'd asked about his life in London and his business. Sometimes talk was more humorous but no less insightful.

"What were you thinking the day I came to the orchard? Right after you'd scolded me for my lack of interest in the estate?" Killian ventured one night after a particularly satisfying bout of lovemaking. He twirled a lock of her hair around his finger, watching it spring back against the white flesh of her breast. They were naked in her bed, warm with the flush of their passion, the sheets riding low on their hips.

Rose smiled wickedly, a finger tracing the aureole of his breast. "You'd stepped towards me and were suddenly interested in the quality of the apple wood. I thought you were going to spank me." Her eyes lit with a seductive blue flame that stoked the embers of his arousal. He was already coming to life again when she added, "And I thought a spanking from you wouldn't be entirely unpleasant."

Killian chuckled. Rose continued to surprise and amaze him at every turn. To discover a woman so confident in her own sensual appetites was a rare find indeed. "You must have thought you'd been very bad."

"Well, I had given you a dressing down that was most out of line."

"Then we have something in common. About that same time I was giving you a dressing down in my mind of another sort entirely." Killian tucked her beneath him and rose up on his arms.

"You're not appalled then? About the spanking thing?"

Killian laughed. "Aroused is more like it. In case you haven't noticed…" and then there was no more talk for quite some time.

But all good things come to an end and Killian's week had flown by filled with the contentment of days spent in hard work and nights filled with unequaled passion.

The orchards were close to picked. Only a day or two remained, Killian noted ruefully as he watched Rose deal with the workers, offering encouragement when a job was well-done, redirecting when tasks were performed less efficiently. The people respected her. She took time to bend close and listen to the things the children told her or to look at a treasure from their pockets as she strode through the orchards. She was less patient with the weather. Several times he'd caught her watching the sky with narrowed eyes as if trying to gauge how much time she had left.

"What worries you?" He asked, coming to stand by her on one such occasion. The afternoon was waning, the sky gray overhead instead of yesterday's blue. It was colder too. He rubbed his hands together and tucked them under his armpits for warmth.

"The frost." She replied grimly, balancing her gaze now between the apples that remained and the lingering hours of daylight. We won't have another day. We'll have to work late tonight. There's no other choice, but at what cost?" Her voice trailed off, fighting worry and desperation. They'd been so close to beating old Jack Frost.

Something foreign and possessive awoke full-fledged in Killian's gut: the sudden recognition that these were his people, *his woman*. If they needed this crop in, if *she* needed this crop in tonight, he'd move heaven and earth to see it done.

CHAPTER EIGHT

THE WORKERS WERE TIRED. She'd lose the women and children when dark fell. Children needed to be fed and put to bed. With the work force depleted, the men would have to work even longer. Killian knew what to do. "Let me take care of this. Can Mrs. Hemburton get torches ready?" He grabbed an older boy by the shoulder as he passed. "Can you drive a gig?"

"Yes, milord." The fourteen-year-old bobbed his head with adolescent pride. He was a big lad for his age, his boast was probably true. "Good, I want you to take the gig and the pony that are in the barn and drive to Pembridge Hall. Tell them you want to speak with Lord Dursley, tell him we need help getting the crop in. He'll take care of the rest. But tell him to hurry."

The boy ran off and Rose began to protest. "Really, we'll be fine. We'll manage something. There's no need." She was full of stubborn pride. Killian recognized it at once as a landowner's pride.

"I know you can manage, but why just manage when we can do it well? He answered with a smile. "Get the torches ready and have Mrs. Hemburton set up the shed as a staging area.

Within three hours, the sun had set and the orchards had been transformed. Torches safely lined the rows and various intervals to give light to the pickers. Trestle tables had been set up the length of the shed, laden with food packed down in hampers from Pembridge Hall. A space had been cleared for a bonfire so that basket carriers could warm their hands before setting off into the orchard with empty containers. Children who were too tired to pick apples up off the ground any more were tucked into makeshift haystacks along the wall of the shed, warm and drowsy.

Outside the shed, Killian silently congratulated himself. It was almost a party-like atmosphere. The little lines of worry that had creased Rose's brow had disappeared and he took a sense of pride in knowing he could take responsibility for that.

Peyton appeared at his side, his shirtsleeves rolled up. He'd been directing the unloading of baskets of apples at the cider press. "I brought you some clothes, by the way."

Killian chuckled. "How did you know?"

Peyton fixed him with a knowing stare. "There are only a few reasons why a man doesn't come home at night." He paused and Killian sensed he was waging a debate with himself. "I hope you know what you're doing. This isn't London and you've been away a long time."

"Rose and I understand each other. She knows this is just an affair and a short-lived one at that." But even as he said the words, Killian heard their emptiness. What did he want after their agreement was over? What did Rose want? Did she want him to leave? Was he only a convenience?

"Just so, Killian, be aware these are dangerous times. There is unrest afoot. They're breaking machinery in Kent and burning ricks. I would caution you not to lift these people's hopes only to have them dashed when you're gone, which will be all too soon for their tastes. The estate is indeed broke, but for your sake I'd still not like to see it burned."

Killian nodded solemnly. The swing riots had started over the summer in East Anglia. In addition to machine-wrecking there'd been accounts of arson and blackmail. The rioters were usually led by people of decent social character finally fed up with the state of the economy and the government's inattention to fixing the problem. The government was too busy these days worrying over the new revolution in France to focus enough of its attention on the rioting poor and out-of-work laborers.

Thanks to Killian's efforts, the evening of work came to a close around nine o'clock, the last of the pickers straggling in from the orchards, tired and dirty. Although it was late, Rose had insisted on paying everyone before they departed. Normally, Killian would have protested, arguing for a payday to be set for the morning. But after Peyton's pointed reminder of the unrest around them, he said nothing, only positioning himself solidly behind Rose's chair at the makeshift pay table and letting her work.

She paid them in coin and in kind. Along with cash wages, workers also received casks of cider and a few bushels of apples, useful food items to have in one's cellar against the oncoming winter. Killian noted Mrs. Hemburton deep in conversation over all the country delicacies one could make from apples. He had no doubt that pantries throughout Pembridge-on-the-Wye would be stuffed with variations of everything from apple jelly to apple butter.

The whole process was quite humbling. The people lined up in front of Rose's table were grateful, the apples and casks carted away like treasures, the coins carefully tied in handkerchiefs for safekeeping on the ride home. The harvest was over, Killian realized. Whatever money these laborers had hidden away at home would have to last them until spring when they could find work hiring on to plow fields and begin the process all over again— six long, cold months away. How did they do it on a few cider casks and coins? Almost all of them had families to care for.

He'd never lived that way, even though his father had not been a wealthy man by ton standards. They'd been rich though, in ways he had not appreciated. There'd been no worry about where the next meal would come from or whether there'd be new warm clothes to wear, and there'd been money for his education. Truth be told, standing there in the dark behind Rose, he felt more than a little guilty, not so much because of what he'd had, but because of what he'd hadn't noticed. Until tonight, he'd been blissfully unaware.

He watched Rose slide an extra coin into the pile collected

by the young boy who'd driven the gig to Pembridge Hall.
She squeezed the boy's hand as she pressed the extra coin
into his palm unnoticed by all but him. "Promise you'll
send for me if your father takes a turn for the worse." She
said in a low voice so as not to shame him.

But Killian was ashamed. Not for the boy, but for himself. He'd been unaware his whole life, but Rose wasn't.
She knew these people, knew their individual needs, like
those of the fourteen-year-old boy who'd been out doing a
man's work in place of a father who couldn't, a father who
must be lying at home worrying about what his family
would do without his wages. She was doing what she could
for them, and as a widow on her own with no substantial
wealth to her name she was not necessarily well-placed
to do it.

Rose Janeway was not rich. Her neat stone manor was
nicely kept, but it was old. He'd taken stock over the week
of her circumstances. Her furnishings were well-worn.
He'd be surprised if the scarred wardrobe they'd made
love against that first morning was less than two generations old. In all likelihood it was probably more. In the
country, furniture was handed down father to son, mother
to daughter. These homes were not like the townhouses of
London's elite, redone according to whim and fashion.

No, Rose Janeway was not rich. But she was doing what
she could with what she had, and Killian guessed she
was doing so at some expense to her personal comfort.
In Kent, the laborers earned fifteen pence per week, and
she'd paid out an average of twenty pence for a week's
worth of work.

At last, the workers were gone. Even Peyton, who'd stayed until the end, had left. A thrill ran through Killian at the thought of having Rose to himself and the sensual celebration they would carry out in private. He was imagining how he would take her on the soft bed upstairs, her hair spread out on the pillow, her body completely naked in the candlelight, her lips wet with kisses, when Rose closed the cash box and held out her hand. "Come with me, Killian."

At her touch, he hardened immediately, but she did not lead him upstairs. Instead, she led him into the cider shed. The sweet smell of apples assailed his nostrils; the shed was warm and crowded with barrels of fruit waiting to be made into the region's preferred drink. He'd never seen so many apples in one place before.

"What are we doing here?" Killian asked, trying to combat the dual senses of urgency (he wanted her desperately) and disappointment (since it appeared they weren't headed directly upstairs).

She turned and smiled at him, a wide, generous smile that fulfilled all his preconceived notions about her mouth. She pressed her body against his and wrapped her arms about his neck before dropping a hand between his legs and squeezing gently. "We're doing *this*." Then she took his mouth in a deep kiss that fired his imagination while leaving nothing to it.

CHAPTER NINE

SHE'D NEVER TAKEN A MAN. Before this week, she'd never taken a lover either. Her husband had been a comfortable man and their marriage solid, but he'd been so much older than she, and there'd been little room for romance amid the practicalities of their daily life. Killian had shown her there was a difference between the two aspects. Whatever else Killian Redbourne could or could not be to her, he was her lover, and, in that sense, her first.

Rose slowly undid the buttons of his shirt, careful not to let her nerves, her excitement, give her away with fumbling fingers. It was warm in the shed, perhaps not warm enough to dispense with clothing altogether, but maybe a few garments.

Access at last! She ran her palms over his chest in smooth circles, feeling his skin and the ridges of the muscles beneath. This was what the body of a man in his prime felt like, all hard muscles and contours. "You're beautiful." She looked up at him. Could he see the awe in her eyes, the abject appreciation? Who'd have thought a man's body was to be worshiped?

"I think there should be more poetry written about a man's body." Rose teased, her voice soft and coy. She let a thumb drift lazily over his nipple, feeling it harden beneath her caress. "I wonder why it is that there's so many sonnets written to a woman's eyes, but the male gender seems to have been missed altogether."

Killian laughed, a warm, seductive sound in their lantern-lit paradise. His arms were linked loosely about her waist in casual intimacy. "Do you suggest an ode to a man's chest?"

"That rhymes. I think you may be off to a good start. I'm beginning to believe you have many hidden talents."

"Like what?" He bent to kiss her, a little nip on the column of her neck that sent her pulse racing. It was incredibly simple to be this way with him, as if they'd been lovers for ages, acquiring an effortless comfort that only comes with long familiarity. And yet it had only been a few days. That was part of his charm, this ability to put a woman at ease.

"You're fishing now, looking for compliments." She replied, dropping her hand back to the waist of his trousers, seeking an entrance to the heat of him.

"I'm not the only one fishing." His voice had taken on the gratifying husky qualities of a man well-aroused. There was a certain power in knowing she could stoke him to readiness. He was a man who could have any woman he chose, and, for the time being, he'd chosen her. But for how much longer? The crop was in. Their implicit arrangement was at an end.

Her hands worked his trousers free, boldly pushing them over narrow hips and firm buttocks. He was ready, but where to put him? She'd not thought of that when she'd begun her seduction. She'd only thought of how warm and wonderful-smelling the shed would be, how lovely to couple with him amid the bounty of the harvest. She'd not thought of any actual place, merely images.

"I think the table would do nicely." Killian whispered naughtily at her ear. He gave it a quick perusal for splinters, but it was a sturdy work table of heavy cherry, smoothed from years of use, and there were none.

He backed up to it and dragged her to him. "Now, I believe you were about to climb on top of him."

"Why I believe I was." Rose laughed, the awkward glitch neatly dealt with before embarrassment could damage the ambience.

His hands were warm at her hips, holding her firmly, guiding her discreetly, she noticed as she stripped out of her own trousers, and she came over him with only her shirt on, feeling the air of the room caressing her bare skin.

"Slowly, Rose. I want this to last. There, sink down now. Take me deep inside you."

She did as she was instructed, feeling decadent and utterly female as she joined her body with his. This was something she'd only dared to imagine. Killian let out a contented "Ah," and she could feel the coarse rub of his man's hair against her bare buttocks.

Rose moved experimentally, but Killian halted her.

"Wait, give your body time to stretch, time to know its mate." His hands were at her shirt front, fumbling uncharacteristically in his haste, making no secret of his rising need. "I want to see your body, Rose, I want to feel the weight of you in my hands as we make love." His eyes were black with desire. Her own need for him spiked at his words. These were not the words of a practiced libertine; his body attested to the truth of them.

His hands were at her breasts now, cupping them in his palms, his thumbs stroking her nipples into an erection of their own. She started to move over him and this time he did not stall her. She rocked her hips gently, back and forth at first as if she were out for a Sunday ride. The first tiny notes of physical fulfillment grew in her, lapping at her core like small waves against a shore. She changed her gait and began to move up and down on his shaft, crying out in wonder when she rubbed a place deep inside that released the most exquisite sensation of pleasure-pain.

A knowing smile took Killian's mouth at the sound of her gasp. "I didn't know..." she stammered.

"Now you do, my dear." But his own pleasure was rising fast, and he could manage no more words.

She delighted in the sound of his moans, in the feel of his body beneath hers giving itself over the primal release bearing down on them both. His hands at her hips urged her on faster now, her breath was coming in pants, their bodies were pushed to the limits of anticipation. Then she took them there, to the top of their pleasure, and they were overcome with the power of it.

She collapsed on top of him, exhausted from the physical efforts of the long day and the emotional wellspring of their lovemaking. She was boneless against him, unwilling and perhaps even unable to move. Why move when paradise was contained on a tabletop, she thought dreamily.

Rose was vaguely aware of Killian rising, assembling his clothes into some decent array and then lifting her in his arms for the journey to the house.

How he managed the trip up the stairs, she could not guess. She was capable of little else but basking in the drowsiness of satiated satisfaction.

CHAPTER TEN

ROSE WOKE SLOWLY THE next morning, her body filled with the lazy exhilaration of knowing there was nothing to do, at least nothing that *had* to be done. The apples were safely stored. There was nothing that could not wait one more day. After the hard work of the summer and the harvesting of the autumn, she could take one day and relax. The thought of a full day stretching out before her with no expectations seemed like a gift from the gods.

Beside her, Killian stirred, his arm seeking her in his sleep. She turned towards him and smiled, reveling in the chance to study her lover up close in the light of day. His hair was loose, falling over his shoulders, dark and sensual, framing his face. Longer hair on a man was undoubtedly sexy, Rose thought. Not that Killian's hair was truly long. It wasn't long at all compared to a woman's. Her own hair unbound reached the small of her back. Killian's hair merely graced his shoulders, enough of it that it could be neatly pulled back without looking straggly.

She stroked a length of it, pushing it back behind his ear. It was enough to wake him. "Good morning."

"You've been watching me sleep." Killian teased in a gravelly voice still filled with the effects of slumber.

Rose propped herself up on one arm, "I've been wondering all sorts of things about you."

"Like what? Or should I be frightened?" Killian traced her hip bone through the sheets with slow hands, and her need for him started to rise at his touch.

"Did you really make Mrs. Dempsey swoon?"

Killian's mouth made a playful, scolding frown. "What a leading question." His hand kept kneading the curve of her hip in a most delightful, possessive manner that would soon render the issue of Mrs. Dempsey de trop.

"Well," Rose pressed. "Did you?"

Killian rolled his eyes. "Suffice it to say, Mrs. Dempsey is a woman with an overinflated sense of her own charms."

"Hmmm." Rose pretended to reflect on the comment, studying him. "Sounds like a certain man I know."

"Does it? I'd agree with the *overinflated* part just now." Killian rejoined. Rose's eyes dropped to his waist, speculating about what she might find if she lifted the sheets. "Lusty wench." Killian grinned, following her gaze. "The problem with you, wench, is that you need kissing. Badly, unless I miss my guess." He drew her to him, the evidence of her speculations confirmed.

"The *problem* with me, is it?" Rose said coyly, laughter rising up with her words

"Thankfully," Killian said in mock seriousness, drawing

a finger up the back of her leg. "I know precisely how to solve your kind of problem."

Rose yelped. "That tickles!"

Killian's eyes brightened, and she knew she'd made a tactical error. "Oh no, oh no, you wouldn't!" Rose cried as Killian launched an avid search for more tickle-spots.

They were wrestling now, kicking at the covers, grappling for pillows, laughing, screaming out their delight in the impromptu tickle war that ensued.

They didn't hear the pounding of booted footsteps on the landing until it was too late. The door flew open and Rose's latest scream died a squeaky death in her throat. She grabbed up a sheet in a belated attempt at modesty, feeling her cheeks heat to a beet-red. Killian merely put down his pillow shield and drawled, "Good morning, Peyton. What brings you out so early?"

They might as well have all been dressed and sitting in the parlor for tea, Rose thought, the ridiculous image causing an embarrassing bubble of laughter to creep dangerously up her throat and threaten to burst. But what Peyton had to share was no laughing matter.

"There's been a fire at a Mr. Franklin's place. The barn burned. He claims there's reason to believe it's arson."

Rose's heart was in her throat, replacing the errant bubble of laughter. It could indeed be arson. She heard the implied message behind Dursley's terse message and all that went unsaid. A barn burnt meant necessities lost: a winter's supply of hay for the animals, perhaps even livestock itself. Franklin was not well-liked. He'd paid his day laborers poorly this year, citing the exigencies of a smaller crop, and had hoarded the profit for himself. People felt he had dealt with them unfairly.

"What do you want me to do about it?" Killian said, his strong gaze matching Dursley's in challenge.

Dursley raised a supercilious eyebrow, a practiced move, Rose was sure he'd done a thousand times. It was no doubt quite effective in getting results. "In case you've forgotten, you're the damned magistrate in these parts now, Redbourne. You need to get out there and handle this before your little part of Herefordshire falls victim to swing riots."

Killian rose from the bed and drew on his discarded shirt, anger simmering in his taut muscles. "You don't need to tell me my duty, Peyton. I know it full well. I'll be downstairs in five minutes."

CHAPTER ELEVEN

"YOU HAVE SOME answering to do," Killian fumed precisely five minutes later in the small parlor of Rose's home. Peyton sat on the worn sofa, one leg elegantly crossed, looking entirely too pleased with himself. "You cannot come barging into someone's home like that and walk into their bedroom, where God knows what's going on."

"Clearly." Peyton said.

"Stop doing that eyebrow thing you do. You're going to do it again, I can tell. I'm not one of your errant brothers, you know."

"Leave my brothers out of this." Peyton said with a coldness that made Killian regret his words. Perhaps he had gone a bit too far with the comment, but deuce take it, he was furious with Peyton for interrupting a most private pleasure and for unnecessarily taking him to task in front of Rose.

"I am sorry, Killian, for barging in. But this news is serious, far more serious than playing Tup the Widow."

"Don't be crass." Killian cut in. "It's not like that."

"Oh? How is it then? You'd hardly been in town two days and you were in her bed and haven't been home since. What do you think this is? She does understand that you'll be leaving as soon as you possibly can? That she's just another notch in your illustrious belt, nothing more than a sidelight compared to your conquests in London."

"I will not be provoked, Peyton." Killian grimaced. "My relationship with Rose Janeway is not the issue on display here. It has nothing to do with these claims of arson."

"If you think that, you've not been a nobleman very long." Peyton took a small measure of pity on him.

"About one week, by my recollection." Killian replied dryly. "I'm a businessman. I know how to make money. I don't imagine I'll ever really be a peer, regardless of what the title says."

Peyton nodded. "A businessman is very bottom-line by nature. You see profit margins and risk, balance sheets where neat columns line up with calculated answers and assurances. A nobleman's view is quite different. A nobleman must see all things as interconnections, interconnections that all, I might add, lead back to themselves. A businessman is a private citizen, but a nobleman is not. He must answer to his subjects on all levels. There is no private sector in this life, Killian. Even my mistresses are fair game for common knowledge. It is the same for you as it is for the rest of us. You're something of a celebrity now. You must go and deal with the question of arson fairly and honestly, if for no other reason than to keep Rose Janeway safe. You would not want to bring the wrath of the rioters down on her head simply because of her association with you." Peyton counseled.

"He's right." Rose spoke from the doorway, pale and worried. Killian had the uncomfortable sensation she'd been standing there longer then he would have liked, perhaps hearing things best left unsaid until matters were sorted and heads cooled. But her shoulders were straight and she'd dressed in a subdued dress of blue wool with tight sleeves and a high neck trimmed discreetly with white cotton lace, her hair netted and tamed in a chignon at the base of her neck.

"I have water on for tea and toast in the oven. After breakfast, we'll go out and settle this matter." She said matter-of-factly.

Killian started towards her. "Rose, I think it would be best if you stayed here."

She shook her head. "No, you need me. You don't know these people. You came here a few days ago seeking me for just that purpose didn't you?" she reminded him in a tone that brooked no argument. "Now, gentlemen, come and eat. Justice is hard to come by on an empty stomach."

One would have thought Rose Janeway was in the habit of entertaining lords in her kitchen from the way she settled them at the long work table with tea and toast and a few sausages she adeptly fried up. Killian found a new level of appreciation for her, watching her in the kitchen. His Rose was quite versatile. She could run a farm, bring in the apple harvest and cook (apparently the redoubtable

Mrs. Hemburton had the day off), to say nothing of the passion she brought to bed at the end of the day.

Quite honestly, he'd never met a woman like her. The women who populated his circles in London were elegant rich women of varying stations, but all were obsessed with the same thing—themselves. Rose's thoughts were for others. Even last night, her thoughts had been for him, for bringing him pleasure. Of course, he'd seen to it that he'd not gone alone into that world of ecstasy. But her intentions had touched him greatly.

Over toast, she briefed them on Franklin, telling them about the low wages he'd paid out and the situation concerning Herefordshire agriculture in general. One thing was clear: desperation levels were on the rise.

Connelly had not lied when he'd told Killian Rose was the one best placed to help him get to know the area. She was an astute farmer herself and a keen observer of human nature. Such traits spoke to the kind of life she must have led as the local squire's wife, Killian thought. A surge of jealous possession went through him. It was hard to picture her as another man's wife. In the time he'd known her, she'd become entirely his, and the recognition of that truth rocked him to his core. He'd never felt such possessiveness over a woman before.

"We're all worried. No one wants the swing riots to occur here, but there's only so much any one of us can do and a mob is a rule unto itself," Rose was saying.

Reflexively, Killian reached out a hand to cover hers where it lay on the table, wanting to give her comfort.

"They won't come here, Rose. You paid more than fair wages last night. People cannot blame you."

"Not philosophically anyways." She gave a weak smile. "But who's to stop them? Philosophy and logic are poor shields against hungry men trying to get justice for their families."

Perhaps she did not mean it as a personal jab, still he couldn't help but feel the sting of her words. A lord in residence might keep the peace simply through his presence. Without him, who would be on hand and willing to step into the breach if disorder broke out? An awkward silence descended on the table.

"Let us go and hitch up the gig for you and Mrs. Janeway." Peyton suggested. He turned to Rose.

"Will ten minutes be enough time? We should not delay longer than needed."

CHAPTER TWELVE

THE BARN WAS A CINDERED remnant of its former self, a
black frame against the sky. Several people were milling
about the wreckage when they arrived. Killian hoped bits
of useful evidence hadn't been destroyed or altered by their
presence. He jumped down from the gig and immediately
strode forward, taking charge.

"Everyone, step back from the remains," he commanded.
"We need to look around to see if we can spot anything that
might have started the fire before we can go further."

Mr. Franklin stepped forward, a bluff, florid-looking
man in his late forties, an expression of smug satisfaction
on his face at seeing Killian. "I'm Pembridge." Killian
said, extending his hand to the man.

"Now we'll get somewhere." Mr. Franklin's voice was
loud and menacing, as if he were threatening those about
him. "You'll all see you can't take matters into your own
hands. I've got a suspect too," Franklin said to Killian.

"Jeppeson over there has been uppity since August, complaining about my wages."

Killian shot a quick glance at the man indicated and raised his brow in questioning disbelief. "And he's come out to help you salvage? That doesn't initially strike me as the action of an arsonist. But I'll reserve judgment until we've established it was even arson at all. Please excuse me, I want to take a look at the site."

Killian strode through the charred debris, kneeling down in places to sift through the ash and burned wood. He was aware of Peyton talking with people off to the side, away from where careless footsteps could further disturb the remains. It took a while, but finally Killian found what he was looking for. A wave of relief swept through him. He'd been ready to prosecute if he'd had to, justice had its point after all. If he was to be taken seriously, he had to act swiftly and decisively no matter what the case. But he doubted Mr. Franklin would appreciate his findings as much as he himself did.

Discreetly, Killian approached Mr. Franklin and walked off into privacy with him. The man had lost a barn, a valued commodity in the country. He deserved to hear the news first and alone. "Mr. Franklin," he began, "it appears a lantern was the cause of the fire."

"A lantern put in my barn by Jeppeson." Franklin said resolutely.

"No, I think that is not the case." Killian pressed on, showing Franklin the blackened metal he'd picked up. "I found this at the hottest part of the blaze. The trademark on the metal is the same as other pieces from other lanterns used in your barn. This lantern is yours."

"How do you know it's from the hottest part of the fire?" Franklin queried, his anger rising.

Killian jerked his head towards the ruined barn frame. "Because it's still smoldering there, and when I bent down to touch the remains, they were still hot, unlike the remains in other places which had already cooled. I will tell you something else too, Franklin. The hottest part of the fire came from the middle of the barn, not from an outside wall where an arsonist would likely start a fire so they could get away quickly. This blaze started inside. It's my conclusion that the peg this lantern was on probably gave way and the lantern crashed to the floor."

Franklin sputtered. "But who will pay for my barn? Where will my animals live this winter?"

Killian didn't have those answers. Franklin would have to decide that for himself. Killian looked around at the people assembled. "Well, there just might be some people here looking for work who wouldn't mind helping you raise a barn."

Franklin's eyes bulged at the prospect. "You don't understand, milord," he stammered in incoherent argument.

Killian placed a steadying hand on the big man's shoulder, remembering the things Rose had shared at breakfast. "Oh yes, I do. I understand better than you think."

Poetic justice, divine intervention, whatever one wanted to call it, Mr. Franklin had been served up his just desserts. If he wanted a barn by winter he'd have to pay those he'd cheated on wages earlier in the year. Killian thought the outcome quite fitting. He'd had his first trial as Pembridge and he'd passed admirably in his opinion.

Others seemed to think so too. By the time they'd said good-bye to Peyton at the turn in the road, and made their way through the village in the gig, he and Rose had picked up a following. By the time he'd parked the gig near the town commons, they were surrounded by merchants and day laborers who wanted to meet the earl in person.

Sensing the prospect of some extra income, the innkeeper discreetly rolled out a keg, followed shortly by a few trestle tables on the commons, leaving no doubt in Killian's mind the day had become an impromptu holiday of sorts. It reminded him of the medieval court days he'd read about in history books with the lord of the manor sitting in judgment over disagreements and quarrels.

He sat at a table, people of the village on all sides of him. Someone thrust a mug into his hand, and he listened. He offered feedback. Then he began to plan. The comments all had one constant theme—the need for regular sources of income that existed beyond the seasonal opportunities of farming. Even the merchants were affected by the seasonal funding of their local economy. If people didn't have money to spend, they couldn't buy the goods stocked in the village shops.

Killian raised the mug to his mouth, expecting to taste ale. To his surprise, it was cider instead—a sweet, smooth cold cider, delicious and wet. He didn't need more than a second swallow to know it was the finest cider he'd ever tasted. He caught sight of Rose moving through a crowd of women, someone's baby on her hip, her bonnet askew from the baby's antics and her lovely hair peeking out.

Red-gold.

The idea he'd been searching for finally came to him in concrete detail. Rose's shed full of red-gold apples. Red gold. She wasn't the only one. Practically everyone grew apples here and made cider. Cider was commonplace here.

Red gold.

The Redstreak apple.

Cider.

A cider cartel.

There was a market for cider if one could get it to the city.

"Do you send cider up to Hereford?" Killian asked, his mind alight with ideas.

"Yes, milord. But that's only one city. There's not too many big cities around here." It was true. Pembridge-on-the-Wye was closer to Wales than it was to London. Killian smiled. A farmer alone could not think of the expense of sending his cider to London. That's where they needed him. He could show them how to mitigate expenses by working together, and once London got a taste of this cider, it wouldn't want to buy anything else, no matter how much closer it was. His mind was spinning fast now. Who was to say they couldn't also go into Wales? Their little cartel could become international, *would* become international once he got done with it.

CHAPTER THIRTEEN

KILLIAN WAS QUIET ON the drive home—all his attention riveted on the horse and the road perhaps? Or were his thoughts elsewhere? Rose wondered. Had he figured out that he didn't need her at all? He didn't. He'd been fine on his own, magnificent in fact. From the moment he'd stepped down from the gig at Franklin's barn, she'd seen a different side of him, a side that made her wince with embarrassment when she recalled the rough dressing down she'd given him that first day in the orchard.

She'd listened to rumors, seen the playful light in his eye and taken that to be the sum of him, a man more interested in the light pleasures of lazy society. She'd judged him on his appearance, determined to find him shallow because he'd been handsome and absent to defend himself against the rumors that had drifted down from London over the years. But Killian Redbourne was much more than that.

Today he'd been the earl. He'd actively sought justice for the fire. He'd given of his time to those who needed his ear. He'd sat for hours with the people, listening to them. When he'd risen from the tables, there'd been a new sense of purpose to the crowd. The grim expressions had been transformed into something more hopeful. Change was in the air.

What did that mean for her? He'd done it all by himself. He had not needed her introductions as he'd feared. The men liked him for himself. Why should they not? His command had been impressive today. She had watched him whenever she could. She could not help but feel proud in 'her man.' But that was where the fantasy ended. He wasn't her man. He'd never be her man. Whatever he'd been before, a businessman of sorts, he was an earl now and out of her league.

"A penny for your thoughts," Rose ventured cautiously. They were nearly home. She mentally cringed. How easy the idea of them together had slipped into her way of thinking. This wasn't *their* home. It was her home, and it would her home after he left.

"I've been thinking of all that needs to be done."

"For what?" Rose felt as if she'd entered a conversation halfway finished and was missing vital information.

"To set up the cider cartel, Rose." He explained the details to her, how they would transport the local cider into cities year-round. "We'll probably have to grow more apple trees to keep up with demand once we get established."

There was no missing the excitement in his voice, and it was contagious. They pulled into the yard and he came around to help her down. She put her arms about him and kissed him full on the mouth. "You're brilliant."

With Killian at the helm of the project, she had no doubt it would succeed in ways local farmers could not hope to achieve.

"I have you to thank for the inspiration." His eyes twinkled as he set her down, still holding her close, the heat of his body comforting and solid against the evening chill. "Red gold you called it, and so it will be. Now, as I recall, we have some unfinished business upstairs from this morning. Shall we?"

There was an extra edge of euphoria to their lovemaking that night, Rose's thoughts of a dismal future without him firmly pushed away in the wake of Killian's ardor and the hope that the cartel might give him a reason to stay. Maybe she wouldn't have to say good-bye after all.

Perhaps if she'd known him longer, she would have sensed the underlying urgency in his lovemaking. Perhaps she'd have realized the ardor that drove him was fueled not only by exhilaration over his plans but by the imminent approach of their good-byes.

As it was, she had a rather rude awakening the following morning.

The bed was empty. Killian stood bare-chested, dressed in trousers before the open wardrobe, carefully folding the spare shirt and clothes Dursley had brought down for him. It took a moment or two for Rose's sleepy mind to register that these weren't the actions of a man called away on an emergency; such a man would be stuffing clothing haphazardly into a valise. These were the actions of a man who'd planned a departure.

"What are you doing?" Rose managed to ask. She'd not expected to wake like this. She'd expected a cozy morning in bed, picking up where they'd fallen asleep last night, safe in each other's arms.

Killian turned from the wardrobe, a smile on his face. "I'm leaving, Rose."

As if that was cause for a smile. Her stomach plummeted. "Leaving? For where? Why?" Rose sat up in bed, shoving handfuls of hair out of her face.

"I can't stay here forever if we're to get the cartel up and running." He shrugged into his spare linen shirt, looking elegant and graceful, a stark reminder that he'd worn clothes far beneath his station since he'd arrived at her doorstep. So this was how it would be. He would return to his rightful station and she would be left in hers. No plans for *them* crossed his lips.

He put on the hunting jacket he'd arrived in and pulled on his boots. Each action led him closer to farewell. Rose's throat tightened. She'd known he would leave her. She'd just hadn't known it would hurt so much. He snapped the valise shut and came to the bed, dropping a quick kiss on her cheek. "Everything will be all right, you'll see."

He was too cheerful for her taste. It would certainly help if he felt even a twinge of sadness at going. Rose merely nodded. "Take care of yourself," she managed. He wouldn't want tears. It would make him regret their time together. Regrets were not what she wanted him to remember.

Rose heard the front door shut and hurried to her window. She'd torture herself a bit longer and see him leave. She pulled back the lace curtain to watch him harness the pony and throw his bag up onto the gig before swinging into the seat. He slapped the reins and was off.

Rose sighed, her breath frosting the window pane. She'd meant to give herself an experience. But he'd taken her heart.

CHAPTER FOURTEEN

IT WAS IMPOSSIBLE TO get Killian Redbourne out of her head,
out of her house or off her land. Everywhere she looked,
there were reminders. Some physical—the dining-room
table where they'd eaten that first dinner together—others
mental images of things he'd said, things they'd done. Even
the orchards weren't safe from memories of him. He was
simply everywhere.

After three days of trying to prepare the press for the
annual cider-making and succeeding only minimally,
she finally gave in and contrived an excuse to drive up to
Pembridge Hall in the old farm wagon. She dressed with
conscientious care, not wanting to look overdone for a
casual call upon a neighbor. She didn't want Killian to
suspect she was moping, pouting or in anyway sulking
due to his absence.

She loaded two small casks of cider in the back of the
wagon and set off under the flimsy pretense that she'd not
yet paid him for his work in the orchards. Not that the earl

needed payment, of course. But he might appreciate the humorous gesture anyway.

Pembridge Hall was a monstrous sprawl of a house, big and intimidating. The old earl had liked to intimidate people, he'd wanted those around him to feel the weight of his consequence. He'd been a skinny, bony bag of a man and had had to do his intimidating through avenues other than his size. Pembridge Hall was proof of that.

She summoned her courage and knocked on the door. A stuffy butler answered it; she vaguely recalled him from the few times she'd visited on formal occasions. "I'm Mrs. Janeway. I've come to see the earl."

"Right this way, please." At least that was something, Rose thought. She'd not been turned away and, in fact, had been easily admitted. Killian didn't plan on ignoring her then.

The butler led her to a small sitting room done up in various shades of yellow, and she sat down to wait, her confidence surging a bit over the decent reception.

"Mrs. Janeway, how delightful to see you again." It was Dursley who spoke from the doorway. Her hopes fell. It was the wrong earl. How awkward.

Disappointment must have shown on her face. "You were expecting Pembridge?" Dursley inquired kindly. "I am afraid he's not here."

Luck was not with her. First the wrong earl, then Killian was out on some errand. It was probably no less than she deserved, traipsing over the countryside hunting down a man who'd made it clear their brief interlude was over.

She'd never thought much of women who made cakes of themselves over men. Now she'd become one.

Rose gathered her dignity. "It's no problem. I brought him some casks of cider. I thought he might need them." She couldn't think of why he'd need them. Hopefully, Dursley would throw her a scrap of mercy and not ask. "If you could tell him when he returns?"

"I will, Mrs. Janeway, although it might not be for a while." Dursley was looking at her strangely. "I can see you don't know. He's gone. He left for London a few days ago."

Rose was thankful she was sitting. Otherwise she might have fallen over completely. Killian was gone? In London? "How long will he be gone?" She couldn't bear to ask the other question on her mind: *Will he be back?*

Dursley shook his head patiently. "I don't know. He didn't say. I'm sorry, I assumed he'd told you."

Rose was numb. Killian had simply disappeared back to London. When he'd said he couldn't stay here, she had thought he meant at her house with her. But he'd meant it in a far bigger sense. He couldn't stay in Pembridge-on-the-Wye. It hadn't been clear to her, but then it had all happened so fast. They'd been making love and then he'd been gone.

She managed to get home before she broke into tears in the privacy of her room. The best she could hope for now was that he didn't mean to betray the villagers who'd believed in his cartel. It was clear to her that he meant to run the cartel from London, from the terminus of the supply line instead of at its onset.

In hindsight, it made sense. He was a man of business with other interests he could simultaneously oversee if he were in London, and he'd said the estate was broke. Dursley must be tying up loose ends for him before heading back.

She knew she should be thankful. Killian had found a way to be the absent earl he wanted to be *and* to help the people find the income they needed. He'd discharged his duty on terms acceptable to all—except perhaps her.

Rose punched the wet pillow. She'd been such a fool.

CHAPTER FIFTEEN

London, November 30, 1830

KILLIAN LIFTED HIS hand from the stationery, setting aside the quill as he debated what more to add. His letter to Peyton was mostly complete. The villagers could celebrate the upcoming Christmas season with glee. He had contracts for cider with over fifty inns in the greater London area, with the promise of more next year. The letter contained the details, along with the delivery date for the first shipments and an order to start the cider presses. Between pressing and carting, they'd have all the work they wanted and more just to fill these initial contracts.

He'd tell them himself except that speed was of the essence, and he wanted to stop along the way home and cultivate a few of the inns that ran along the Herefordshire-London road. The letter would arrive before he did, and the villagers would need all the time they could get.

Killian felt well pleased with his efforts. But he felt more pleased with the idea of going home. For the first time in his adulthood, he had a place he wanted to call home. He picked up his quill and hesitated again. He wanted to add a postscript for Rose, to tell her he was on his way home, on his way back to her, that he'd missed her tremendously. Time without her had provided him with a perspective on what she'd come to mean to him.

He decided against it. This letter would be passed around, everyone wanting to hear the details of the cartel. This missive was not the place for personal disclosures.

"Milord, the messenger is ready to leave." A footman entered the room to collect the letter. There'd be no time to write a second one privately. Killian carefully folded the heavy paper and closed it with the Pembridge seal, something he was still getting used to.

He wished he was leaving with the letter, but he still had another day in town before he could depart.

Killian closed his eyes and leaned back in his chair. He was tired of London. Even with all the comforts of his own home, Killian longed for the simple pleasures of Rose's soft bed

The visions of her in his mind were strong. He could see her in the fields, all boots and trousers, her hair tucked up beneath a cap, challenging him. He could see her beside him in the gig in her blue dress with the lace at the throat, ready to stand by him and ease his way if need be. He saw her amid the women in the village, respected as a leader in her own right. He saw her at the coin box, in the cider shed on the work table and in his arms up against the wardrobe, her hair loose, her passion exposed. And he saw her rumpled with sleep that last day when he'd kissed her good-bye.

She did understand, didn't she? He was coming back. She did understand he wouldn't leave her? He hadn't said good-bye because it wasn't good-bye. He'd be back for her. How could he not be? One did not throw away a piece of one's soul. But he worried. He had no explicit guarantee. He had only the implicit promises their bodies had made each other, the implied bonds of their midnight conversations.

In his excitement over the cartel, the scene that last morning had not resonated with him at the time. But now, as he played it back in his mind, the exhilaration of the cartel subdued, he wondered what it had looked like from Rose's perspective, and prickles of doubt began to nag at him. Had she thought he was saying farewell to her? To them?

More than ever, Killian wanted to get home.

Fate conspired against a speedy journey. It was December now, after all, and the roads were muddy. What wasn't muddy was slippery. He was thankful for the Dursley equipage, the finest available. The traveling carriage was well-sprung and had all the best refinements. But Killian wanted speed, and he chafed at the slow progress of his journey. He felt helpless sitting for hours on end, doing nothing. He couldn't read. He couldn't think. He wanted Rose in his arms. He wanted to know she was still his.

He wanted to see her face light up and her blue eyes glow when he gave her the little gift he'd found in London.

He'd brought other gifts for her too. He'd spent his last day in London shopping for her. He wanted to strip her out of the silk negligee (what there was of it) that he'd purchased and make slow love to her. Alas, now he was alone *and* aroused. This was possibly the most miserable trip he'd ever been on.

Three miles out of Pembridge-on-the-Wye and dark coming on fast, a wheel axle broke, proving even the Dursley wealth was no match for Mother Nature, though it had given her a hell of a run for her money. Killian swore, and jumped down to lend a hand.

The driver and his nephew, along with Killian's muscle, were able to get the carriage to the side of the road. But there was no question of going further without help. They unhitched the horses, agreeing to ride the rest of the way and send a team back for the carriage later.

Despite the setback, Killian's heart soared at the sight of the town steeple coming into view in the dusky twilight, the lights of the main street glowing. His town. It took an effort of supreme will to ride past the turn to Rose's and keep going towards Pembridge Hall, but he had his duty to Peyton. He couldn't leave Peyton's carriage lying in a ditch. Killian chuckled to himself. His duty to Peyton did have its limits though. He'd tell Peyton about the carriage and then let him deal with it.

Peyton laughed at his report. "Apparently, you find humor in the wreckage of your very expensive carriage?" Killian said, doing a fair imitation of Peyton's lordly eyebrow-raise.

"No, it's you that has me laughing. You can't wait to

be off to Mrs. Janeway's. So it's finally happened, has it? The legendary Killian Redbourne has fallen in love?"

There was no sense in denying the truth. Killian shrugged. "It would seem so. But I wouldn't laugh too hard. It will happen to you too, just wait and see if it doesn't."Peyton looked dubious over this pronouncement, but Killian was too happy to care. He was free at last to see Rose.

She wasn't at the grange. The house was dark. Disappointed, Killian stopped in at the pub. The innkeeper would know where everyone was. As it turned out, he didn't need to ask. The pub was thronged. It took Killian a moment to realize the pub's patrons weren't the usual. Tonight, there were women and children, families, gathered around the tables.

He grabbed one of the barmaids. "What's going on?"

"We're celebrating our cider contracts, sir!" Then she paused, recognizing who she was talking to. Killian imagined he didn't look quite himself after days on the road and forgave her for the oversight.

"It's him, everyone! It's Lord Pembridge!" She shouted in her excitement.

All eyes swiveled towards him. Killian smiled, although this was not the discreet homecoming he would have wished. He'd have preferred something more private with Rose. But as Peyton had said, his was a public life now. He searched the crowd for the only set of eyes that mattered. He found them at the back of the room. He started moving towards her, shaking hands and clapping shoulders, accepting good wishes, acutely aware that he'd truly come home, that he was building his future here.

But, always, he was moving forwards. He wouldn't really be home until he reached her.

Rose's breath caught. Killian was back! He looked dirty, his greatcoat spattered with mud at the hem, his dark hair loose and tangled, his beard stubbling on his chin. He'd never looked more handsome to her, and Rose very physically felt her hard-won control shatter. She'd had a month to make all the necessary justifications to herself, a month to relegate Killian Redbourne to the status of an unforgettable experience. But that was the problem with the unforgettable. One always remembered. And now he was here, walking toward her with a look of single-minded determination in his coffee-colored eyes.

His purpose was clear: he wanted her. He'd come back for her, cartel notwithstanding. What should she do? She had only moments to decide. Could she risk her heart again knowing that he could not offer all her heart demanded? Would he make her choose between him and Pembridge-on-the-Wye?

Killian stood in front of her, tall and strong, desire pulsing through his frame. He took no pains to hide it. Rose bit her lip. No wonder Mrs. Dempsey had swooned. Any woman would kill to be looked at thusly by a man.

Killian took her by the hand in front of all those assembled. "I need a word with you." He said softly, although Rose knew everyone would have heard him even if he'd whispered. He led her to one of the private parlors and shut the door firmly behind them.

"Killian, what…" She did not get any farther. He

enveloped her in his arms, his mouth possessing hers, her body held tightly against his, and she gave herself over to it. There was no denying the joy her body took from his. But it was more than that. There was a joy in being with this man that transcended the physical. She knew instinctively no other could provide her the joy she found with him.

"I missed you. I don't want to be apart from you like that again." He whispered between kisses, "I didn't like wondering if you were still mine. I realized I might have left my intentions unclear."

"I thought you weren't coming back." It had to be said.

"It occurred to me, rather belatedly, that you might think that. So I've brought you something to convince you otherwise." He reached into his pocket and pulled out a small velvet-covered box.

"What's this?" Rose asked, her emotions threatening to get the better of her. The evening had turned into a whirlwind of surprises.

"Open it," He pushed the box into her hand.

Rose slipped open the lid and gasped. It was an exquisitely crafted brooch—a ruby shaped in the form of an apple lay on black velvet, a sliver of jade carved to represent a leaf. "It's beautiful." She said softly.

"It's for a countess who's crazy enough to let her husband run a cider cartel." Killian's voice cracked over his next three words. "Marry me, Rose."

Rose looked at him in amazement. By the saints, the

great Killian Redbourne, possessor of swooning kisses, was nervous. And that was all the persuasion she needed.

"I'll never be a fashionable countess." She said.

Killian smiled, relieved hope starting to creep into his expression. "But you'll be mine. And we'll be here in Pembridge-on-the–Wye together. London's had me for fourteen years. You can have me for the rest." His hands shook slightly as he pinned the brooch to her dress. "Say you'll be mine?"

"Yes, Killian, I'll be yours." Rose grinned up at him, her arms about his neck. What an extraordinary man she'd found. He'd understood her dilemma before she'd even voiced it and had removed it from consideration. She cocked her head in contemplative fashion. "Do you think they'd miss us, if we slipped out the back?"

Killian gave her a stare of mock seriousness. "Yes I do, which why I propose we stay right here. But don't worry, I have it on good authority that tables can be put to several diverse uses."

"I wish I'd thought of that." Rose tugged impatiently at his waistband.

Killian winked, moving down on top of her. "Someone once told me wishing makes all the difference, my dear, between expectation and hope."

* * * * *

The Captain's
Wicked Wager

MARGUERITE KAYE

Born and educated in Scotland, **Marguerite Kaye** originally qualified as a lawyer but chose not to practise—a decision which was a relief both to her and the Scottish legal establishment. While carving out a successful career in IT, she occupied herself with her twin passions of studying history and reading, picking up a first-class honours and a master's degree along the way.

The course of her life changed dramatically when she found her soul mate. After an idyllic year out, spent travelling round the Mediterranean, Marguerite decided to take the plunge and pursue her life-long ambition to write for a living—a dream she had cherished ever since winning a national poetry competition at the age of nine.

Just like one of her fictional heroines, Marguerite's fantasy has become reality. She has published history and travel articles, as well as short stories, but romances are her passion. Marguerite describes Georgette Heyer and Doris Day as her biggest early influences and her partner as her inspiration.

Though she continues to write regular pieces for a number of Scottish magazines and also publishes short stories in women's weeklies, romances are her passion. When she is not writing, Marguerite enjoys cooking and hill-walking. A confirmed Europhile who spends much of the year in sunny climes, she returns regularly to the beautiful Highland scenery of her native Argyll, the place she still calls home.

Marguerite would love to hear from you. You can contact her at: Marguerite_Kaye@hotmail.co.uk

Author's Note

Gambling has long been the vice of choice for the rich and famous, from horseracing, the traditional sport of kings, to today's televised celebrity poker tournaments. It is easy to see the attraction. The heady mix of glamour, money and drama is both alluring and seductive. This was certainly true in Regency London when the Ton and the *demi-monde* flocked to hells of St James's and Piccadilly in search of illicit thrills and excitement.

But what if more was at stake than money? What if someone was driven to gamble with their body, their feelings, even their virtue? What if losing became more appealing than winning? Freed from society's conventions and constraints—for how can there be guilt when one has placed one's fate in the hands of the gods—what might the gambler learn about his or her secret self?

This is what I wanted to explore through Isabella and Ewan's story, where a turn of a card, a throw of the dice decides how shockingly they must behave, what sensual acts they must indulge in. And at stake love, the ultimate prize, can be either won or lost.

I hope you enjoy reading this, my first ever **Undone**, as much as I enjoyed writing it. I'd love to hear what you think. You can e-mail me at marguerite_kaye@hotmail.co.uk.

"If ever any beauty I did see,
Which I desired, and got, 'twas but a dream of thee."
—John Donne, *The Good Morrow*

For J, who makes any room our everywhere. Just love.

CHAPTER ONE

London, 1785

THE GAMING SALOON WAS PACKED, the clientele mostly male but with a fair sprinkling of women present, too. Thanks to the notorious Duchess of Devonshire, playing deep was very much *à la mode* for the fairer sex. The air was stifling, the atmosphere redolent of hair powder and scent, brandy and wine, mingled with the musky smell of too many bodies crowded into too small a space. Candles sputtered and flared, casting distorted shadows on the walls.

"Eight wins." The large woman in charge of the faro bank glowered as she pushed a pile of counters across the table.

Isabella Mansfield, her attention focused on trying to calculate the value of her winnings, ignored the woman's growing animosity. Faith, but it was hot! The fan she wore tied round her wrist provided her with precious little relief. The unaccustomed hair powder irritated her scalp. The rouge she had so carefully applied to her cheeks and lips prickled her delicate skin. The folds of her dark blue polonaise dress and the ridiculous layers of undergarments required to hold the shape in place at the back all contrived to make her distinctly uncomfortable.

Though they also, she reminded herself, served to ensure that she blended in, looked just like every other woman present. Aside from her complete lack of jewellery that is. Her great-grandmother's pearls, the only thing of value she owned, had been discreetly sold to provide her stake for this evening. Two more wins, if her luck continued to hold, and she would have enough.

Captain Ewan Dalgleish watched with interest as Isabella pushed her entire stack of counters onto the two, causing a crackle of excitement to fizz round the throng of eager onlookers. There was something driven about her demeanour, quite different from the recklessness of a genuine gambler. She was clearly nervous: long fingers plucking at the sticks of her fan, her eyes fixed on the dealer's card box as if it contained the key to her very destiny. Which, he thought, raising his eyebrows as he calculated her stake, it most probably did. He was intrigued.

On the anniversary of the day he had resigned his commission following his father's death, and on his thirtieth birthday to boot, he had come to this newest hell made popular by Fox and his cronies in search of diversion. In the past year he had sampled every pleasure, licit or otherwise, the town had to offer, kicking over the traces and flaunting his newly-inherited respectability in the faces of his critics with gusto. Sport, women, sprees like this latest outing—they all provided temporary excitement, but nothing matched the visceral thrill of battle, the gut-clenching intensity of combat. He was coming to believe that the army had leeched all feeling out of him. An intense *ennui* threatened to overwhelm him.

He'd had the devil's own luck with the cards tonight, but it meant little. The fortune his father had left him was immense. And as for the brandy he had imbibed—his mind might be somewhat befuddled, but the abrasive edges of his poisonous mood had been in no way smoothed. To hell with all of it! Even his burning desire to try to right the wrongs of the world offered little solace. What he needed was something more exotic by way of an antidote.

The beauty at the faro table was most definitely that. Despite the regulation paint and powder, there was something distinctive about her. Winged black brows sat above cobalt-blue eyes fringed with long black lashes. There was a spark of intelligence there. A mouth wider than the fashionable rosebud, the bottom lip full. The long line of white throat swooping down to a luscious swell of bosom. The same flawless white skin on her arms, delicate wrists and long fingers. Slumbering sensuality combined with a haughty touch-me-not air. A challenging and enticing combination.

At the faro table Mrs Bradley, the banker, was declining the beauty's bet, clearly afraid it would break the bank. Her many chins wobbled as she shook her head. "I'm sorry, madam, that is twice the maximum stake permitted."

"But…" Isabella looked up, embarrassed to find all eyes upon her. Impatient. Speculative. Inquisitive. Leering. Under her rouge, she blushed. Not all the women here were ladies of the *ton*. Not all the gamblers were gentlemen. With a heavy heart she took back half her counters. At this rate, she would never win as much as she needed. She must have the full funds by the end of the week or all would be lost. She simply had to win enough tonight.

"With the bank's permission I will cover the bet, and any others the young lady cares to make." The deep voice had just the trace of a Scottish lilt.

Startled, Isabella looked up into the most striking pair of eyes she had ever seen. Amber tinged with liquid brown, the colour of autumn leaves. For a moment they clashed with her own, causing a flicker of excitement to shiver down her spine. A sculpted mouth curled in a half smile.

"Captain Dalgleish," the banker exclaimed in surprise. "This is most unusual."

He flashed her a smouldering, flirtatious smile. "Unusual, Mrs Bradley, but I'm sure you can find a way to accommodate me."

The banker smiled coquettishly. "Captain Dalgleish, I'd wager there's scarcely a woman in London who wouldn't be willing to accommodate you in any way you saw fit. If I was twenty years younger I might even be tempted myself."

A ripple of laughter spread through the onlookers.

Ewan's eyes twinkled mischievously. "Madam, that is a regret we will both have to live with." The crowd roared its approval. "Perhaps this will ease the pain somewhat," Ewan said, passing her a sweetener which she quickly palmed, indicating her acceptance with a coy fluttering of her lashes.

An air of heightened excitement eddied round the room at this new, unexpected development. Jaded gamesters tilted back their straw hats to stare. High class birds of paradise and raddled society *grandes dames* alike peered curiously from behind their painted and lace-trimmed fans. Into the brief silence blew a flurry of whispered asides.

"Rescued the climbing boy himself. They say he whipped the master." "Apparently, he's no stranger to the Roundhouse at St Giles. Locked up overnight with common thieves more than once." "They say he found an escaped slave begging on the streets, set him up as an apothecary, no less."

Captain Dalgleish drew the attention of the whole room inexorably towards him with all the natural and unconscious ease of a magnet pointing a compass northward.

In common with everyone else, Isabella stared. When she had first heard tell of him he had been new to town, as famed for his daring exploits on the battlefield as he was infamous for his public condemnation of the American war in which he had fought. Now he was just as notorious, but for his hell raising. Ewan Dalgleish was not a man who lived by society's rules. A rebel in every sense, she thought enviously. Why on earth would he want to cover her bet? But unless he did—no, she would not allow herself to think of the consequences of failure.

She watched him covertly as he placed a roll of notes

onto the table. He was tall, with his coat cut in the new fashion buttoned tight across his chest, showing off the breadth of his shoulders, the severity of the rich black velvet cloth lightened only by the glimpse of a dove-grey waistcoat, the fall of white linen with just a hint of lace at his throat. The deep copper of his hair glinted bright as a new-minted penny in the candlelight. It was a memorable face. High cheekbones with a small scar visible on the left one, a sabre cut no doubt. A strong, determined jaw. His colouring gave him an untamed look. The perfection of his tailoring somehow served to draw attention to the muscles hidden underneath. A mountain lion, Isabella thought with a shiver. Strength and power barely concealed under a veneer of sophistication. A fierce Highland warrior in the sober garb of a gentleman.

She smiled at herself for being so fanciful and then flushed as she caught the echo of her smile returned from across the table. For a second she met his glance haughtily, amber clashing with cobalt-blue. An almost tangible current of awareness crackled between them. She dropped her eyes.

"Madam?"

Mrs Bradley's voice recalled her to her purpose. Isabella pushed all of her counters onto the table. The watching crowd craned ever closer for a better view.

The banker's card was a six of diamonds. The *carte anglaise,* the winning card, was hers.

"The lady wins," Ewan Dalgleish said softly in his husky Scottish burr, pushing her counters back towards her and adding the same amount again from his own

supply. He had just lost a fabulous amount, yet it seemed
he was content to do so. A quirk of his mouth, a quizzical
eyebrow formed the unspoken question.

Isabella took a deep breath and returned the entire total
to the table, raising an audible gasp from the audience. It
took all her courage, such a fortune as she had before her,
but it would not yet suffice. Coming up short was not an
option. A life depended upon it. Heedless now of everything but the game Isabella clenched her hands together.
One more turn of the cards. Just this one.

Ewan did not take his eyes from her. Her face was a
mask of concentration, her eyes focused on Mrs Bradley's
hand, which rested on the dealing box. Whatever she was
playing for, it was not the thrill of it. He was conscious
that a part of him wanted her luck to hold, no matter that
he would be the poorer by thousands.

The cards were dealt and the colour drained from
Isabella's face as they landed face up on the baize. A small
sound, like steam escaping from a pot, hissed round the
table.

She had not even a stake left with which to continue.
Blindly, Isabella got to her feet. The gilded chair on which
she had been seated fell backwards. The lace at her elbow
had become entangled with her fan. *Her gloves...where
were her gloves?*

Suddenly, he was there in front of her, handing her the
gloves and her wrap. He took her arm firmly. "Come with
me."

"No, no, I…"

But it was to no avail. A strong hand guided her away

from the curious faces of the onlookers. She was propelled out of the crowded room and into an unoccupied one across the passageway.

Ewan closed the door behind him and pressed her onto a chair by the fire. A glass of fiery spirit the same colour as his eyes was handed to her. "Drink this," he said firmly.

Isabella drank. The brandy made her gasp, but it also revived her spirits. She took another gulp.

"Slowly, take your time."

The amusement in his voice served to rile her. Defiantly, she drained the glass. "What does it matter if I'm drunk? You've already made me penniless."

"It was your choice to play so high, not mine," he said pointedly. "If you are now penniless, you have no-one but yourself to blame."

The truth of the remark hit her like a deluge of ice-cold water. Isabella slumped back in the chair. What had seemed, when she started out tonight, like an inspired solution to her problems, had left her worse off than before, for now she did not even have her pearls.

"You are right. I beg your pardon," she said, shakily placing the empty glass down on a side table. "You are the winner, and I the loser." She rose to leave.

"You don't have to be." It was a crazy notion, but he felt fate had sent her to him. He could see his own concealed desperation reflected in her beautiful eyes. And something else. Defiance in the face of defeat. He recognised that, too, from the battlefield. Unusual in a woman. Admirable. And very, very desirable. Like a call to arms.

Isabella eyed him uncertainly. "I've already given you all my winnings. I have nothing else to offer."

He towered over her. There was an animal grace in the way he moved. She was conscious of the palpable maleness of him. His laugh was like a low growl of pleasure. It made the hairs on the back of her neck stand up. "The sum you've lost means nothing to me. In any event, I'll wager you have much more need of it than I."

Her smile was twisted. "You can have no idea."

A long finger under her chin. Amber eyes looked deep into her own. "You can have it back if you agree to my terms."

She held his gaze proudly, her heart thumping. "I am not a courtesan. I won't be bought."

Ewan placed the money casually in front of her. "I don't want to buy you. All I ask is that you agree to take part in another, different sort of wager."

Isabella tore her eyes from the money to his face. "What kind?"

Aware he was behaving outlandishly, conscious that his mind was excited from brandy, Ewan eyed her speculatively. Her lovely countenance was flushed. Excitement there was in her striking eyes, in the rapid rise and fall of her breasts. Defiance and daring, too. Beautiful. And highly alluring.

It was an impulse, nothing more. He wanted to see how far she could be pushed. Had no real intention of seeing it through, though he knew deep down even then, that whatever it took he could not let her go. "You spend three nights with me. The outcome each night will be dependant upon the fall of the dice. The winner to decide what happens between us. Anything…" he heard himself say, unable quite to believe he was uttering the words "…or nothing at all, if your luck holds. What do you say?"

Ewan's smile entreated trust, but Isabella was not fooled. He had the look of a lion confronted with a wary prey. She swallowed her instinctive flat refusal and forced herself to think rationally. The money would allow her to fulfil the plan which brought her here in the first place. This was her last chance, and she knew it. In the past three months she had exhausted all other avenues. But what price might she pay in the three nights which lay between now and then?

The man in front of her was a complete stranger, known to her only by reputation, and a disreputable one at that. If he won, and the odds were that he would on at least one occasion, she would have to give herself to him. Shocking to even consider it. Scandalous. No lady in her right mind would. And yet were not the circumstances so extreme as to justify the gamble? Would it not be more scandalous still to let this unexpected final opportunity to provide desperately needed salvation slip through her fingers?

In any event, the fates might favour her and allow her to win all three throws of the dice. She had been lucky tonight, until the last. She might be again. And if she was not? She probed deep, but could find only a strange quiver of excitement at the prospect. What was convention after all, when the stakes were so high?

"Why not, Captain Dalgleish?" she finally said, with a shaky laugh, "I agree to your wager."

He took her hand and raised it to his lips, soft against her skin. "Ewan," he said, "my name is Ewan. And what might yours be, my fair opponent?"

"Belle," she replied instinctively.

"Belle," he whispered. "I would not have had you for a Belle, but it describes you well enough." Now was the time to laugh, to pass it off as a jest. Now was the time to step back. Instead, he kissed her, and in doing so hurtled both of them irretrievably beyond the point of no return.

Gently, he kissed her, his lips cool against her own, his fingers tangling in her elaborate coiffure to tilt her head up. Isabella stood compliant, her mind numbed, conscious only of his mouth, his fingertips, the nearness and heat of his body. She was alarmed by the power she sensed there, yet reassured by the gentleness of his touch. Strangely, detachedly, exhilarated by the sensations he was arousing in her. A craving for more awoke in her but he stepped abruptly back.

"One thing you must know," he said, taking her hand, "I will neither harm you nor hurt you. I have already seen enough cruelty to last me a lifetime. Come then, I'll have them call my carriage."

What had she done? What on earth had she let herself in for?

CHAPTER TWO

SITTING BESIDE EWAN in the carriage as they rattled their way along the cobblestones towards the imposing, recently-built mansions of Cavendish Square, Isabella tried to quell her jangling nerves. Whatever happened now, she reminded herself, she had secured the funds she needed. But it was not this, the much longed for achievement, which caused the fluttering in her stomach.

The carriage lurched over a hole in the road surface, throwing her against Ewan. A strong arm righted her. She could see his eyes glowing in the soft light. Nervousness turned to anticipation. Guiltily, she realised that the prospect of winning was not the only option which held allure. She had the sense to realise she had best keep such thoughts to herself.

An impassive servant opened the door to them. Handing over his hat and sword stick, Ewan gave him his instructions in a soft undertone before leading the way to a small saloon upstairs. Long curtains of heavy green damask were drawn against the night. A fire crackled in the grate, the light from the many candles reflected in the two long mirrors hung on the walls between the windows.

The reality of her situation struck Isabella with the force of a hammer. Whatever happened now, it was irrevocable. She was not sure she could go through with it. She knew she *should* not.

Something of her panic showed in her face. "You do not have to do this," Ewan said abruptly.. "I will understand if you want to reconsider now, before it is too late."

"No," she said with a defiant tilt of her chin, throwing the last seeds of caution to the wind. "I will not renege on our terms—you need have no fear of that."

"I don't," Ewan replied, confident now that the rules of engagement were understood between them.

His touch sent a shiver up her arm. His extraordinary amber eyes glinted down at her. Desire. Confidence. Knowledge. As his gaze flickered over her face down to the neckline of her dress, Isabella flushed. Her breathing quickened.

"Shall we," he said seductively. "You may have the honour."

Isabella picked up the dice, running her tongue over her full bottom lip, where traces of rouge lingered. "Five," she called, throwing a six and a three. Ewan was watching her, catlike. Devoured. She would be devoured, she thought with shocking relish.

"Six", Ewan called with assurance before he threw. A five and one rolled obligingly onto the table.

Expressing neither surprise nor disappointment Isabella

turned towards him, her eyes almost navy blue, dark with the rush of anticipation. "You win."

Without a word he led her from the room, along the corridor and through a doorway at the end into another room. Candles were lit on the mantel, another branch on the large inlaid chest which stood in the corner. A bottle of champagne and two glasses sat waiting atop a small table as Ewan had requested, so confident had he been of victory. A chair and a chaise-longue sat at right angles to each other in front of the grate. Crimson hangings covered the windows. The polished floor was strewn with rugs, soft silk and rich wool. The room was dominated by a large four-poster bed, the hangings of silk damask the same colour as the curtains, the counterpane of velvet strewn with tasselled cushions.

Isabella sat on the chaise and took the glass of champagne he poured, her hands trembling.

"Wait here," Ewan said, opening a door in the panelled wall which presumably led to his dressing room.

She sipped on the ice-cold drink, feeling the bubbles sparkle and burst in her mouth. The unaccustomed alcohol relaxed her. She felt as if she was in a dream, observing herself from a distance. Disconnected. Isabella waiting in the background to see what Belle would do in the fore. She poured herself another glass of champagne, drinking it quickly down.

Ewan returned clad in an exotic banyan of Chinese silk tied loosely around the waist. As he sat down on the chair beside her, she eyed him cautiously. A long muscular leg emerged from the folds. A well-shaped calf. A glimpse of thigh. He was clearly quite naked underneath his robe. Isabella dragged her eyes upwards. A sprinkling of hair at his throat, a darker copper than that on his head. A strong neck. His hair, unfashionably untied, reached his shoulders. It suited him. Like a mane. She tilted back her glass, surprised to find it empty.

Long fingers relieved her of it. "You have a debt of honour to pay. I would have you sober enough to deliver it properly."

Beneath the cool tones his rich Scottish timbre served to threaten and entice at the same time. She glared defiantly at him. She was his prey, but she would not be his victim. "I am perfectly aware of my obligations sir. You have me at your disposal."

Ewan reached out to clasp her hand. Long fingers. Pink nails. Pulse fluttering visibly on her wrist. He kissed it, his tongue touching her flesh. Inhaled the light flowery scent there, feeling his own pulse pick up a beat in response. "Not at my disposal, Belle. At my command."

For a fleeting moment he thought he detected fear in her expression, then it was gone. "And what would you command me do," she asked somewhat breathlessly, rising to the challenge as he had known she would.

"Undress for me. But do it slowly, I want to enjoy the spectacle."

Isabella stared in consternation.

"You cannot deny me. I won, remember."

That mocking smile of his riled her. So confident he was. Toying with her, she could see that now. It was a game. She could not allow herself to be defeated by her inhibitions. *She would not allow it!*

Ewan sprawled back on the chair. The sash on his banyan had loosened. Isabella's eyes widened as she took in the rapidly hardening length of him nudging against the embroidered silk. He saw her looking. She must not turn away. She tried instead to imagine how it would feel inside her, but could not. A frisson of almost-fear surged through her.

Slowly, she started to disrobe, embarrassed and self-conscious as she tugged at the lacing behind her dress. The silk gown spilled at her feet, leaving her in her shoes and underclothes. Blushing, she snatched a look at him. Broad shoulders, a muscled torso tapering down to where the belt tied, then up to his unblinking gaze. She heard his breathing, quicker surely than before?

Relief washed over her. He liked what he saw—was anxious to see more. *Slow, she should slow down.* Postpone his pleasure. Delay her own unveiling. Turn it into a performance, a contest.

Belle untied her petticoats and bustle, trying to make a drama of each button and string, stretching and bending to conceal and reveal. Embarrassment dissolved as she gave rein to her instincts, her confidence growing as she watched the effect on her audience through her lashes. Shocking. Her behaviour was outrageous, yet gratifyingly effective.

She stood before him in her stays and chemise, the ribbons of her stockings fluttering against her knees. When he reached for her she stepped back, and knew it for a turning point. She had learned how to tease. Pain and pleasure intermingled. She saw it in his eyes. Felt it take a tentative hold on herself. Ewan was not the only one enjoying her show.

Slowly, she twirled for him, like a dancer on the stage. Posing now as if for a portrait to show off the line of her throat, the curve of her spine, conscious of her breasts rising and falling in the confines of her stays. Discarding her inhibitions with her clothing. A transforming. She was not Isabella stripped. She was Belle revealed.

In front of her Ewan no longer smiled. His face was a mask, eyes golden slits of light, lids heavy. Belle's glance flickered down to his manhood. She had never seen a man naked before. It was strangely beautiful, smooth and curving, like a separate being. She wanted to touch it. To run her fingers along its length. To caress it.

Her muscles clenched in anticipation. Her breath came faster. Ewan's gaze locked onto hers. Watching her watching him. A reflection of desire. And in the reflection a multiplying. Sure of her instincts now, she stepped out of the garments at her feet. Deliberately turning her back to him, she rested her foot on the chaise-longue, provocatively stretching over so that her chemise was pulled tight against her bottom. A shoe removed. Her stocking followed. She could hear Ewan breathing. She could smell her own scent. Salt and spice. Her other foot on the chair. Shoe. Stocking. She turned and walked towards him, the urge to touch was almost irresistible but she managed to restrain herself, presenting her back to him.

His hands on the laces of her stays. His fingers running

down her spine, setting every nerve end on fire. She stepped away again. Slowly, she pulled her chemise down. The soft material felt strangely coarse on her nipples. Distracted, she touched one curiously with her finger. It was pebble hard. Amazingly sensitive. She closed her eyes at the spark of feeling. Opened them again as she heard Ewan's intake of breath.

"Sit down and do that again," he said, his voice ragged.

Embarrassment briefly flared. Mortification threatened. Then she remembered; *perform.*

Belle sat naked on the chaise-longue. Tentatively touched her nipple. That strange feeling again. Abrasive. Pleasure and pain. Like the teasing. She closed her eyes as her untutored touch sparked a connection, from her fingertips to her nipples to the knot in her belly and the heat between her legs. The damask covering of the seat had a deliciously abrasive quality. She writhed against it.

"Lower," Ewan rasped.

Her eyes flew open, startled. She must be mistaken. *Surely, she was mistaken?*

He raised his eyebrows, patiently waiting. The tussle for supremacy was almost tangible between them. She would not surrender so easily. He would not be the only one to exercise control.

She knew with shocking clarity what he wanted of her. *She could not!* But to deny him would be to admit defeat. She would not be defeated. In his eyes she was already a wanton, after all. Why not complete the illusion?

Closing her eyes, Belle sprawled back on the sofa. Released from shame by his command, she touched herself. She was in uncharted waters, navigating by intuition, steered by Ewan's visceral reaction. Tentatively, she allowed her finger to slide over the most sensitised part of her, dipping down, inside, then back. Slippery. Swollen. A feeling like waves rolling into the shore, like breakers ready to foam. Astonishing and yet somehow completely natural.

Then, a hand on her wrist. Her eyes flew open. Ewan was standing over her, his face hard planes and rigid control. "Not yet," he said harshly, placing her hand onto his erection.

Belle sat up. Giddy. Disoriented. Edgy. She touched him. Skin like velvet. A pulsing vein running up to a hot tip. She ran her fingers over it, felt him shudder and ran her fingers back down, mimicking the way she had touched herself. Trailing and fluttering. Now cupping. Feeling him contracting against her, feeling the roughness of hair on her palm, enjoying the contrast of his satin smoothness in her other hand.

"Like this," he said, wrapping her fingers around him.

She watched, fascinated by his response to her touch, and smiled with satisfaction at the pleasure she was giving, for in his pleasure lay her victory. She looked down, lest she give herself away, moving her hand more purposefully. Feeling a shifting response in herself she moved closer, grazing her breasts against him.

Ewan pushed her back onto the chaise-longue. Unresisting, Belle lay waiting for his next move. She did not know, but she knew. He had won the throw, and in the end she must capitulate. She did not care, as long as there was an end, and soon.

He pushed her legs apart to kneel between them. He touched her. A whisper of sensation in the delicate crease at the top of her thigh. The heel of his hand between her legs, cupping her as she had him. She pushed against him. Harder, she wanted to say, but didn't. His finger eased her open, as if separating the petals of a flower.

His touch sliding over her, she felt gripped as in a vice. She struggled to breathe. Clenched to resist him. Hold on, she thought desperately, but she wasn't sure she could. Sparks of heat flickered out from where he touched her. She no longer cared what he did, so long as he did. It was profoundly different from her own caress. A change of tone and note.

Ewan plunged his finger deep into the honeyed flesh spread out in front of him, relishing the way she bucked up against him. Relishing the pleasure he could see etched on her face. Exulting in the knowledge that he caused it, controlled it.

Belle moaned, pushed, writhed. With every stroke she curled tighter into herself. She wanted only to complete this journey, to release the clutching, pleasurable tension between her legs.

Ewan rubbed and dipped and stroked. Faster. Then slower. She could not bear to wait. She reached down to grab a fistful of his hair.

He shook her away with a strange smile on his face. Vaguely, she recognised it as victorious. A sweeping, stroking, pressing movement, and she held it, clutched at it like something which would fall—and then she did, holding tighter, taut, resistant, until she could hold it no more and set it free like a bird soaring from her, flying high with a shattering pleasure, moaning, mindless.

Ewan pulled her onto the floor beneath him and entered her with one hard thrust, pushing into the hot, wet centre of her. So tight. So ready. He paused, his breathing ragged.

Beneath him, Belle said something inarticulate, her muscles gripping, holding, urging. Moving again, he was pushing hard into her, thrusting, a welcome sensation high inside her. So hard, questing, pushing in until she was sure he could not go further, but still he did. Her legs lifted over his shoulders. Pulled tight against him. Thrusting, all of him now, all of him, and she could feel every inch. She tried to hold him, feeling her own excitement build again as he moved. Harder. Higher, until she felt she would die of the tension. She wanted to scream from it, and just as she thought she would, it snapped, different from before, a sheer exhilarating drop.

Ewan could not think, his mind filled with the image of her spread out for him, creamy white thighs, full breasts, the nipples hard and dark, black curls hiding the hot pink centre into which he thrust again, oblivious now of everything save his own pleasure, holding her by the waist to pull her into him. Sharp nails dug into his buttocks, long legs curled round him. His eyes were screwed tight shut as he climaxed, pulsing into her, relishing the feeling of power and pleasure and release all rolled into one. He lay spent, breathing hard against the soft white flesh of her body.

Belle felt as if she were floating on a cloud somewhere. Sated. Now she understood the word. She could feel Ewan's breathing slowly return to normal. She had done something irrevocable, but she had enjoyed it. Relished it even.

Ewan raised his head to look at her and smiled. "Come to bed," he said, sweeping her up effortlessly in his arms. "To sleep," he added in answer to her questioning look. "Tonight's wager has been settled in full."

CHAPTER THREE

HE WAS AWOKEN BY THE grey light of dawn creeping in through the gaps in the curtains. Sitting up groggily, he was startled to find an extremely beautiful naked woman lying asleep next to him. Then he remembered. Belle. Ewan groaned. He must have had far more brandy than he'd realised. He searched his mind for regret, but could find none.

She lay on her back before him, a picture to drive any man wild with desire. Lips swollen from kissing. Lids heavy and slumberous. Full ripe breasts. Hair strewn out on the pillow behind her. "Perfect antidote, I knew you would be," he muttered to himself.

Slipping out of bed, Ewan threw on his robe and padded silently from the room, closing the door quietly behind him.

Isabella awoke to the appetising smell of fresh chocolate and warm bread. She rolled over in bed, wondering what on earth she had done to merit such an unaccustomed treat. Sitting up, she rubbed her eyes and shivered with the cold, realising with astonishment that she was naked and not in her own bed.

"Charming," a deep voice said.

Ewan was standing by the bed, holding a tray and smiling appreciatively at the vision of her black hair glinting through her powder and tumbling down over her back, her shoulders and her breasts.

Isabella grabbed the sheet, blushing furiously, images of the night before whirling through her mind like leaves in a gale. She had behaved shamelessly. She risked a glance at Ewan, busying himself with the chocolate pot. He looked tired, but showed no other outward signs of last night's events. It occurred to her that *she* must look different, changed somehow. Of a certainty she felt it.

Ewan handed her a delicate china cup patterned with dragons. Isabella took it gratefully, mumbling her thanks without meeting his eyes. She had no idea how to behave.

"I am no more familiar with the situation than you," Ewan said, echoing her thoughts. "I don't make a habit of letting women into my home. In fact, you are the first."

He stood by the bed in a heavy brocade dressing gown, smiling mischievously down at her. In the light of day she could see streaks of gold glint through his copper mane of hair. The stubble on his chin was the same dark shade of copper as the hair on his chest. The animal magnetism which had drawn her last night seemed enhanced by his dishevelled state. Really, he was quite unfairly attractive.

"Belle?"

His voice interrupted her reverie. There was an edge of amusement in it which made her certain she had been staring. She met his gaze. "I beg your pardon."

"I was asking if you regretted our wager."

Isabella eyed him speculatively. "And if I said I did?"

He laughed, sure now that she did not, for there was no indication of either tears or recriminations. "And do you?"

She shook her head. "I had no choice."

"You prefer the illusion that you are acting under duress. You will not admit you are enjoying yourself."

"The only thing I am interested in is my money," she said firmly.

"You are being less than honest, Belle."

Her winged brows rose. Her mouth quirked. It was as if they were redrawing the battle lines for later, and she knew she had to muster every advantage. "I was your prize. I did as you asked, nothing more."

Ewan remembered now what it was about her which had drawn him to her in the first place. Defiance in the face of adversity. A determination to win against the odds. He liked it. And in the luminous daylight, she was quite simply breathtaking. He was intrigued as well as aroused. "Let us call a truce for now. Have your breakfast, and then join me in the garden. You will find clothes in the chamber next to this one. My sister's. She is recently married, and left them behind when she bought her trousseau." He noted her sceptical expression. "I may have a reputation but I don't lie, Belle, you may count on that."

He disappeared into his dressing room. Isabella took her

time, enjoying the rich hot chocolate, nibbling hungrily on the bread and butter as she pondered her own feelings. Had it not been for the extremity of her circumstances she would not have dreamt of entering into such an outrageous bet, but having done so she could not regret it one little bit.

She had secured the funds—that was surely all that mattered. Even as she thought it, she knew it was a lie. Last night she had discovered something shocking about herself. She had relished every minute of what had taken place. The memory of it aroused her now. More shocking still was the admission that she wanted more, and with it the understanding that it wasn't just the physical act she had enjoyed. She had pleasured herself before, but it had never felt like that. So intense. So gratifying. So primeval. Ewan's touch was part of it. Having Ewan inside her was another part—and a very large one, she remembered with a saucy smile.

But it was more than that. It was seeing him wanting her. It was about teasing him and taunting him and flaunting herself in front of him. It was knowing she was desirable and desiring to be more so. A heady mix, made all the more complex by their sparring.

Power was at the root of it all. And confidence. She trusted him enough to expose her secret self to him, though she could not have said why. She knew he had done the same. He was a stranger, yet he was familiar. As if she had always known him and somehow forgotten.

It was with a renewed sense of anticipation that Isabella dressed in a robe *à l'anglaise* of pale blue muslin. With her coal-black hair free from powder, she looked much more like her true self. Last night she had crossed over into a new world. Or so it felt to her. She was surprised to see no evidence of the journey reflected back at her from the mirror.

Tripping lightly down the stairs, she let herself out of a side door and into the walled garden at the back of the house. It was clement for the time of year, with the sun shining high in a pale blue sky scattered with puffy white clouds. A paved path meandered through formal beds, the edges bordered with lavender and thyme which brushed against her skirts as she made her way towards an arbour at the centre of a rose garden where she could see Ewan waiting.

He was looking serious, but rose to greet her with a warm smile she could not but return with one of her own. He was so handsome, and the day was so perfect, and Isabella was so glad to have escaped the worries and sadness of the last few months. She felt released. Free.

"I'm sorry, Belle, but there is something I must ask you," Ewan said as they wandered arm in arm towards a small fountain playing in the middle of a lawn at the bottom of the garden. "What need have you for such a large sum of money?"

Isabella hesitated. "To pay off a debt," she replied cautiously.

He raised his brows. "That is a lot of debt. May I ask how you incurred it? Surely, not through gambling. Despite your best efforts you had not the look of a seasoned gamester."

"And yet, in a sense it is a gambling debt none the less," she said sadly. "My father's, originally. And now my brother's."

"Tell me," Ewan said gently.

They had reached the fountain, a frothy confection of nymphs and seahorses disporting themselves playfully. Isabella sat on the stone basin, trailing her hand in the icy cold of the water. The urge to confide in him was strong.

"My father was always a bit of a dreamer. Always full of hare-brained schemes to make our fortune. When my mother was alive she kept his reckless impulses in check, but she died five years ago and since then—well, suffice it to say he was not inclined to listen to my advice."

"You mentioned a brother. Surely, he had some influence?" Ewan sat down beside her on the stone basin.

Isabella smiled. "Robin is my twin. I love him dearly. We are very alike to look at though not at all similar in character, I'm afraid," she said with a rueful smile. "Robin had rheumatic fever as a child, which left him with a weakened heart. His delicate constitution combined with his natural inclinations make him even more unworldly than our father."

"Leaving you to look after them both?"

"Not any more. Robin is married now. To Pamela, last year. She is a good wife, she nurses him devotedly. They moved to the country when Papa settled an annuity on them, his wedding gift. They are very happy."

"So happy that they did not enquire how your father funded his gift, I gather," Ewan said dryly.

Isabella looked at him in surprise. "You're quite right, they didn't. It was another of Papa's schemes of course. His grand design, he called it. Said it would shape our future. He was certainly right about that." She was silent for a moment, staring off into the distance. Continued in a curiously flat tone, as if reciting something by rote. "The scheme involved buying ships and speculating on the value of the cargo of precious spices and the like they could pick up in the West Indies. I tried, but nothing I said could dissuade him. In fact, the more I begged him to back out, the more determined he became to prove me wrong. He borrowed an enormous sum—privately, of course No bank would have given him the money. He sailed with the ships. They were attacked by pirates. The ships and cargo were taken and Papa killed in the melee." Isabella's eyes filled with pain. "Poor Papa. He may have been foolish but he only wanted the best for us."

She straightened her back and shrugged her head as if to cast off unwelcome thoughts. "That was some months ago. As his heir, poor Robin inherited the debt, which is far beyond what could be recovered by the sale of his property. He has tried, God knows, to find some means of generating sufficient funds, but without success. Now we have run out of time. We have until the end of the week, or Robin will go to prison." She swallowed, brushed impatiently at a tear. "The doctor has made it clear my brother would not survive the harsh conditions of prison.

It is as good as a death sentence. So you see, I had to do something."

"Does your brother know of your actions?" Ewan asked harshly.

"No, no, of course not. I will think of some tale to satisfy him, you needn't worry."

"He does not deserve you," Ewan said, anger on her behalf warring with a kernel of guilt. With her hair unpowdered and her face free of rouge Belle looked younger and far more innocent than he had taken her for last night.

"I won't have you judge my brother," Isabella said vehemently. "You know nothing of him. And I won't have you judge me, either."

Ewan disarmed her by kissing her hand. "I would not dream of judging you. You have my deepest admiration, Belle. It is myself I would judge."

"I don't regret last night if that is worrying you. I have already told you that." Unwilling to have him question her motives further, for she was not ready to examine them herself, she gave him a challenging look. "Do you?"

Here at least he was on firmer ground. Ewan smiled. "Not if you don't. I knew the moment I saw you that we would give each other pleasure."

She blushed. "Don't be ridiculous."

"Come on, Belle, you felt it, too, admit it."

She shook her head, turning aside to hide her smile. "That is the second time today you have tried to make me do so, but I won't. I needed your money. That is what I found attractive."

He touched her, a finger on the shell of her ear. His

voice became low and husky. "You wanted me as much as I wanted you. I felt it in your kisses," he whispered, his mouth on hers. "And in your touch," he said.

She brushed his hand away. "You are quite right, I did," she said, looking at him with the determined tilt of her chin he already knew well. "It was not just your money I wanted, it was you. But not for the reason you think."

"My instincts tell me you are about to launch an attack. Yet still I would know. Tell me," he said with a sardonic smile.

She crossed her arms defiantly. "It's simple. I was curious. I am four and twenty, with no prospects. I do not want to die a virgin. I wanted the experience without creating an obligation. The terms of our bet made that possible."

He had known, of course he had known, that he was her first. It was inappropriate, but he could not help it. He was gratified as well as confused. "You should have told me. I would not have…"

"What," she interrupted, anxious to stall the guilt she saw looming in his eyes, "what would you have done differently? I knew the risks. I accepted the odds. I put up a creditable performance—at any rate, you seemed to enjoy it. That is what it was, though, a performance." She shrugged with what she hoped was nonchalance and turned to go, but a strong hand on her arm wiped the triumphant smile from her face.

"I wonder, though, my lovely Belle, why you waited so long? Had you made your need for a candidate to deflower you known, any man on earth would have been willing. Yet you chose me. Why?"

She licked her lips nervously.

Ewan laughed. "Take some advice from an experienced campaigner and retreat while you're ahead, Belle."

Isabella glared at him furiously, but could think of no retort.

Ewan took her arm. "It's gone one o'clock," he said, his tone more conciliatory now.. "I find a night such as the last makes me uncommonly hungry. Let us go in search of sustenance."

With her nose studiously in the air and her temper simmering, Isabella walked with him back to the house.

But it was not in her nature to sulk, and over a repast of cold cuts and hothouse fruits, Ewan set out to charm her. Since he touched not on the personal, and his opinions happily coincided with her own on an astonishing number of topics, this he did very well. He had a dry humour and pithy wit which Isabella found most invigorating. He made her laugh. She realised it had been many months since she had done so. His tales of his army days were fascinating, recounted with a modesty and humour which made her warm to him all the more.

"You're very self-effacing about your exploits," she said teasingly.. "I had heard you were quite the dashing hero."

"I prefer to let my actions speak for me, rather than words," he replied with a shrug.

"Tell me," she asked, "what turned you into such an avid supporter of Mr Fox and the Colonists—Americans, as I believe they like to be called? Having fought so loyally for the King, it seems a rather paradoxical stance to take."

"Some would even say traitorous," Ewan said bitterly.

"Not I," Isabella said firmly.

He looked at her searchingly. "Thank you for that."

Silence reigned for a few moments and Isabella held her breath, aware that the matter was important to him and deeply personal.

"I suppose it started at Bunker Hill," Ewan said in a low voice. "I was just twenty, too young to question why I was there, nor to doubt that I was fighting on the right side. We won, but it was a pyrrhic victory, the casualties were severe. You can have no idea how..."

His grim expression bore testimony to the dark memories crowding his mind. Isabella took his hand.

"Anyway," Ewan continued, "it was horrible for both sides. And that's when I began to realise it was wrong, too. We British were the trespassers, the usurpers. I realised that, but I could not do anything about it. Soldiering was my life. Loyalty to my colonel unquestioning, even if I did question the cause. Then our old enemies the French joined the Americans, and confused the issue. It was only years later, after Washington took our surrender in Yorktown, that I had time to sort out my feelings. And only when I left the army could I speak my mind without being disloyal."

"You certainly did speak your mind," Isabella said, remembering that even her father had called Ewan a turncoat.

Ewan shrugged. "Much good it did. I was cut by a

number of my comrades. I featured in one of Mr Gillray's caricatures as a wild Scotsman in a kilt, and now Fox looks like he'll be stuck in opposition to Mr Pitt for the rest of his life."

"Have you no desire to take a more active part in politics?" she asked curiously.

Ewan shook his head. "Words and posturing are not for me."

The ormolu clock interrupted their conversation by striking five, taking them both by surprise.

"We should take the opportunity to rest before dinner," Ewan said with a wicked glint in his eye. "With any luck it's going to be an eventful night."

A frisson of pure anticipation coursed through Isabella's veins. What would the fates have in store for her this time?

CHAPTER FOUR

BELLE DRESSED SIMPLY for dinner in a gown of pale green muslin worn open over a white slip, the sleeves tight to her elbows, below which the ruffles of her chemise billowed. Green ribbon formed a sash around her waist, and was also tied artfully into her hair, one long ebony curl allowed to trail over her shoulder. She studied her reflection in the long mirror with satisfaction. *Au natural,* a veritable milk-maid in the style made popular by Queen Marie-Antoinette. With a frisson of excitement she headed downstairs to the dining room. Whether she won or lost, she was determined to have Ewan in a fever of wanting.

He was different in the candlelight. Less approachable in his dark evening clothes. More self-contained. She felt a quiver of apprehension. Or was it some less admissible emotion?

They sat adjacent to each other at the oval table. Ewan dispensed with the servants and served her himself. She took claret, he burgundy. Roast woodcock met with her approval. Expertly, he carved the game bird and placed a portion on Isabella's plate.

White teeth nibbling on the tender meat. Fingers first licked, then sucked clean, one by one. A luscious mouth dabbed delicately with the table linen. A glimpse of pink tongue. Ewan shifted uncomfortably against the high back of his chair, feeling himself stiffen against his breeches. He could not but help imagining her mouth on him. Licking. Sucking.

"What have you in mind for me if you win again tonight," she asked, fixing him with her gaze.

He grinned. "It does not do to depend upon winning, for that way disappointment lies."

"So you would be disappointed if I win," she teased.

"I would not be the only one."

"Sir, you flatter yourself."

A hand grasped her firmly by the chin. "At least I am honest with myself, Belle. I want you. If I win the throw I will have you, and you will be willing. But if you win, what then? 'Twill be a frustrating night, for you will spite us both."

She pulled back, anger sparking in her eyes, not wanting to hear the uncomfortable truth. "For you perhaps. I told you earlier, you have already served your purpose for me." She pushed back her chair impatiently. "Come, let us settle it at once then, since you are so clearly unable to wait."

Ewan laughed softly and followed her wordlessly upstairs to the small saloon where the dice box lay waiting on the table.

* * *

Isabella looked blankly at the dice when they stopped rolling. "It seems you have won, Captain Dalgleish. Once again, I am at your disposal. What would you have me do this time?"

"Come here, Belle." He could see her breathing through the thin muslin of her dress. A long curl, glossy black, trailed down over the white skin of her neck. So lovely.

She stepped closer. He smelled of clean linen and soap, a hint of wine on his breath. She looked up, found his lips close, felt his breath warm on her cheek, an arm snaking round the ribbon at her waist. She could feel her nipples harden against the cotton of her chemise. Wanting flared in her, a need she had not known until yesterday and which since then had stubbornly refused to subside.

Her wrists were captured, tugged tight behind her back. She was pressed close to him, chest to chest, so close she could feel the buttons of his coat digging into her. His smile was cruel but she was not frightened.

"So I have served my purpose have I? You do not dispense with me so easily, Belle. I will make you ache for me."

His words served to boost her determination to deny him. "You may try, but you will not succeed," she said with a taunting smile. "There is nothing singular about you, Captain Dalgleish. What you can give me, I don't doubt I could have from any other man of my acquaintance. You said as much yourself."

"As I also pointed out, you chose to wait for me," he reminded her. Her wrists were released abruptly.

Ewan strode over to the door of the saloon. The lock clicked home.

He moved purposefully towards her. "Turn around."

The ribbon from her waist was untied and placed around her eyes as a blindfold. "What are you doing?" Belle asked, a tremor in her voice.

"Proving a point. Since you cannot see me you are free to imagine me whichever man of your acquaintance you choose. But you will not be able to, Belle. No matter what you may say, I know you want only me. And you will admit it."

"I am at your command. I will say anything you would have me say."

"No, Belle, you will say it because it is true."

Strong hands on her. Her dress untied. Her petticoats, her stays, her chemise, all expertly removed. The pins taken from her hair. She could feel it cascading down her back. She stood, vulnerable in her stockings and slippers, unable to see, afraid to move, yet unafraid.

"I won't say it because it isn't true," she said, knowing she was lying, knowing he knew it, too, knowing that the battle of wills enhanced the wild excitement of the battle of the flesh.

Nothing happened for a few agonising seconds. Time seemed to stand still, the sense of anticipation almost unbearable. Suddenly, she felt a hand touch her head, long fingers combing through her hair, fanning it out over her shoulders. He was standing behind her. She could feel the cloth of his coat. His mouth on the nape of her neck. Cool lips on hot skin, on the lobe of her ear, trailing kisses down to her shoulder. Fingers kneading her flesh. Hands reaching round to cup her breasts, trailing down to the curve of her waist, a tantalising flicker on the soft skin at the top her thighs. Belle stood motionless, her mind floating, empty of thoughts, allowing sensation to take over. Cloth on skin. Cool on heat. Dry on wet.

Ewan guided her towards a sofa and arranged her there on her stomach, running his hand along the perfect contour of her spine, curling into her waist, curving out to her bottom. Such skin, such softness. curves and flesh, all so different from his own. She smelled of flowers and spice. As she shifted restlessly under his caress, he caught a glimpse of black curls curtaining flesh darkened by arousal. Desire twisted like a knife in his gut.

Quickly, Ewan divested himself of his clothing. To take her, possess her utterly was what he most desired. But first he needed her, more than he cared to admit, to put the evidence of her own desire into words.

The delightfully ticklish sensation of something unbearably light being trailed over her back raised goose bumps on already over-sensitised skin. Belle shifted on the sofa. Between her thighs now, whispering down, on the backs of her knees, her ankles. Back again. She arched her bottom up, pressing her knees into the sofa to give her purchase, inviting the soft caress back, down, between.

A quite different sensation now. A tongue, licking down the curve of her bottom, velvet soft, dipping into the curve of her thighs, away again. She tried to imagine another man as he had commanded, but it was impossible. She did not need to see him. Her body knew it was Ewan. Could only be Ewan.

Something else now, playing on her skin. Silken, hard, nudging against her thighs. "Ewan," she said, arching against him.

Cold space. "Say you want me, Belle," Ewan whispered.

Silence.

His erection was nudging against her, sliding against her. She felt the tip of him part her. Feelings almost painful in their intensity. Deprived of her sight it was as if all her other senses were enhanced.

"Belle?"

Silence.

Cold again. She was turned over. Sprawled on the settee, one leg trailing on the ground. She wanted to touch him, reached out blindly for him, found her hands pushed away.

Her legs parted. That tantalisingly ticklish sensation again. A feather…that was it. On her thighs. Between her thighs. Brushing her heat. Tickling her curls. Now fingers doing the same. Now a gentle breath. His tongue. *Oh,, his tongue*. Licking her thighs. Closer. Flickering round the edges of desire. Then not round the edges. A gentle touch…too gentle. A sweeping movement now, hot on hot, wet on wet. Such sweet pleasure, she was melting. Belle pressed herself against his mouth. More.

Instead, his voice, insistent now. "Who is it you want, Belle?"

Edgy, he sounded edgy. Passion, but it could be

anger. She could not tell. She bit back the urge to plead with him.

Tongue and mouth again. Sucking and licking. Twisting and clenching. Throbbing. She was so close. He stopped. "Ewan." Her voice was husky with passion and need. Her fingernails dug cruelly into his shoulders. "Ewan, for heavens' sake, I want you. Now." Co-operation, not defeat. There was a limited pleasure in resistance and she had expended it.

For what seemed like eons nothing happened. Belle waited impatiently in the enforced darkness. Then suddenly he was kissing her—a hard, insistent kiss. She could feel tension in his shoulders but it was not anger. He was as desperate as she was. All of a sudden, she wanted to give him what he needed. "I chose you. I wanted you last night. I did not care about the bet. I want you now."

The blindfold was torn from her, and she saw amber eyes gazing at her, dark with passion. A mouth sculpted into a victorious smile. She cared not, secure in the knowledge that she possessed him as much as he did her. Her nails dug harder into his flesh.

Ewan knelt between her legs. No teasing now, he licked her roughly, unerringly, tugging and sucking with just enough friction to drive her into a frenzy, pulling her hard against his mouth as she climaxed, pulsing into him, onto him. Waves turned to ripples and he licked again, turning the tide back from ebb to flow, pulling her to her feet, bending her over the sofa. She could feel him behind her, the hard length of him nudging against her.

Ewan rubbed himself against the perfect white cheeks

of her bottom, his hand cupping her, feeling her rippling, so achingly arousing on his palm. He could see her, dark pink and wet as he entered, slowly, pushing in between layers of heat and damp, her muscles pulling him in, feeling her parting, gripping, holding him as he pushed in and in and in, all the while watching himself as he thrust into her, feeling as if every fibre of his body was being set ablaze.

Belle clung to the back of the sofa. Her knees were pressed against its edge. Ewan's legs pressed into the backs of hers. Rough hair. His breathing heavy. His hands clutching. Higher than before he was going, more and more until there was no more and he paused tantalisingly. She pushed back against him, gripped him, experimentally rocked back and forth, loving the way even such a tiny movement rippled inside her. He felt thick and hard and high.

Ewan withdrew then plunged in again with that same deliberate, excruciatingly exciting slowness. It became another battle; the need to keep him inside her, to stop him withdrawing, to hold him. And she was winning. He was thrusting harder now, faster. She could feel the delightful slap of him against her bottom as he bucked. She could tell from the way he seemed to expand inside her that he was close. She felt her own muscles contract in response. An echo of her climax or a continuation or something new, she didn't care, except it whirled her away unexpectedly, and immediately she felt him shuddering in response, a thrusting becoming a pounding becoming a release, and she felt him spilling into her and she moaned his name without realising, holding him vicelike to feel and feel and feel as he spent himself.

Afterwards, he was tender, sitting her down beside him on the sofa, holding her close, stroking her hair as she nestled into the hollow of his shoulder. They sat thus for a long time, neither willing to break the spell. Later still he took her by the hand and led her to the bed chamber. They lay in the dark together under soft cotton sheets gazing without seeing.

"Is Belle your real name," Ewan asked unexpectedly.

"Why do you ask?"

"A feeling. At times—these times—you seem to be Belle. But in the day when I speak your name, you look at me as if I am talking of a stranger."

"You're right in a way." She felt as if their love-making had reshaped her. "Belle is a shocking creature. She has dark thoughts and dark needs. Isabella, my real name, the real me, knows nothing of them."

"Isabella. I like it—it suits you. We all have a dark side," Ewan said softly. "It's just that most people do not have a name for it."

"Some abuse it," Belle said with a shiver.

Ewan pulled her close. "Yes, some do. I have seen it in the aftermath of battle many times. But that is not what I meant."

"No, you meant what we have together," she replied with growing understanding. "We clash because it enhances the defeat as well as the victory. Like tonight, there is as much pleasure in submission as there is in domination. Provided we both stick to the rules, of course."

Ewan ran a possessive hand down her spine. "That is it exactly. I knew when I saw you that you would understand me, though, I could not have articulated it so. And you knew, too, you will admit that now?"

Belle smiled into the dark. "Why not? You won after all," she teased.

"Yes, I did. And I am not finished with you yet," he said with a growl, pushing her onto her back.

Afterwards, she slept deeply and dreamt she had been shipwrecked, drifting at sea alone. In the distance, at last, she could see safe harbour.

CHAPTER FIVE

SHE AWOKE IN THE MORNING alone and feeling strangely contented, as if she had emerged from a dark tunnel into the light. New. Replete. For the first time, Isabella examined Belle cautiously in the light of day, like a scientist surveying a new-found species. Alien but familiar. Part of her, once caged, now set free by this game of theirs. Like an alchemist, Ewan had conjured something new from two separate elements.

Something destined to be short-lived, she realised poignantly. After tonight it was a part of her which would forever go unnourished. Without Ewan, Belle would surely wither and die. The thought squeezed her heart, and she banished it. Plenty of time for pain on the morrow.

After dressing, Isabella found Ewan in the library reading *The Spectator*. He held out his hand in greeting, looking much younger in the daylight, almost boyish. Welcoming. She remembered her dream. Here was a man to keep confidences. A man to trust. A man of integrity, so different from the dark soul she crossed swords with at night. And yet...

Two Ewans; one for Belle, the other for Isabella. Opposite sides of one coin. Like her. Exactly like her. Like an animal with hibernation in mind, she stored up this comforting crumb for the bleak months ahead.

Wandering aimlessly about the room, Isabella spotted a large map of America laid out on the desk. "Is this the New World?" she asked excitedly. "Tell me about it, Ewan."

He described cities and plantations, a land of contrasts and plenty. "But no words can convey the sense of space the sheer size of it," he said with a sweeping gesture.

Isabella ran her finger over the vast empty space to the west of New England. "The Frontier, they call it. Think what that could mean. The chance to start afresh, without the prejudices and constraints of England."

"That is precisely why the early settlers went there in the first place. But it is a life of hard work and many dangers, too," he cautioned.

"Think of the rewards, though," Isabella said with a glowing smile.

"You are serious," he said wonderingly.

Her smile faded abruptly. "A dream, that's all." She was silent, frowning down at the map. "As a woman, I am allowed no ambitions," she said bitterly. "But you can do anything you want. You are marking time with your hell raising I think, but it does not satisfy you, does it?"

"You're very perceptive. It's not the danger I miss, nor

even the battles—it's the challenge, the unpredictability. I had forgotten what that felt like until I met you."

"Your dark side," Isabella said, flushing. "You will need to find another outlet for it after tonight."

He was hurt. "And you, too," he said roughly, testing her reaction.

She shook her head. "Tomorrow, perhaps even tonight if I win, Belle will be gone forever."

"Don't talk like that," he said, putting a hand on her wrist.

She brushed him away. "This is not real life, what has transpired here between us. It is a game. A necessity for me, a diversion for you." She stood, brushing out her skirts, and left the room, seeking refuge in her chamber. She would not give house room to this stupid sentimental feeling the day-time Ewan aroused in her. He was her adversary. For if he was not, then what was he?

The question would not go away. As she bathed and dressed in an evening gown, as dusk fell and night ascended, Isabella and Belle waged war in her mind.

It's ridiculous to imagine an acquaintance which can be measured in hours could amount to anything important. I hardly know Ewan.

I know the important things. I have known those since almost the moment I set eyes on him.

Extreme circumstances brought us together. I am here only to save my brother.

I came here for Robin but I am staying for my own reasons.

I am simply in thrall to my own passions then...that is it, surely?

This chemistry between us is a symptom, not a cause. My passions are the result of my feelings, not the other way around.

So I am in love with him?

Yes, I am in love with him. Deeply, irrevocably in love with him. There, it is said!

I am not foolish enough to think my love returned, though.

No. And I do not want his pity, either.

My opponent he must remain then, Isabella said.

My opponent, Belle agreed sadly.

But by the time Belle faced Ewan over the dinner table, her mood was black. She would be gone in the morning. She wished she could be sure Ewan would miss her. She wished she did not care whether or not he did. She wished she could stop wishing. She cut viciously into the capon on her plate.

"You have the look of someone with a hunger food won't satisfy."

His words cut into her thoughts. He was not smiling, but he was laughing at her all the same. Pettishly, she pushed her plate away. "You flatter yourself if you think it's you I hunger for," she snapped. "You are a skilful lover, and you have taught me a few tricks, but I am a quick learner. I don't need you. Rather it is you who has need of me."

Her words were meant to hurt him. He knew that, but they hurt all the same. He could not read her mood. When she had left him earlier, he told himself it was part of their game. But she was still angry; so angry with him, and he did not know why. With the curtain up on their final act, it was as if he was in the wrong play. He had not thought of the ending, but he did not want *this* ending. "Isabella," he said urgently, "it doesn't have to be like this, you know."

"Yes, it does," she said at last. "We agreed on the rules at the outset. And you must call me Belle, not Isabella," she added coldly.

As he followed her for the last time to the upstairs parlour, uncertainty made him apprehensive. He had convinced himself that the fall of the dice tonight was irrelevant. He realised he had been horribly wrong. He picked up the ivories. "Three," he called, for the nights of their wager. "No four," he amended superstitiously, casting the dice reluctantly.

Belle watched unblinking as they landed. Five and six. When it was her turn to throw she looked at Ewan, not the dice. "Three," she called, and three is precisely what fell.

He could not believe it was over. Striding over to the silver salver standing on the table beside the fireplace, Ewan poured himself a large brandy and downed it in one draught.

"Slowly, take your time," Belle said, in a deliberate echo of his own words that first night. "I would have you sober. You have a debt to settle, Captain Dalgleish."

Ewan looked up. Blue eyes, alight with something. Mouth curled up in a mocking smile, a direct imitation of his own. "But you won," he said stupidly.

"Indeed I did. Which means that I decide what happens." She crooked her finger and swept imperiously from the room.

Ewan followed, his heart thumping with anticipation. By the time they arrived at the door of her chamber he was already hard. Never had he wanted something so much.

"Undress," Belle commanded him, busy rummaging for something in the tall chest of drawers set against the far wall.

He did so. She turned to find him magnificently naked before her. She caught her breath, allowed her eyes to travel slowly over him, from his flaming mane down past the breadth of his shoulders, his chest, the rippling muscles of his abdomen, his powerful thighs, her breath coming shallow and fast as she took in his aroused state. She forced herself to continue down the length of his legs, the beautifully defined muscles of his thighs and calves. Standing thus, there was no trace of the sophisticated gentleman; he was all raw power and overwhelmingly male. Untamed. But not, she hoped, untameable.

She wondered if it was possible to tease a man in the same way as she had been teased. Brought to the brink of pleasure and suspended there, time and again. She was resolved to try.

"Well," Ewan demanded, more aroused than abashed by her scrutiny. "Do I pass muster."

"You are a fine looking specimen," Belle said dismissively.

He laughed, genuine amusement rippling through his

stomach muscles, making his eyes crinkle attractively at the corners.

She could not help it; she returned his smile.

"Come here, Belle."

His words brought her up short. "No! It is for you to do my bidding tonight. Lie on the bed."

A quizzical look, but he obliged. "What do you plan to do with me?"

She looked down at him, trying to etch his image in her mind. Anger gave way to tenderness. Desire, as ever in his company, lurked in the wings ready to take a leading role. "Tonight you are the vanquished. My prisoner. I intend to make use of you. Raise your arms."

Warily, he did so, watching as she produced two silk ribbons, sashes from dresses, he realised, and tied one around each wrist. When she concentrated her tongue peeped out between her lips. He wondered if she knew. He wanted to kiss her. As she tested her knots and began to tie the other end of the sashes to the bed posts, he relaxed. She wanted revenge, but it was not his demoralisation she sought; it was the upper hand. In this dark part of themselves were they not made of the same clay? Tonight, she needed him to resist before he submitted. A reversal of last night. He understood that, too.

Belle surveyed her handiwork with satisfaction. She stood in front of him to unhook her dress, recalling how much he had enjoyed watching her disrobe that first night. How much she had enjoyed it, too. Watching his excitement mount served to increase hers, she had learned. Provocatively, she paraded in front of him, casting silk and lace and cotton and ribbons aside. Naked, she reached up to loosen her hair, stretching her arms above her head to tauten the line of her breasts, watching Ewan through half-closed lids with immense satisfaction. He was positively devouring her with his eyes. A curl of excitement knotted tight in her belly.

Ewan strained at the ribbons. Forced himself to relax.

Belle laughed for the pleasure of it. She climbed onto the bed between his legs. Leaning over him, she allowed her nipples to graze the skin of his abdomen. She shivered at the contact and stooped down to lick him, tracing the line of his rib cage with her tongue. Stopped to watch him.

His eyes darkened with desire. She felt him strain at the ribbons again. "Kiss me, Belle," he whispered huskily.

She shook her head. Leaning over him again, she traced a path with her tongue down his stomach, cradling his length between her breasts, teasing him with her nipples, relishing the feel of their hardness against his silken skin. Down she licked; the inside of his thigh then the other, revelling in the heat and maleness of him, feeling herself tight and wet, aware of his breathing becoming harsh and quicker as she lingered on the crease at the top of his leg.

"Do you like being my prisoner, Ewan?" she asked, her mouth against his skin.

Silence.

Her finger fluttering along the length of him. Circling the tip. Her tongue now, repeating the action, licking her way up, lingering, circling. Ewan groaned.

"Tell me you surrender, Ewan," she whispered.

"No," he managed through gritted teeth, straining at the ribbons.

Belle licked again. More than anything she wanted his hands on her, his lips on her, but that way lay capitulation and she was not ready for that. Not yet. Daringly, she put her lips around him and sucked gently. Silence of a different sort. She sucked again. Breathing so rapid she thought he was in pain. Looked up. Saw his eyes fly open.

"Don't stop."

"Say it," she insisted.

Her lips on him again. He thought he would die with the pleasure. Now butterfly kisses and fingers stroking, her lips again. Now looking at him, demanding. Ewan closed his eyes and looked away, praying she would have pity.

She remembered last night. She could do the same to him. She could have him without allowing him to have her. It was a powerfully erotic image. Ewan was looking at her. She could see the plea in his eyes, though he would not say it. She touched him with her fingers, stroking until she could feel the blood pulse, stopping as it did, glorying in the exquisite pain she could see etched on his face.

She put her lips around him again, drew him in as much as she could hold. Sucking purposefully now, feeling him engorged in her mouth, aware of him straining, breathing, saying her name, but caught up in her own powerful need to control him, feel him, and then he came, and finally she heard him, over and over again, saying the words, *I surrender,* but she didn't care anymore and it didn't feel like a victory; it simply felt right.

She lay on his stomach. She could feel his heart beating hard. She was conscious of her own arousal, and wondered what to do about it. She could make him tend to her as he had last night, but that was not what she wanted. She wanted him inside her. Cautiously, she touched him. Wondering.

A throaty chuckle. "Give me a moment."

She looked up. "Fighting back, Ewan?"

He shook his head. "Simply trying to do your bidding, but I need time to recover. If you untied me, it would help."

But she would not. And it did not take so very long after all. ;

Lowering herself onto him, shivering as she felt him enter her, satin smooth and hard in contrast to her soft and wet core. Slowly, she sheathed him until he filled her, and she held him without moving.

"Belle," Ewan said urgently.. "Belle, untie me."

She shook her head. Even that tiny movement reverberated inside her.

Ewan strained at the ribbons holding him but to no avail. Belle moved again, up, down, slow, too slow, tilting herself forward on top of him, nipples grazing his chest. She was doing something else now, so that he was caught in a vicelike grip inside her. He felt the blood rushing. "Let me go, Belle."

Still she denied him, squirming on top of him, enjoying the friction, enjoying the power she had over him, enjoying the power she had over herself. She lifted herself up again, then down, then writhed.

She could feel herself unravelling. She leaned forward using her elbows for purchase and thrust again. Ewan pushed up to meet her. His eyes on hers, dark amber, watching her, waiting for her, she realised. Finally, she kissed him. Deeply. Passionately. Her tongue hot in his mouth. She thrust, could hold it no longer, came around him, gripping his shoulders, like a complicated knot untying, and felt him climax almost at the same time, so that she was lost, unable to tell which was her and which was he as they fell, glided, and soared.

Little kisses nuzzling her back to consciousness... Abruptly, Belle sat up. Reluctantly, she pulled herself away. She untied him.

Ewan smiled at her lazily. "How does it feel to win?"

"How does it feel to lose?"

"Surprisingly good." He sat up, massaging his wrists.

To her embarrassment, there were red wheals where the ribbons had been pulled too tight when he had strained against them. "I'm sorry," she said contritely. "I didn't mean to hurt you."

He shrugged and pulled her down on top of him. "It's of no consequence."

His hands stroked her back, pulled her close, so close she could hear the thump of his heart. Her head fitted snugly onto his shoulder. How could three days have passed so quickly? Why could not the night last longer? She was dreading daybreak.

"Belle, about tomorrow," Ewan said.

"There is no need to say anything," she mumbled into

his chest, unwilling to hear any reminder of their terms or, God forbid, his thanks or his excuses. She would leave without betraying herself if it killed her.

Assuming they were in perfect accord, Ewan smiled contentedly. She was right. There was no need for words to frame something so fundamental. But he would say them all the same in the morning. Unconventional this courtship may have been, but it must be formally sealed. He slept deeply and dreamt of their future together. When he awoke she was gone.

CHAPTER SIX

"WHY DID YOU LEAVE without so much as a word?"

Ewan pushed passed the maidservant and slammed the door of the small parlour firmly behind them. He was clearly angry. It showed in the hard glitter of his eyes, in the rigid way he held himself, leaning against the door, muscles tensed as if waiting to pounce, holding her in a gimlet glare she dared not break.

Isabella shook her head helplessly.

"I thought things were understood between us," Ewan said harshly, pushing himself from the door and closing the distance to her with three long strides. "Last night, you said we need not say anything, I thought you realised—" He stopped abruptly, ran a hand over his unshaven jaw, up to his hair, copper and gold in wild disarray, in tune with his mood. "Isabella, have you any idea how I felt? I did not even know where you live."

She smiled nervously. "We did not get around to such common place information."

"No. What we shared was rather more fundamental," he said, taking her hand. "Luckily, the footman who summoned the hackney for you this morning has an excellent memory."

Hope flickered in her breast, but she could not yet turn it into belief. "We certainly reached a—a frankness in a very short acquaintance which few people achieve in a lifetime."

Navy blue eyes met amber. Each searching desperately for reassurance. It was Ewan who spoke first.

"Two days and three nights that is all, yet I feel I know you. I feel you know me, too."

He was frowning, his mouth a tight line. It was a look which could have been frightening, so fierce it was, but she was not frightened. Uncertainty, need, too, were reflected there. She had never seen him look so anxious. Never heard that note in his voice, not even at the height of their passion. She recognised it all. A reflection of herself.

But still she sought reassurance. "You said last night we had no need for words."

"You thought I meant no regrets," he said, understanding slowly dawning.

She gave a ragged laugh. "I thought you were reminding me of our terms. That you had had enough of me. I could not bear to say goodbye."

A smile lurked at the corner of Ewan's mouth. "Goodbye! One word we will never say. No, it was not that. It was just—something so elemental as we share, it seemed to me sacrilege to speak it."

"Elemental," Isabella whispered. "That is how it felt."

"An irresistible force. We called it a battle, but it was more like an explosion, so powerful it was, that thing which brought us together." He pressed her hand between his,.then.knelt at her feet. "We fought for control, when we should have simply surrendered. We are two halves of one being, Isabella. One creation far more powerful than its components. Do you not realise that?"

She knew only too well. "*My face in thine eye, thine in mine appears*," she quoted softly. "I know that I love you, Ewan, if that is what you mean."

"I look at you and see me. That, my lovely Isabella, is exactly what I mean," he said. "And though our wooing has been rather unconventional, that is what it was after all, a wooing. So I would beg you in the most conventional way to be my wife, for the most conventional of reasons, that I cannot live without you and my life would be empty without you."

She fell to the floor beside him, wrapping her arms around him. "And I must reply in the most conventional of ways that I will, I will, *indeed* I will."

"I love you, Isabella," he whispered into her ear. "A mere three days we have spent together, but we have been meant for each other since the beginning of time."

Finally, his lips met hers. Tongues tangling. Breath mingling. Hot, hard kisses. Arms entwined. Bodies pressed so tight together nothing could ever come between them.

A mere two hours they had been wed. They left on the morrow for the New World.

"You're shivering," Ewan said, running his hands down his wife's arms.

"I'm nervous," Isabella replied. "I know it's foolish, but I feel as if this is the first time."

"It is. Before, we indulged in love-making. Tonight we will be making love. I am as nervous as you are."

Shyly, she untied the fastening of her chemise and let it fall to the ground. She came towards him, white skin, black hair, blue eyes, pink mouth.

"Beautiful," Ewan whispered. "Beautiful Isabella." He ran his hands down the line of her spine to cup the curves of her bottom, pulling her close against him. "My wife. I love you."

"My husband," she whispered, rubbing herself sensuously against him. "I love you."

He kissed her, and his touch sent a jolt of fire through her. Ewan's hair clenched in her hand. Herself pushing, arching her hips into his, relishing the hardness of him against her. He lifted her onto the bed. Touching. Stroking. Licking. Sucking. Her mouth. Her breasts. Down to the heat between her legs. She moaned his name. Began to fall. Then he was on top of her, kissing her, thrusting deep inside her as she climaxed, arching against him, feeling him spill into her at the same moment, kissing, clutching. Calling her name. Calling his name. Drifting weightless, dispersed like a thousand stars into a new sky.

One. They were one. That is how it ended. And that is how it began. In a new world.

* * * * *

Seducing a Stranger

CHRISTINE MERRILL

Christine Merrill lives on a farm in Wisconsin with her husband, two sons and too many pets—all of whom would like her to get off the computer so they can check their e-mail. She has worked in theatre costuming, where she was paid to play with period ballgowns, and as a librarian, where she spent the day surrounded by books. Writing historical romance combines her love of good stories and fancy dress with her ability to stare out the window and make stuff up. You can visit her website at www.christine-merrill.com

Author's Note

Since I like to think every new project is an adventure, it was a real treat to do my first **Undone**. My goal was to see how much story I could fit into a few thousand words, while keeping the relationship hot and still getting to the happy ending that we all love. It was a chance to take a break from plotting a full book, to let both my imagination and my characters run wild.

I hope you have as much fun with it as I did.

Happy reading,

Christine Merrill

To Mohawk the cat, who gave selflessly of his time by teasing the dog to hysteria and sleeping on my keyboard. Without his help, I would never have been able to finish this story in August. I'd have been done in June.

CHAPTER ONE

THE ABBESS MET VICTORIA Paget at the door of the brothel welcoming her in without a word. She did not ask Victoria's name or her reason for seeking out a specific man. She showed no loyalty to her customer, nor did she seem to care overmuch what the strange lady on her doorstep wished to do with her time or her reputation. Victoria suspected that the Earl of Stanton had paid the woman well to insure her lack of curiosity.

And what did it matter, if she was forced to play the whore to discover the truth? It would be worth any sacrifice, if it meant that she could put her husband's death behind her. If a subordinate's betrayal had brought about his end and she knew, and yet she did nothing? Then she failed him as a widow, just as she feared she had as a wife. Until she was sure that poor Charles rested easy, she would have no peace herself.

The woman led her through the main salon and down a hall hung with red curtains and bawdy art, and opened one of the many rooms for her. "I know the man you seek, and I know his tastes." She turned a critical gaze on Victoria, as though she were inspecting merchandise before displaying it. "There will be no difficulty in getting him to come to you, if you have the nerve to meet him." She waited to see if Victoria expressed shock or hesitation. When she saw none, she said, "Tom Godfrey is known by the girls here to be clean and gentlemanly. You are in no danger, spending an evening in his company." The woman gave a small satisfied smile. "In fact, there are those who would be jealous of your good fortune."

Victoria sincerely doubted it, but said nothing.

The abbess gestured her into the small bedroom before them. Then she turned to a silk curtain next to the door and pulled it aside to reveal a brass-bound peephole. The woman offered no further explanation, but Victoria could guess what was expected of her. Lieutenant Godfrey would be led down the hall, toward this room. The abbess would pull aside a portrait or a drapery to give him his first glimpse of the woman who awaited. She was to beguile him with her movements, allowing them both to pretend that she was unaware. She nodded to the abbess.

The woman nodded back. "Wait here and I will see to it that he finds you." Then she departed, closing the door behind her.

Victoria examined her surroundings, surprised that it was no different than a common bedroom. The walls were covered in cream silk, but there were no paintings or any sort of ornament. The room was empty but for a wardrobe, a small dressing table and mirror, and a great soft bed with virginal white sheets.

She wondered if this room had a specialized purpose: the loss of innocence. Surely this was not the place for her. She had lost that, long ago. And yet? As she hung up her cloak, a shiver went through her that had nothing to do with the temperature of the air.

When she had gone to see her husband's friend, the Earl of Stanton, with her unusual request, he had first dismissed her as foolish. Perhaps her husband had suspected that there was a spy in the midst of his company. His death did not prove the fact. Soldiers died. Surely she knew that. She had followed her husband to the Peninsula and seen the results of battle, had she not?

She had argued that her Charles had died not in battle as he should but because of false intelligence. His men had been unprepared when they were ambushed on the road. Her husband had often remarked about the strange behavior of Lieutenant Godfrey and insisted there was something not quite right about him. It must be more than coincidence that the man who her husband suspected was the only one to escape unscathed from the massacre.

Stanton had argued that she had no real proof. That the man's reputation had been sterling, right up to that moment. And in any case, he was no longer the army's concern. He had been badly wounded in another engagement, retired from the service and returned to London. Then he had thought to tease her, and made the outrageous suggestion that she find the man and ask him herself.

When she had eagerly agreed to this, he had changed

his tune and tried to frighten her. Godfrey did not inhabit the sorts of places that a respectable lady might go. Did she mean to frequent bawdy houses, looking for him?

She had squared her shoulders and said, "If necessary."

And necessity had brought her here.

Victoria reached behind her to undo the modest gown she wore. She had cast off her mourning before coming here. Though black might suit her mood, it did not fit her disguise. Red had seemed too obvious. So she had chosen a green dress. She favored the color, although she had worn nothing so frivolous since before her marriage. Now she removed it and hung it on a hook at the back of the wardrobe.

She stood in petticoats and shift, staring at her own white face in the little mirror. It could not do to look frightened, when he came for her. Stanton had argued that she would be horrified at what was expected from a woman in such a place.

She lifted her chin, examining her reflection and pinching her cheeks to get some color back into them. She had informed Stanton that she was no longer a schoolgirl, and was not in the least frightened of a thing that she had done many times before.

Her frankness had made the poor man blush, and he'd pleaded with her to cry off and to forget everything he had said on the matter.

Of course, she had refused. Given the suspicious nature of his death, her husband would have expected her to act on what he had told her. Although Charles had been a good man, sometimes he had treated her no different than he treated his soldiers. He expected loyalty, obedience and courage, as well as her devotion. If the Earl of Stanton did not mean to pursue the matter, then she must. And she would be better off under his guidance than acting on her own.

When he had seen that she would not be swayed, he had shaken his head and given her the address of this place. He had promised that although it was against his better judgment, all would be arranged.

She froze. There was a whisper of air against her bare arms. It seemed to come from behind the draperies on the wall behind her. He was there, watching her.

She turned so that her back was to her supposed observer and touched her own neck, running a finger along the skin, and up to remove the pins from her hair. Then she took up the brush from the dressing table, combing out the curls as though she were preparing for bed.

Her hair was her pride and joy, now that she was back in London. She'd cried when Charles had made her cut it, saying that if she was to follow him to Portugal there would be no time for feminine nonsense. But it had grown back as full and lustrous as it had been before her marriage. She wondered if the man who watched cared for it, or if he thought her foolish as well. She twisted the locks in her hands, spread them and let them fall down her back.

Victoria stared into the mirror again. If she took too much time with her clothes, he would know that she dawdled. She took a deep breath and undid her petticoats, letting them drop to the floor, stepping free of them and taking the time to brush away the wrinkles before hanging them beside her gown. She had not bothered with stays. They hardly seemed necessary, considering what she was likely to do tonight. Now, she wondered if they should have been present as part of the ceremony of undressing, or if he preferred the glimpses of her body through the thin shift she wore. The knowledge of an anonymous watcher and his opinion of her was like a bit of ice drawn slowly over her heated skin, bringing sensitivity wherever it touched.

She sat down upon the bed, ignoring the way the shift's hem rode high to reveal her legs. She removed her slippers, dropping them on the floor. And then she undid her garters and rolled her stockings down, pointing her toe and flexing her bare legs. She shifted on the mattress until her back was against the wall at the head of the bed and felt the hem creep almost to her waist as she did so. And for the first time that evening, real fear took hold of her. She felt exposed, vulnerable.

Then she banished the feeling with a false smile. She knew what she might have to do, when her quarry entered the room. In comparison, the task of the moment could hardly be considered frightening. She was still alone.

It was not as if, even when alone, she had allowed herself to behave with abandon. It was not proper. But she was in the last place in the world where she would have to concern herself with propriety.

She reached up, tentatively at first, and touched her own breasts through the lawn shift that covered them, shocked at how sensitive they felt. Her nipples tightened in response to the pleasure and the coldness of the room.

She closed her eyes to hide herself from her circumstances and cupped her hands under them, pushing them tight to her body so that they almost spilled from the neckline of the shift, enjoying the weight of them.

She let her hands drift lower, to catch the hem of the shift and draw it completely out of the way. She bit her lip as though in desire, and blocked the last of her fear in her mind. Then she let her legs fall open, exposing herself to anyone who might be watching from the hall.

From some hidden place, there was a sharp intake of breath, and the slow hiss as it was released again.

The sound sent a tremor of awareness through her. Was the man on the other side of the curtain the man she sought? Perhaps it was some other stranger. Whoever her audience might be, they were expecting her to continue.

And suddenly, her body trembled again, and she wished it as well. She spread herself with her fingers, and began to play.

Tom Godfrey looked at the woman sitting on the bed and tried to disguise his shock into something within the realm of expectation or eagerness.

The abbess touched his arm, to silently ask if this was the sort of woman he had been looking for.

He placed a hand over hers and nodded. Not only was the chestnut hair just as he had wished, and the eyes bright green, but the shape of the face was the same as well. There was the short nose, the gently rounded cheeks and the small dimple in the chin.

He had not seen her body in the little miniature his

captain had carried. But he had imagined it: the pale skin dusted with gold from the sun of Portugal, with long legs, high breasts and a trim waist flaring into soft round hips. His imagination did not do this woman justice.

The madam smiled and nodded, gesturing to the door at her right and pressing a key into his hand. He pressed a coin into hers in return. Then, she retreated.

He stood there for a while, staring into the little window, enjoying the clandestine view it provided. The woman was very like the one he longed for. And with his desire came the faint feeling of guilt.

Though why he should feel guilty about thoughts not expressed, he did not know. It was not as if he had ever bothered Victoria Paget with his opinions of her. He had never even met her. He had not even sent the briefest of condolences, along with her husband's personal effects, fearing that some stray comment in it would lead her guess to the truth. He had done nothing to be ashamed of.

But while his actions had been blameless, he regretted his uncontrollable thoughts. Captain Paget's descriptions of his wife's spirit, and her unfailing loyalty and courage had moved him to envy. The devotion of his own fiancée waiting in London for him had seemed ambivalent in comparison. And then, Paget had shared a glimpse of the little portrait that he had so often admired himself.

Tom had felt the first stirrings of jealousy. Perhaps it was because he doubted that Paget deserved such a wife as the one he'd described. At times, he had spoken of her as he might of a particularly good soldier, and not a woman who was worthy of respect and tenderness. And though the captain had claimed to have a great fondness for her, when the war parted them he had shown no particular desire to be faithful to her in the way he swore she was to him.

Perhaps it was merely covetousness on Tom's part. He had seen the peace it brought Paget to look on the picture before a battle. And he had wanted some bit of that peace for himself. He had longed for reassurance that someone waited for him and cared for his survival. The few pitiful letters he'd received from his supposed love filled him with doubts about their future. And his fears had been proven true soon after his return to England.

But worst of all, there was lust. He had seen the picture, and wanted the woman in it. When the captain had died, Tom had searched his pockets for it, out of a sudden shameful desire to keep it for his own. That he could have it to gaze on each night, before he slept. And to imagine…

It had repelled him that he could have such thoughts about the widow, with the husband barely cool on the ground before him. So he had bundled the miniature up with the captain's few personal effects, tucked the lot into his haversack to keep it safe from the soldiers who were looting the battlefield, and sent it back to camp with the next courier.

When he had arrived there on a stretcher almost a month later after another skirmish had shattered his leg and his career, he had wanted to meet with her and to explain the circumstances of her husband's death. But she was already gone back to London. Disappointment and relief had mingled with the pain of his wound.

Grief was an indulgence not always followed by the women in the camps. Although it was rare in officer's wives, there were some women who put greater store in being married then they did in the identity of their husband. An unfortunate death in battle meant that there would be a drumhead wedding to someone when the company returned.

If the opportunity presented itself, how would he have been able to resist an inquiry? He was not even free to make the offer. And worse yet, suppose she'd married someone else?

But, no. She would be brokenhearted, he was sure. She would have thought him coarse beyond words to suggest that she wed again so quickly. Now that he was free, perhaps he would seek her out, after a respectable period of time.

In the waiting for the opportunity, the desire for her had only grown in him. He had come to a brothel for relief. And now, he found himself peering into the boudoir of a woman who could easily be the double of the girl in the portrait.

But not in nature. Even in his wildest imaginings he had not dreamed of seeing her like this. She was touching herself. She cupped her breasts, and then sat back upon the bed and spread herself wide before him, letting her fingers sink into the curls of hair between her legs before settling into a rhythm against her own body.

Tom swallowed and tried to still his breathing. She must know that he watched. There was a sly smile upon her lips as though she could imagine the effect that her play was having upon him. And then it was forgotten in a gasp as she shuddered and made a faint noise of pleasure released.

The effect was exquisite. He was hard for her, almost to the point of pain. He fingered the key in his hands for a moment, watching as she arched her neck and gave another shudder of satisfaction from her own touch.

Then he went to the door, opening it hurriedly, entering and locking it behind him again.

CHAPTER TWO

VICTORIA SMILED IN triumph as a man limped into the room, for it was obvious that she had been right. He had watched. She could see it in his eyes. And it was plain that she had aroused him with her behavior.

His cheeks were flushed as though from too much wine. But it was not drunkenness. Desire, of course. She had expected that. But embarrassment? Watching and knowing that she knew. She had been told he was no stranger to houses of ill fame. But perhaps he was not usually a voyeur. He was younger than she had expected, little older than herself, but ten years younger than Charles. And though the sight of him locking the door should have scared her, his appearance did not match the dark villain she had expected. Tom Godfrey's hair was brown, touched with gold from too much sun, and it fell in his eyes as he looked at her. He reached up and brushed it away.

"Do you fear interruption?" she asked, glancing at the locked door.

He dropped the key into his pocket. "I certainly do not wish it." His voice was pleasant, almost defying her to enjoy the sound of it. He approached the bed, and she resisted the urge to close her legs. Instead, she leaned back against the pillows, stretching her arms over her head and clasping her hands together. She could feel her breasts draw tight, straining against the chemise as she moved.

He shed his clothing quickly, as though there were little time to waste. And judging by the state of him, perhaps there was not. She felt an inappropriate frission of desire at the sight of him. He was a soldier, body hardened and marked by battle. There was an angry red scar high on one leg, which explained the hitch in his gait as he walked.

But he seemed healthy enough. And aroused he was almost frighteningly large.

It had been a long time since she had been with a man, she reminded herself, trying not to stare. And while she had no reason to want this particular man, her body's reaction to his was normal, and not the least bit traitorous to her husband's memory. As long as she did not dwell on it.

He smiled at her, and climbed on to the bed, reaching for her. As he took her into his arms, she felt the tingling friction of his bare skin against hers, and dropped her arms to circle his neck. Heat rose in her at the contact, and she fought down her guilt. What was about to happen meant nothing. She must separate physical response from more tender emotions. She would lie back and close her eyes and it would be over in no time.

And then, his lips touched hers.

She shied away from his kiss, turning her head. The man might expect no more than a lack of struggle in the actual act, but there would be no way to hide what she felt for him if they kissed.

He pulled away as well. "I'm sorry." He glanced around the room. "Have I misunderstood? Because if you are unwilling…" He was hard against her leg, but very still, as though he awaited her permission to proceed.

The reaction surprised her. He was strong, and she'd been afraid he would force her cooperation if she did not give it. "I am willing," she said softly. "But not to kiss. Not upon the lips, at least."

He smiled. "Why ever not?"

Why indeed? "There are some things best shared between true lovers. And I wish to save some small part of me, for that."

He seemed puzzled. And she wondered, did he need to fool himself that an encounter in such a place meant something more than it actually did? It was a sign of a romantic nature, a weakness that she had put long behind her after the hardships of even the happiest moments of the last few years. To reassure him, she said, "There are other things, very pleasant, I assure you, that I am quite willing to do." She ran a hand down his body, slowly over the chest, and followed the trail of hair on his belly lower, until she could take him in her hand.

The act was all it took to render him incapable of further questions. The confusion on his face was replaced with a dazed smile and he closed his eyes and sighed. She had imagined a coupling almost brutal in its suddenness. But it appeared that he was content to let her be the aggressor.

It was strange and exciting to have such power. She could set the pace, and the action, and perhaps she could avoid joining with him at all.

Victoria pushed lightly upon his shoulder, rolling him onto his back. Then she knelt between his legs and slowly massaged his member, from shaft to tip and back, spreading his own moisture upon him, feeling him pulse beneath her hand, and an answering pulse in her own body.

He groaned, and covered her hand with his own. "Darling, your touch is heaven."

A wicked thought occurred to her. And as she stroked him, her curiosity grew to insatiability. What better place to give over to such a whim then here? She bent over him. "Then what shall you think of this?" And she gave him the kiss that no man could resist, taking him gently into her mouth, surrounding him with her lips and running her tongue along the tip of him, feeling smoothness, tasting salt.

His hands clutched the sheets on either side of her head, as though he were afraid to reach for her, lest she stop. She moved her mouth over him, taking him deeper, and his back arched as muscles tightened in growing excitement. His moan stopped suddenly, his teeth closing with a snap. "Please." The word was shaky, little more than a gasp. "Oh, yes." He trembled. She could feel his control slipping, and it caused an answering tremor in her own body, before she reminded herself that what was happening between them had no meaning.

"We have not been introduced," he ground out, with a desperate laugh. "My name is Tom Godfrey."

She withdrew slightly, and purred against his skin. "Thomas."

He groaned as though the sound of his own name was as exciting as her kiss. Then, he reached out a hand and stroked her hair. The gesture was strangely tender. "Your name. Please. I must know…"

She gave one last whirl of her tongue against him, and said, "Victoria."

He gave an almost convulsive shudder and rolled away from her, spilling his seed into the sheet beside them.

For a moment, she felt strangely bereft. She missed the feel of him against her cheek and in her mouth, and the warmth of his body close to his. Had she really been alone so long that even the touch of an enemy was welcome?

He was curled over with his back to her. And his shoulders were shaking with what looked to be silent laughter.

It angered her to think that he found her performance so amusing. Was she really so unskilled that her actions were laughable? She buried the feeling, and reached out a hesitant hand to his shoulder, as though from concern. "Is something the matter?"

He was definitely laughing, for his words escaped after a chuckle. "An old gun does not usually have a hair trigger."

"Old?" At first it made no sense. Then, she realized he spoke of himself. "You are hardly thirty."

He rolled back to her, still smiling, and touched her cheek. "That is old enough to have learned control. But you quite overcame me. I embarrassed myself like a greenling on his first trip to a brothel. Unlike some, you are too kind to comment upon it."

Perhaps, if she had truly been a whore, she would have known the correct response to what had just happened. Should she have laughed at his joke, to put him at ease? She must do something quickly. If she wished information, she could not have him pulling on his boots and leaving her. "We could try again."

"My thoughts exactly." He leaned forward to kiss her.

Without thinking, she turned her head from him again, causing him to draw back.

"You are a most curious woman, Victoria." He was staring at her as though he was the one who had come to search for truths. "I cannot decide what arouses me more, what you will do, or what you won't."

"That was not my intent."

He ran a thumb from her cheek to touch her lower lip, and then drew it slowly down to stroke her throat. "Liar. I think it is in your nature to drive men mad." He leaned forward to kiss her throat at the spot where his thumb rested, and she felt a jolt of excitement.

"Please, do not."

"You do not like it?"

It would do no good to lie. "Of course. But…"

He kissed her again. "It will be some few moments before I am ready again. If you will not spend it in kissing, then I must find another way to pass the time."

Now he was ringing her throat with love bites, as though tracing the path of a necklace as his hands roamed over her breasts. His touch was hard, possessive, just as his kisses were. And it was not the only thing hardened, for she could feel his body growing eager to join with hers. She gave a weak laugh. "Dear sir, I think you are quite ready enough, now."

"Do you?" He dipped his head to take the tip of her breast in his mouth through the cotton shift. "But I wish for you to be ready as well."

"I do not require satisfaction." She gasped, for his hands were between her legs, tugging at the curls there. "At least, not in that way."

"You hurt me, darling, to make me think that it is my money that matters to you. You might not require this. But you certainly deserve it, after what you just did to me." As his mouth slid down her body she had a fleeting fear that his actions were as much about control as hers had been.

And she could feel it slipping away as he moved closer and closer to where her body wanted him. She tried to pull away, but he wrapped his arms around her waist, holding her fast. "Please sir, no."

"You will not let me kiss you on the lips." He sighed, but did not release her. "So you must allow me to imagine what it might be like." He dipped his tongue into her navel. "To whisper into your ear and touch it like so. To kiss my way along your cheek." He trailed the kisses along her belly. "Until my lips find yours." He settled himself carefully between her legs and barely touched her with his mouth. "Gently at first. Ever so gently. Just a touch."

The shock of it was too much, and she gave another

shudder. What had the abbess said, about the jealousy of others working here? If this was how he was in the habit of treating them, then she understood. His kiss was rougher now. And as he thrust his tongue into her, his fingers crept up to stroke.

Victoria put her own fingers into her mouth and bit down, trying to stop the scream of pleasure that she knew was coming. But the feel of them, the intrusion and the sharp pain of her bite along with his repeated invasion of her body tipped her over the edge into another cascade of pleasure.

Yet, his kiss did not cease. She struggled against it for a moment. But it was all too much, too good, and she was unable to think for wanting more.

Only when she was sure that she must be spent did he obey and release her, to slide his body up hers. "And now, I think you are ready, are you not?" He hovered for a moment at the entrance to her body, before beginning a slow thrust into her. He stopped. "Unless you do not wish it."

His hesitation was almost painful, for she longed to be filled. "Please." Later, she could regret asking him. But now she was so close to coming again that it was impossible to do other than beg for more. "Please. Oh yes. Please."

He pushed into her with a sudden, hard thrust and she gasped. She had not expected it to be so...

He withdrew and thrust again.

...different. The act was familiar and yet new, because her lover was different. The intense pleasure she felt was from the novelty, nothing more. Or so she told herself, as she dug her fingers into the muscles of his shoulders and moved her hips to match the strength of his thrusts, eager to feel him deep inside.

Sensing her need, he was not gentle. He raked his fingers down her back to clutch her bottom and pounded into her with a strength that demanded nothing less than her total surrender. Then he buried his face into the side of her neck, his teeth grazing her skin, and he licked hard at the muscle on her shoulder until she moaned in response.

At the sound, he rolled so that she could be on top of him and squeezed her hips to urge her on.

And she rode him, squeezing her legs together around him, tightening her muscles about him to feel how impossibly hard he was until she heard his answering groan and his body began to arch. As he lost control, he reached to the front of her, rubbing her with his thumb to bring her over the edge with him, shattering.

She collapsed on top of him, sprawling across his body, her cheek against his chest. It made her feel alive again to lie still for a moment, as passion receded and sense returned. He was taller than she had expected. His body big and solid under her, and still inside of her, undeniably male.

It felt good to be wanted. To be desired. And not to be alone.

He wrapped a hand around her waist. His grip was weak at first, little more than the weight of his own arm, as though exhausted by his own climax. Then slowly, he curled it possessively around her, the hand angling up toward her shoulders in a caress.

She could not see his face, but could tell his smile was gone by the tone of his voice. "I know who you are," he said.

CHAPTER THREE

VICTORIA PAGET WAS lying in his arms, spent from love-making, just as he had always imagined her. It should be a dream, but now that the act was done, it was set to turn to nightmare.

Why had he asked her name? The question tortured him. He should have remained in ignorance, convinced that he was with some nameless bit of muslin. Or perhaps he should have left at the first moment of suspicion, when he'd stood outside the room.

Of course, that would have left her at the mercy of the next man to come along, and the thought of that haunted him even more. She was the object of his desire. A desire that had bordered almost on obsession in the months he had spent recuperating from his injury. He had hoped to exorcise the demon of her memory in a harmless game of pretend. A woman of experience would have him without complaint, scars and all. And the madam had assured him that in dim light, the girl she'd found would pass for the one he dreamed of.

She lay still against him, as though waiting for him to speak. "I know who you are." There. It was out and said.

"Wh-what do you mean?" There was the barest hesitation in her words, before her face returned to tranquility. He had startled her, but she was pretending ignorance.

It angered him that she thought she could still fool him with lies. "You are the widow of Captain Charles Paget, are you not?"

She said nothing, but glanced quickly toward the door and back. Did she fear him enough to run?

"I recognized your name," he said, not caring about her fears. He tightened his hand on her back, still gentle, but enough to forestall an escape.

"It is a common name," she argued, making no move to leave. "And I gave you no surname."

"Perhaps. But it does not signify. You are Victoria Paget."

"I did not think that you...that anyone would realize." He could feel her budding resistance fade. Her eyes dropped, probably in shame of what she had become.

"I served under him. He spoke of you often, with much pride and affection." And yet, she had come to this. He made no attempt to hide his disappointment. "He showed me the miniature he kept with him. I was there on the road with him, when he died. It was I who gathered his effects and returned them to you."

"Why did you bother?" There was bitterness in her tone as well, to answer his.

"It was the least I could do. Not enough, I know. I could not save him. Nor could I help the others." And now, he was the one who felt shame. What sort of monster was he, to offer words of condolence on a brothel bed? He rolled to the side, so their bodies could part from each other. "If it gives you comfort to know it, his death was sudden. The pain was brief. If he had time for a final thought, it was of you. But I did not want to see his possessions taken by looters. They were rightfully yours."

"And much good they did me." She drew even farther from him, fumbling for the sheet as though it would be possible to hide from him, after what they had done.

"What brings you here?" Had Paget left her nothing but that damned picture, that she had been driven to this on her return to London? "The abbess said you were new to this place. But that is a common lie."

"In this case, it is true. Just this night. For money," she said simply, as though it explained all. And it did. After all his fine talk of his stalwart wife, he'd thought the captain would know enough to set a portion aside for his widow. But some men expected to live forever and sort out the finances after the war.

He reached out and clasped her hand. "I could not save Charles. But I will save you from this, if you let me."

"How would you do that?" She looked at him with a slanted cat's gaze, as though weighing his intentions.

"Come away with me. Now. Tonight. You need have

no fear of the mistress of this house. She will not dare to cross me. Once you are settled in my rooms, you can send for anything you wish. Or I will purchase what you need."

God knew how. He could little afford a ladybird, should her tastes prove extravagant.

She thought for a moment, and then nodded. "I have nothing but the clothes I came with. I will dress, and then we may go." Her lack of expression surprised him. He had expected some display of emotion, either enthusiasm or argument, or perhaps an embarrassed speech about how this was not normally her way. But she did not seem overly bothered by what had happened between them. Nor was she relieved or upset by his offer, just as she'd not been bothered by the knowledge that a stranger had watched as she'd touched herself. Perhaps she had been seeking a protector, all along.

Fool that he was, he had imagined the captain's widow wrapping herself in grief and propriety. But the true Victoria Paget was mercenary, to an almost military degree. Her cold blood was almost as disturbing as the truth of her identity had been.

She was dressing as he waited. Strangely, the sight of her becoming clothed was more arousing than the sight of her naked had been. He wanted to peel the clothes away again, and touch her skin to assure himself that the event of the evening had truly happened. He turned his head, trying not to look at her. "You are sure you have no possessions?"

"There is nothing for me here." Her cloak hung on a peg in the corner of the room, and he reached out for it, dropping it over her shoulders, then he escorted her from the room. As they left, she did not look back.

They rode in silence toward his flat, and he wondered if her feelings toward him would warm, given time. Would her opinion change in regard to kissing him? It did not seem so. When the carriage door was closed he had touched her chin as a prelude to turning her mouth to his. And she had looked away again.

What did it matter that she felt no tenderness for him? She had agreed to come with him, knowing what it would mean. He could have her again, soon. Tonight perhaps. And as often as he liked hereafter.

Bought and paid for.

The words echoed in Tom's mind as the carriage stopped and he helped her from it and up the few steps to his apartment. His manservant looked up as he entered, with some small surprise that he was not alone. Tom gave the smallest shake of his head to indicate that he would explain in time, and the man went about his business as though there was nothing strange.

Then he said with some embarrassment, "I am sorry that my quarters are so small. Just the sitting room and the bedroom. My servant, Toby, sleeps by the kitchen fire. I do not have even a cot to offer you. In time, you shall have your own room. Or an apartment, if you wish it."

How silly. Of course she would wish. What sort of idiot

offered a carte blanche to a woman he could not afford to keep?

"You shall have a maid. Dresses. Anything you wish. But it is rather late. In the morning…" They were rash promises, and he had no idea how he would manage, but he would give her anything she desired, if it meant he could touch her again.

"Of course," she said. "I understand." And then she fell silent.

It worried him that he did not know what to say next, other than to repeat the pathetic offers he had just made. There was so much more to be said, so much that he wanted her to understand. And in turn, there was much he wanted her to answer for. But he doubted that either of them wanted to hear the truth. For now, he would let his body speak for him. He stepped forward and reached for her.

She took the slightest move away, as though his touch was unwelcome, now that she had what she wanted. And then she said, "When did you recognize me?"

The suddenness of it stunned him. Perhaps she wished to defend what was left of her honor, now that she had seen the humbleness of his quarters. It was a harsh thought, and he did not wish to believe it of her. But better not to act like a besotted fool, lest she announce that she had no wish to lie with a cripple if they would be forced to share the bed after.

He retreated to neutral hospitality, taking her cloak and leading her to a chair by the fire, then signaling his man to bring them a brandy. Once the servant had retired to the kitchen he said, "I did not know you at first. Not until you said your name. If I had known, I would not have allowed you to do what you did."

Liar. He'd known in his heart exactly who she was from the moment he had laid eyes on her. But he had not been able to resist having her.

"Once I realized the truth, I could not stand by and leave you in that place, to God knows what fate. I owe it to a brother officer, to see to it that his family does not suffer. And that is why I brought you here."

"After the fact," she said, bluntly. And for a moment, there was a light in her eye that made him wonder if she sensed the truth of what had happened the day her husband died, and had come to him to exact punishment for it.

Or she might simply be expressing the obvious. His own guilt pricked sharp, like needles inside him. It had been so much easier to be angry and to blame her loose morals for what had happened tonight. But he had wanted her long before he had any right to, and he had taken her the first chance he'd got. Then he'd convinced himself that her desperation was a sign of unworthiness, and that his lust was somehow her fault. No wonder she was cold to him. He sighed. "What I did was unconscionable. But once things were begun, I did not know how to stop them, or how to explain myself." He bit his tongue, and began again. "That is not true. Once we had begun, I did not wish to stop. I was selfish, and thoughtless of all but my own needs. Because of my injury, pleasure has been infrequent, and to find myself in the company of such a beautiful woman?"

He shrugged as though it were possible to minimize his attraction to her. "But that is no excuse. Although it is too late to take back what I have done, I will not trouble you further with my attentions. I only wish to know that you are safe, and that you are not forced to debase yourself further because of misfortune."

"Oh." There was a crease in her forehead, as though she were puzzled. Or perhaps she was disappointed, although that hardly seemed likely. "Thank you for your kindness." She sipped from the drink she had been offered.

He thought for a moment that she meant to explain how she had come to the state she was in. But she said nothing and he had no right to inquire. Perhaps there was something even more horrible than what she currently experienced.

Then she looked up at him from over the rim of her glass. "But I cannot accept the terms you offer. If you wish to give me your protection, then I must give you something in return. It makes no sense to pretend modesty, and refuse you companionship." She touched the neckline of her gown.

He was mesmerized by her hands. How graceful they were. Long fingered. Supple. His body remembered how it had felt to be touched by them, and grew hard in response. And he knew that his attempt at nobility was for naught. She had offered. And he would take from her again.

It hurt him to know that what was about to happen would

mean nothing to her, other than a bartering of services. She was not the woman he imagined her to be, and her husband's shining description was little more than the fondness of long association.

He set his drink aside and reached out to take her by the wrist, drawing her to her feet and toward the door to the bedroom. And as he did so, the glass shook in her hand, and spilled a few drops of brandy onto the silken flesh above her breasts. He took the glass from her and threw it onto the hearth, listening to the crystal shatter as he pulled her into his arms, burying his face against her throat, chasing the drop of liquor down to catch it on his tongue. When the bodice of her dress blocked him, he reached behind her and undid the fastenings, pushing it and her chemise out of the way until he could reach her breasts, taking the nipples by turn into his mouth to suckle them until the skin puckered and the tips grew hard.

He felt her fingers in his hair, a gentle, almost fearful touch holding his mouth against her body. And then she pulled her hands away, and he could feel her arms go rigid at her sides.

He lifted his head and put his arms on her shoulders, pushing gently until her back was to the wall. Then he dropped his hands to cover her, rubbing his thumbs against the sensitive tips and watching her eyes widen in response. Perhaps she was not such a dispassionate schemer after all. Was it fear he saw on her face? Or could it be desire? He gave the flesh beneath his fingers a gentle pinch, and she gasped and bit her lower lip as though she could bite back the response.

He smiled and stared at her mouth. "If you truly do not wish me to kiss you, you must stop that immediately. You are tempting me beyond endurance."

"I did not mean to," she whispered.

He laughed and leaned forward to catch the lobe of her ear between his teeth, nipping it as she had her own lip. "Of course you did. From the first moment. Lying on that bed, offering yourself to me. You are temptation itself."

"No. Not that. I did not…" She gasped again as he bit harder, and wrenched the truth from her. "I did not mean to enjoy this."

He could feel his body straining to pleasure her, just as hers strained to resist him. "Is that so?" He released her breasts and fumbled with the buttons on his trousers.

She glanced down, and then over her shoulder at the door behind them. Her mouth was a perfect O of shock. "The bedroom?"

He shook his head. "Here. Now. You do not wish to enjoy this. And I do not wish to wait." He could see by the eager way that she lifted her skirt that his pretense at brutish behavior was as exciting to her as anything else they had tried. He touched her between her legs, spreading her with his fingers, stroking for a moment before pushing one inside of her. She was wet and ready, bracing her back against the wall, bearing down on his hand and shuddering with delight. He pulled his hand away and fitted his body to hers, pausing for just a moment before pushing slowly into that wonderful tightness.

The fear disappeared from her face. Now it shone with the light of pure bliss. And then she shut her eyes, as though she thought she could hide it from him.

He withdrew and thrust again, even slower than before, trying to ignore the dizzying rightness of being inside her. He pressed his body tight to hers, one of his hands trapped between them so that he could clutch her breast. With the other hand, he touched her face, running a thumb along her jawline to tip her face toward his. "Open your eyes."

She blinked up at him, looking as dazed by what was happening as he felt. Her lips were parted, swollen and red, and he longed to kiss them as he thrust again. "Tell me what you are feeling," he said, and rubbed his knuckles against them.

She touched his hand with her tongue, and he sucked in a breath, not wanting to lose control too quickly. She hesitated, and he thrust again.

She let out a little squeak of surprise that made him smile.So he kissed her cheek, tantalizingly close to those lovely lips, and said again, "Tell me."

At last, she murmured, "It has never been like this." And as he moved in her, her breathing became irregular, muddling her words. "I have never...more than once... and the way you look at me...and your body...it makes me...every time."

He could feel her losing control again, her body tightening on his. He squeezed her breast and felt her back arch, her hips rock forward into his, her arms wrap around to hold him as she began to tremble. So he enjoyed her perfect body and imagined her perfect lips, and spent himself in her again.

How many times had that been tonight? He smiled to himself, hugging her to him, trying not to lean too obviously upon her. Damn, but he was weak as a kitten. Standing had been a mistake. His leg was aching, and he must get the weight off it, or he would be too stiff to rise in the morning.

From his shoulder came a soft sob.

He lifted his head to find her face wet with tears. He reached to stroke her hair, wondering how he had ever thought her cold. "What is it, love? Tell me."

"I am a terrible wife," she whispered back.

He almost laughed. "Right now, you are no wife at all." Although perhaps she ought to be. At the rate they were going, there would be a babe soon. Surely a wife was easier to keep than a mistress.

And then the weight of her words hit him, and with it, the old guilt. He held her close, not wanting to let a ghost come between them. "He is gone. You are free."

"But I should not behave in this way. And with a man I barely know. With you, of all people."

So that was it. She'd given herself to a lesser man. He focused on the ache in his leg, for it was easier to deal with the physical hurt than the pain her words had caused. He straightened, taking back his own weight, pulling her gown up to shield her body, and offering her his arm.

"How you behaved this evening was little fault of your own. It is I who should be ashamed. I owe you reparation for my base behavior. You honor me by accepting my protection." He swallowed his nerves, for he knew what he truly owed to a lady, even if his words were met with scorn. "And you would honor me still further, if you would agree to wed me."

CHAPTER FOUR

VICTORIA GAVE A SMALL, surprised laugh to cover her confusion, putting a hand to her throat to keep her gown from slipping again. "Marriage?"

"I dishonored you by my actions. As a gentleman, I wish to make it right again," he said, as though it were the most reasonable thing in the world to marry a woman that he had met in a brothel.

"But between us?" She had convinced herself that she should come home with him to gain time to search his possessions and question his servants. But he had so little. Suppose there was nothing to find?

What if Tom Godfrey was innocent? A part of her dearly wanted that to be true. If he was not, how was she to reconcile her feelings when he touched her with the suspicions she had held for so long? She stalled. "How shall I explain the suddenness of it to my friends?" And how would she explain to Lord Stanton? He thought her mad already. What would he think of this turn of events?

Tom smiled. "It will hardly be seen as a nine day's wonder if you marry a soldier. I am a cripple and of inferior rank to your late husband. But we share a common past, we have mutual friends, and I am sympathetic to your plight. Tell anyone who cares that we met in London. Our previous acquaintance led me to offer for you out of concern for your safety and a desire to know that you are well provided for."

"But marriage?" It did make sense, as he described it. But suppose she had been right, and her second husband was hanged the murder of her first?

"For my part, my friends will congratulate me on my extreme good fortune in catching you. You are a very attractive woman, Victoria. And…" He seemed about to say something, and then muttered, "We do share a certain physical compatibility."

He grinned at her. And the grin widened as he saw her blush. Then he grew serious, again. "I understand that you do not love me, and that what I suggest will seem as sudden to some as it does to you. But I would do everything in my power to bring you pleasure by night, and to make you happy by day. Please allow me to help you."

Her intended victim was all but begging that she come close enough to betray him. But if she had been wrong, how could she ever explain to him? Or was there some way that she could avoid the truth? At last she said, "It is all too much for my poor mind to grasp. May I decide tomorrow? I am quite tired." Perhaps in the morning, she could come up with an answer. She let her voice trail off

as if to confirm her words, and glanced toward the bedroom door.

"Of course. It is late. Until then, will you accept my
hospitality?"

She gave a slight nod, and he led her into the other room.
He turned back the covers on his bed, offering his place
to her. Then he went to sit on a small couch in the corner
of the room. "Until you decide, I think it best that I sleep
here." He smiled and added, "To avoid temptation." He
took off his coat and boots, lay down and rolled his face
to the wall.

As she prepared for bed, she stared across the room at
him. Despite her doubts, she could feel her body longing
for his. She could not fool herself into thinking that her
enthusiastic response to him had been caused by loneliness, or because she had forgotten how wonderful it felt
to be with a man.

It had not been like this with Charles. Not ever. Her
father had assured her that it was a good match, and that
she had nothing to complain about. And he had been right.
Charles Paget had been a good husband to her. And she
had loved and respected him, and wished always to make
him happy.

But he had never looked at her with the hungry intensity
that Tom Godfrey did. She had certainly never been loved
to completion multiple times in a night. And Charles,
God rest his soul, would have told her to leave off with
her nonsense and obey him immediately, had she ever
dared to refuse him a kiss. From the moment she had said
her vows, she had known that while it was important to

love one's husband, to honor him was more so. And total obedience trumped them both.

But Tom had taken her refusal to kiss as a challenge. Her body burned hot at the memory of it. He had been a generous lover, more concerned with her pleasure than his own.

She could not remember the last time that her pleasure, her wants or her desires had been important to anyone. Not even herself. She had learned to ignore them, to postpone them or to do without. Perhaps that explained her sudden and extreme attraction to Tom Godfrey.

And with that, she felt an unexpected pang of guilt. She had insinuated herself into his life to spy upon him. Perhaps she was in the right, for she had done it for England and her husband's memory, instead of for French gold.

But if she had accused an innocent man?

And there was the rub. His behavior toward her was— she struggled to find a word. It was gallant. She felt safe in his company, from the way he wished to rescue her from the brothel, to the foolish gesture of sleeping on a bench, when his own bed was just across the room. Would it not pain the wound in his leg and side to sleep in such a cramped way?

The Tom Godfrey she had imagined was a coward who had sacrificed all around him for personal gain. But from the first moment this stranger had touched her, she'd trusted him. She had given of herself and in ways that were new to her, sure that no matter what they tried, he would not hurt her. That trust had been at the heart of their lovemaking, and her response to it.

On the other side of the room, Tom let out a sigh, and rolled again, to face her. And in the barest whisper he said, "You are awake, aren't you?"

"Yes." She sat up in bed and stared across the room.

He sat up as well. "It is quite hopeless. I meant to bring you here, and to care for you, hoping that I could avoid what I must say. But I will not get a moment's sleep if I do not just admit the truth."

She bit her lip and gave a little nod, suddenly afraid that she might hear the very thing she had expected.

He took a deep breath. "The day Captain Paget died my horse was losing a shoe. He favored a leg, and I was lagging behind, trying to nurse him along. If I had been ahead on the road, as I should have been, they would have had warning. It would have been I and not he." His eyes grew vacant for a moment as he remembered it.

There had been no mention of this in any of the accounts she had heard. But it explained how he had come to retreat, as the rest advanced to their doom. "What became of the horse?"

He looked at her as though it were the maddest question in the world. "Shot in the battle. Poor dumb beast. It was all for naught. In the end, I spared him nothing. I should have ridden forward with the rest and died."

He touched his wounded leg. "Until I met you, this wound seemed a sufficient punishment for any wrong I committed. But now?" He shook his head. "That day, I took your husband from you with my carelessness. And I took your honor tonight. If you will have me, I will do everything in my power to make this right."

Something inside her eased, as though a weight had been lifted from her shoulders. And without thinking of what had brought her to this place and this moment, she let out a sigh of relief. Then she patted the mattress beside her. "I do not think I need 'til dawn to make a decision, after all. Come to bed, Thomas."

CHAPTER FIVE

HE REACHED FOR HER again in the night, touching her skin and smiling in wonder as though her presence beside him was miraculous. She touched him in return, laying her hand against his cheek, tracing the planes of his shoulders and back, learning him in a way that was quite innocent, compared to their earlier coupling.

He paid attention to the details of her body, kissing the hollow of her shoulder, the crease of her elbow, her finger tips, and running his thumb along her spine to find a place on her back that was surprisingly sensitive. It made her gasp, and he smiled, continuing to stroke the spot as he bent his head forward to nip her throat and her breasts. Tom was setting a leisurely pace, as though they had all night to pleasure each other. He gave another flick of his finger, which he combined with a slow pull on her nipple that made her arch against him, clutching his hair to hold him tight to her, clawing with her other hand, down his side to search for him, stroke him and spread her legs for him. Her need grew more urgent the slower he moved. She could feel him laughing in triumph as she shuddered against him, so she pushed him onto his back and straddled him, impaling herself upon him, pressing his hand against her most sensitive place, forcing him to give her more pleasure as she bucked against him, her body clenching and releasing him, as she squeezed his hips between her thighs. She heard the moment when his laughter stopped and he relinquished control to her. His breathing quickened, his body thrusting in response, until he whispered her name and lost control inside her again. The sensation was rare, and she closed her eyes as she savored it. The risk of children born while on campaign had been too great to allow such completion. Now, she might have it whenever she liked, and the children as well.

But when she looked into her lover's eyes, she saw pain as well as pleasure. "Your leg?" She pulled away so that he could withdraw.

He nodded, but laid a steadying hand on her arm. "It is all right." His eyes seemed to glaze for a moment, and then he smiled, and said through clenched teeth, "No. It was marvelous. Well worth a twinge or two."

But all the same, she disentangled herself carefully to lie beside him, careful not to stress the wound.

He put his arm around her shoulders, and kissed the top of her head. "That you would be willing to lie with me at all is pleasure enough. But that you have accepted my offer is quite amazing as well. There have been others who were not so generous."

She frowned. "How strange."

He laughed at her confusion. "My dear, I am not whole. It is quite obvious to you."

"But for the pain in your leg, you seem well enough." She had the temerity to blush, and he laughed again.

"In our case, perhaps it is better that you lie with me before you wed me. The woman I expected to take to wife on my return from the war was none too sure about me. Her father told her that the location of the wound might have rendered me unfit as a husband. And while his daughter had no qualms about my entering the military and was quite taken with the sight of the braid on my uniform, there was something less than heroic about my homecoming, when it could not be made on two good legs."

"But that is horrible. To have served your country is an honorable thing. And to have suffered as you did is a cause for increased respect and not rejection."

"I knew you would understand. You of all women..." He said it reverently, as though she were precious beyond words to him. Tom reached out and touched her lips with his fingers with such gentleness that it startled her. If her eyes hadn't been open, she'd have sworn that he'd kissed her.

And then, with a smile, he closed his eyes and fell asleep.

Victoria wrapped her arms around him and laid her head close against his side, wishing she could take the pain away. She had been so very wrong about Thomas Godfrey. He had suffered at the hands of the French and from the faithless woman who would not take him back.

And he had suffered from her actions as well. She had

defamed him to the Earl of Stanton, putting doubts in the man's head that had no place there. Tomorrow, she would write a letter to Stanton, explaining what she had found, and the strange turn of events that things had taken.

And she would never speak of it again. For much as Tom Godfrey seemed to think he owed her happiness, she owed him a similar debt. She would make up for her lack of faith by being the wife that he longed for her to be.

When she awoke the next morning, Tom was already out of bed, washed and preparing to go out. As though he sensed her return to consciousness, he turned to look at her with an encouraging smile. "Did you sleep well?"

"Yes." Surprisingly, she had. Her decision had given her an easy rest.

"I have no female servant to assist you. If you wish to wait, I can have my valet send for someone. Perhaps there is a girl in a neighboring flat. Or I..." He broke off shyly, holding his open hands in front of him, to show that he was at her service.

"That is all right. I have learned to manage." Her clothing was simple for just this reason. And compared to some of the places she'd stayed with Charles, this meager room was a luxury.

He nodded. "I must go out. And until more things are settled, it is hardly proper for us to be seen too much together. We will see if there is a way for your things to be sent for, discretely."

"No!" She had forgotten that there were details of her life that could not be filed away and forgotten. It would not do for him to see how she lived. At least not just yet. How could she explain her presence, apparently downcast in a house of ill fame, once he saw that she lived better than he, with more space, more comfort and more servants? "I will take care of sending for what I need. I need no help."

He looked surprised at her sudden denial. But then he shrugged as though he did not want to broach a topic that she might find embarrassing or painful. "Very well. I will trust to your own judgment in such matters. But be mindful of appearances, and take care not to be seen, should you leave."

"Why is that?"

He raised an eyebrow, and smiled. "I should think it would be obvious. Your reputation is as precious to me as it is to you. I should hate to have to challenge some young buck to a duel, should he see you creeping from my rooms with the dawn."

She colored. She had been so long married, and out of London society, that she had almost forgotten that anyone might care.

He grew serious again. "You do still wish to wed, do you not? For if you have had a change of heart?" He ran a hand through his tousled hair. "It quite changes my plans for the day. I had meant to procure a special license."

Again she felt the unfamiliar ripple of pleasure, to see him so eager to wed that he could not wait for the banns. "No, I have not changed my mind."

And now, he was smiling broadly at her, as though the reassurance had brought him immeasurable pleasure. He stepped forward, drew her up to sit, and kissed her on top of the head. "I am glad. And I will work to make you comfortable. And happy again, if you will let me."

Happy. What a curious idea. In her old life, she had been content, certainly. But had she been happy, traipsing about the Continent after Charles? Not really. She would have preferred her townhouse, the company of friends. A regular bed and regular meals. And perhaps a regular husband. "That would be nice. Thank you." She hoped he had not been expecting some declaration of love, for it seemed too soon to use that word. But to have a man to love, just an ordinary man, and not a soldier? And to have that man be as devoted to her as Tom Godfrey was? The possibility shimmered before her for a moment, like a beautiful dream.

"I had best get to it. If you are sure that you can manage?"

She gave him an encouraging smile in return. "I will be fine."

"Then I will go and make arrangements. And in no time at all, you will be Mrs. Godfrey."

CHAPTER SIX

TOM SMILED THROUGH clenched teeth as he climbed the steps to his final destination. The pain in his leg had not been so very bad as he had gone about the tortuous process of applying for the special license. But he did not wish to show weakness before the Earl of Stanton at the Home Office. He tried not to lean too heavily on his cane as he spoke to the clerk in the front room, and politely insisted that he had served under the earl when he had been simple Captain St John Radwell. Surely, a brief visit from an old comrade would not be unwelcome.

He heard a bark of affirmation from the door behind him, and words of welcome. But when he turned to face his old superior, the look in the man's eyes was wary. It seemed, after the disaster that had befallen his last captain, Tom would have to prove himself again to this one.

Stanton reached out and grasped his hand, pulling him into the office, but did not bother to shut the door behind him. "What brings you here, Tom? Are you doing well since your return? How is the leg, man?"

He shifted his weight to prove its strength. "As well as can be expected. It will never be right. But slowly, it improves. But other things?" He could not help the grin that spread on his face. "I suppose they are both very good, and most difficult."

"How so?"

"I have it in my mind to marry."

The earl looked startled quite beyond what he'd expected. "Marry? I had not heard…"

"That is because the decision is sudden. Fast as lightening, some might think."

"Do I…know the woman involved?"

The question stopped him. Perhaps Victoria's fears were justified. "I do not see why you should. She is the widow of a friend of mine. I hesitate to mention the name until the announcement is made. It is as sudden for her as it is for me. If she has people, they should hear of it before I go trumpeting my good fortune about the town, tempting though it may be to brag."

Stanton nodded, although there was strange hesitation in his reply. "That is probably wise. If there is a reason to cry off, it will save embarrassment."

And how little confidence in him did such a strange comment betray? "I am not worried on that account. We are in total agreement."

"But you spoke of a difficulty?"

"Simply that I had not thought to marry so soon. While I can manage to provide for her, it will not be as easy as

I might like. I seek employment. I wondered if perhaps there might be some use you could find for a man who has already proven his loyalty to the crown."

And just as he feared it might, a shadow flickered behind the other man's eyes. He must have heard the rumors. Tom had no wish to deny the charges before they were spoken. When half a company died around a man, there were bound to be those who thought him responsible, through negligence or connivance.

Stanton shook his head. "I am sorry, Tom. But I have nothing to offer you. I will keep you in mind, of course. And if the occasion arises, I will be in touch. Leave your direction with my man. But now, there is simply no need of another body."

Tom nodded, and tried to keep the bitterness from his voice. "I understand. Better than you think, perhaps. What you believe about me is not true. If I can find a way to prove it to you, I shall. And then, God help whoever has put these foul rumors in your head. I shall see they pay for their lies."

The earl shook his head. "Then God help you, Tom. For I cannot. Good day to you."

With that dismissal, Tom exited the office, back stiff with shame and the pain of fruitless exertion. Stanton shut the door behind him with a snap. And as he proceeded to the outer room, the little man who had tried to prevent his entrance now moved to block his exit. Tom raised his head to look and the clerk gestured to him, with a barest crook of the finger. "You seek employment?"

Tom nodded.

"And he turned you away, did he not?"

Tom nodded again.

The clerk gave a grim smile and whispered, "There is work enough here, should he chose to take you on. But he does not trust you. It is a shame. But I know of someone who is seeking men with knowledge that they would share. And although you are not as valuable as you might be, if you could return quietly to this office while still in his service, there are some tasks that would suit your abilities."

"Might suit me?" Tom said, a little dumbly.

"I heard, just now, that you wished to take back some of your own against those who have put you in this unenviable position. You are crippled for doing what you thought was right. And now you have been discarded by those in whom you put your trust. I offer you the opportunity for revenge." The man smiled. "And profit as well." He scribbled a few words on paper and pushed them hurriedly into Tom's hand just as the door to the earl's office opened again. Stanton looked at him with only the mildest curiosity, and turned his attention to the clerk.

While they were both distracted, Tom slipped quietly from the room.

Victoria sat in the little chair by the fire, awaiting her lover's return. Tom's manservant would not leave her alone, since he'd caught her going through the drawers of the little desk in the front room. He'd enquired if there was anything he might get for her. And asked again if she wished to send for her possessions.

She'd shaken her head, smiled and assured him that there was nothing she needed. And still, he watched her with sharp dark eyes that said his master might be easily gulled by his feelings for a beautiful woman, but the servant was nobody's fool.

She had wanted pen and ink to write to Stanton, and enough privacy to do it unobserved. With the servant hovering behind her, how would that be possible? And she could still find no way to explain the comfortable life she had been leading just a few short miles across town.

The more she had seen of Tom's civilian life the more guilty she felt for suspecting him. He lived simply, just short of poverty. If he had turned coat for the French, than they would have rewarded him in some way. There was no sign of the zealot in him that might make her think he'd done it out of loyalty to Boney.

And now that she had seen the scars on his body, she could not convince herself that he had staged a minor injury to disguise his perfidy. What kind of fool would come near to sacrificing his leg just to throw the hounds from his trail? It had rendered him unfit for duty, and for many forms of employment.

She had wanted to believe him innocent last night, as he'd held her and slept. But in the morning she had viewed the problem from all angles, lest her judgment had been swayed by sweet words and soft touches. As she weighed the bits of evidence against each other, no matter how she looked at it, it appeared that she had been wrong.

If only she could have come to the conclusion a few hours sooner, she might have slipped away from him last night, and avoided the painful admission she might have to make today.

But she had not left because she had not wanted to, just as he had not stopped himself in the brothel. When he learned the truth he would turn her out, and she would be well punished for her playacting and foolish suspicions, because she would never again feel as she did when he held her in his arms.

As she worried on it, Tom burst in through the door of his room, tossing his hat and gloves aside, but keeping his stick as he dropped into the chair beside hers. "Toby," he called to his servant, "paper and ink. Immediately. Sharpen a pen, and bring the writing table closer to the fire for me. Then, prepare yourself to deliver a message to the home of the Earl of Stanton. You are not to leave until you see the man. Put the paper I give you into his hands and no other's. He will hear me out on this, damn him, if he cares for his country."

"Tom, what are you about? What has happened?" The mention of the earl made her mouth go dry. But Tom seemed more elated than angry. Proof that whatever he had learned it was not the whole truth.

He flexed his bad leg and sighed. "It has been a most curious day. I procured the license, or at least set things in motion to make the damned thing procurable. And then, I went to visit an old friend in the Home Office. The Earl of Stanton was my captain, before your husband. If we are to make a go of it, I cannot lay about here, mooning over the past. I need employment." He was grinning at her as though he thought it the most wonderful thing in the world to toil for her, and she could feel her heart breaking a little.

He shook his head. "But he would not have me. It seems I am not trusted. There were rumors, you know, after the incident. Some thought me a coward, and others a traitor for my damned luck on that day."

She cringed at his casual mention of the very thing that had preyed on her mind. "Perhaps the people who doubted did not know you as I do now." And she would find a way to make it right, now that she had seen the truth.

He smiled and gave another shake of his head, this time in amazement. "No matter. Today, I think it has all happened for a reason. Stanton's secretary was quick to take note of the cold reception, and made me a most unusual offer. I think he hoped that there was some bit of information that I might wish to sell, or that the enemy had some use for a desperate and angry man."

"No." She almost moaned the word. It would be a sad thing if her presence had made him the very traitor she hoped to catch.

He placed a hand on hers. "Do not worry. I am not tempted. But I kept mum about the fact. And now, it seems I have information that would be most valuable to Stanton, and he will be forced to apologize for turning me out." His eyes narrowed. "As if I would turn so easily to help the lot that gave me this gamey leg." His hand tightened on hers, as though he could shield her from the pain of the past. "I know we are barely met. And this all must seem most curious to you. But if asked, I will spy for Stanton and meet with these men to divine their purpose. Perhaps

I can lead them to reveal others. If I can deliver them into the very hands of those they seek to betray, it will be most satisfying. I will lie if I must, and appear to be a rogue and traitor. But you must believe that I am as true to my country as I will be to you." He brushed the hair out of her eyes. "I will make an excellent spy, since it is so easy for most to believe wrong of me."

"Don't." The proof of his innocence hurt almost as much as the fear of his guilt.

He was holding her hand almost painfully tight, as though he feared she would leave. "If we are to be together, you will hear what people say of me. But know that it is all lies. For you, I have nothing but truth. If there was any sin I was guilty of, in all the time on the Peninsula, it was of envy. For Charles told me of you, and I…" He took a breath. "I loved you long before I met you. But I never meant to act on it. At that time, I thought I had a future of my own, even if it was not so bright as his. I would never have hurt him, for doing so would hurt you. And I never could. Not in all the world."

So his last secret was that he loved her better than she knew. And he did not want her to think him dishonorable, should he resort to spying. She could feel the tears welling up behind her eyes. For how was what he was planning any different than what she had done to him?

Other than that she had been wrong.

"What is it?" The concern for her was echoed in his eyes, his voice, and every line of his body, as though he strained from his very soul to put her at ease. It only made her betrayal of him worse. She could feel the sob breaking, and was powerless to stop it.

His arms were around her. "There, there. I have upset you."

"No. It is I who was false to you. You will hate me when you know."

He stroked her hair, letting her cry. "What could you ever do that would make me love you less?"

"The rumors about your disloyalty came from me. I went to the Earl of Stanton. It was I who put the doubts about you into his head. I hoped that I could trick you with my body into revealing the truth."

There was a horrible pause before he spoke. He went still and his face became blank. "And so you have. After less than a day, there is not a secret left in me that you do not know."

"I hate myself for what I have done."

"For giving yourself to me?" His hand moved ever so slightly on her.

"No. That was…" What good did it do to lie and protect the feelings of the dead, when it would further wrong the man who held her? "Perfect. When we are alone? It is unlike anything I have known and I do not regret a moment. But I wronged you with my words, and I lied to you, even after I knew I had been mistaken about your guilt."

"You never needed my help. Not even from the first?" He gave an incredulous laugh.

"I was in the brothel only to trap you. I would never… I do not need money, or the protection of any man. I could have lived out my days alone in comfort. But I had to know...."

"And now you do." His back stiffened, but he did not release her. "Charles was right. Your loyalty to him knew no bounds. Not even those of propriety, if you were willing to lie with me just to prove my guilt."

She opened her eyes and looked up into his. "All I found was that you were a better man, and more honest and noble than I could possibly imagine."

"And now, I am vindicated?" He said it as though it were a small comfort. "And when you accepted my offer of marriage?" There was no rancor in his voice, only a gentle prodding to get to the truth.

"I knew in my heart that it would all end once you realized what I had done. But I could not manage to say no."

He released her and leaned back in his chair, rubbing his hand over his eyes as though befuddled by her answer. "If I had behaved as a man of honor when we met, we would not be in this muddle. I should have walked from the room as soon as I suspected the truth of your identity. But I wanted you, even when I thought you would sell your body to any who would have it. I thought you a common whore, who would leave as soon as she saw how little I had to offer. But I could not let you go."

"You offered yourself. And it was more than I deserved."

"And what you did to me was done out of loyalty to your country, and to your husband. What sense would there be to punish you for believing what everyone else thought true?" He sighed again.

"You do not mean to cast me off, then?" she asked in a small voice, fearing what his answer would be.

He gave her a wan smile. "You must know, Victoria, that it is up to you to decide whether to keep me or cut me loose. A gentleman does not cry off of an engagement."

Without meaning to, she laughed, and then gulped to swallow the sound and covered her mouth with her hand. There was nothing funny about the predicament they were in. He had not been a gentleman, nor had she acted like a lady. She was a spy and wished she wasn't. He was ready to become one to earn money that she did not need. And nothing she'd assumed about him was true. He was sweet and kind and he had loved her before she'd even known him. And perhaps, there was a chance she might love him as well.

"Money does not matter," she whispered, afraid that she might offend him. "I have enough for both of us. But I will be happy without, if you wish me to."

He gave a dry chuckle. "I am not so great a fool as to wish for poverty to salve my pride. You may keep your money, and I will not be as useless as I have been, once Stanton gets my letter. I am sure we can find a happy medium, and live quite comfortably." He paused. "If you still wish to make a go of it."

"If I wish it?" She scarcely dared breathe. For after all she had told him, he still spoke as if a promise made in the dark was an unbreakable oath. "If I did not want to release you?" she whispered. "If I wished, with all my heart, that there was a way to take back the terrible things I said and thought?"

"Then you know what you must do." He was staring at her as though it should be perfectly obvious what he expected.

Was it an apology he wanted? It was his. "I am so sorry. So very sorry, that I hurt you. That I did not take the time to understand, or to know you for who you truly are."

Still he stared at her, unmoving and expectant. There was something else.

And then she realized. There was a way that he would know that it was truth. She leaned forward and reached for him, putting her arms about his neck and her mouth on his. "Let me begin again," she whispered against his parted lips. She slipped her tongue between them, beginning with barely a touch. It was one more thing about him that was different. He tasted...

"Mmm." She smiled to herself as her tongue touched his. For without thinking, she'd made a noise of satisfaction before delving deeper into the kiss.

Suddenly his hands caught her by the waist and dragged her body close and into the chair with him to sit on his lap. She wrapped her arms even tighter around his neck as he kissed her in return. And she decided, if there had been a secret he was hiding from the world, it had nothing to do with loyalty and betrayal, and everything to do with the skill of his kisses.

He broke from her and muttered, "Now I know why you denied me that, when we first met. How could I leave your bed, after such a kiss?"

She laid a hand on his shoulder, tracing the seam of his coat with her finger. "It would not have been like that, at first. I did not want you to know the contents of my heart."

"But now you do?"

"I would like nothing more." And she kissed him again.

* * * * *

*Tainted with
dishonour, undone
by passion*

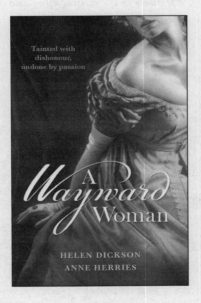

Two women destined for ruin, but can
they be rescued by love?

Available 18th February 2011
www.millsandboon.co.uk

REGENCY
Collection

*Let these sparklingly seductive delights whirl
you away to the ballrooms—and
bedrooms—of Polite Society!*

Volume 1 – 4th February 2011
Regency Pleasures by Louise Allen

Volume 2 – 4th March 2011
Regency Secrets by Julia Justiss

Volume 3 – 1st April 2011
Regency Rumours by Juliet Landon

Volume 4 – 6th May 2011
Regency Redemption by Christine Merrill

Volume 5 – 3rd June 2011
Regency Debutantés by Margaret McPhee

Volume 6 – 1st July 2011
Regency Improprieties by Diane Gaston

12 volumes in all to collect!

MILLS
BOON

www.millsandboon.co.uk

REGENCY
Collection

*Let these sparklingly seductive delights whirl
you away to the ballrooms—and
bedrooms—of Polite Society!*

Volume 7 – 5th August 2011
Regency Mistresses by Mary Brendan

Volume 8 – 2nd September 2011
Regency Rebels by Deb Marlowe

Volume 9 – 7th October 2011
Regency Scandals by Sophia James

Volume 10 – 4th November 2011
Regency Marriages by Elizabeth Rolls

Volume 11 – 2nd December 2011
Regency Innocents by Annie Burrows

Volume 12 – 6th January 2012
Regency Sins by Bronwyn Scott

12 volumes in all to collect!

MILLS
BOON

www.millsandboon.co.uk

HISTORICAL

Regency
LADY FOLBROKE'S DELICIOUS DECEPTION
by Christine Merrill

Lady Emily Longesley married the love of her life and hoped that he would learn to love her. Instead, he upped and left! Confronting her errant husband three years on, she sees that Adrian, Earl of Folbroke, has been robbed of his sight! If she plays his mistress by delicious deception, can he finally learn to love his wife?

Regency
HOW TO MARRY A RAKE
by Deb Marlowe

Heiress Mae Halford has mended her heart after her friend Stephen Manning's rejection. She's ready to find herself a husband, but the first man she bumps into at a Newmarket house party is Lord Stephen himself!

BREAKING THE GOVERNESS'S RULES
by Michelle Styles

After being dismissed from her post as governess for allowing Jonathon, Lord Chesterholm, to seduce her, Louisa Sibson has rebuilt her life. She lives by a rulebook of morals—and will not allow the devastating Jonathon to break them again!

On sale from 4th March 2011
Don't miss out!

*Available at WHSmith, Tesco, ASDA, Eason
and all good bookshops*
www.millsandboon.co.uk

0211/04a

HISTORICAL

HER DARK AND DANGEROUS LORD
by Anne Herries

Exiled Lord Stefan de Montfort rescues Englishwoman
Anne Melford from the sea and takes her to his château
in Normandy. Anne fires within Stefan a disturbing,
forbidden desire. Could such a lady ever marry a dark
and dangerous scoundrel like him?

SIERRA BRIDE
by Jenna Kernan

Wealthy Sam Pickett is used to getting his way. So he is
baffled when Kate Wells, a feisty little hellion who steps
between him and a bullet, isn't interested in becoming
his wife. If he can't make her his bride, then he'll
most certainly make her his mistress!

BREATHLESS
by Anne Stuart

Ruined beyond repair and shunned by London society,
Miranda Rohan rebelliously embraces the freedom of having
nothing left to lose. This dangerous course throws her under
the power of the darkly enigmatic Lucien de Malheur—
known as the Scorpion...
The House of Rohan

On sale from 4th March 2011
Don't miss out!

*Available at WHSmith, Tesco, ASDA, Eason
and all good bookshops*

www.millsandboon.co.uk

04a   0211/04b

"The arrogance! To think that they can come here with their town bronze and sweep some heiress or other to the altar."

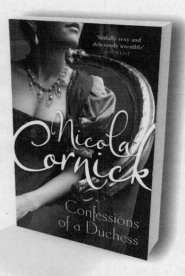

'Sinfully sexy and deliciously irresistible'
BOOKLIST

Nicola Cornick

Confessions of a Duchess

When a feudal law requires all unmarried ladies to wed or surrender half their wealth, the quiet village of Fortune's Folly becomes England's greatest Marriage Market.

Laura, the dowager duchess, is determined to resist the flattery of fortune hunters. Young, handsome and scandalously tempting Dexter Anstruther suspects Laura has a hidden motive for resisting his charms…and he intends to discover it.

www.mirabooks.co.uk

MIRA